The Personal Trainer

A Tale of Pain, Gain, Greed & Lust

DAVID L. HERBERT

Published by

PRC Publishing, Inc.
In conjunction with The Personal Trainer, LLC
P.O. Box 35791, Canton, Ohio 44718

Cover model for The Personal Trainer: Trisha N. Rich Yocom, formerly of Santa Monica, California, now Owner of The Buckeye Bounce Club, LLC, Powell, Ohio.

Cover designed by Laurance C. Herbert, lherbert.freelance@gmail.com.

ISBN 978-0-9894012-0-3
Library of Congress Control Number: 2013908122

AUTHOR'S NOTE

The Personal Trainer is a work of fiction in its entirety, and all of the characters, companies, and organizations in this novel are the products of my imagination. By way of example, the characters of Anthony James Piccini, Mark Trudeau, and Judge Charles Davis — and the company called FitAgain Corporation — are wholly invented. The only exceptions are public institutions such as the state court in which my imaginary lawsuit is tried, and these public institutions are used fictitiously. The story I tell here is not about any real people, companies, organizations or institutions, and any similarity between the fictional contents of my novel and any real people, companies, organizations, institutions or events is strictly a matter of coincidence.

DEDICATION

To Lynda.

ACKNOWLEDGMENTS

Thank you for editorial and production assistance to:
Vickie Rice, Bonny Ammond, Pam Archer,
Molly Romig and Kathie Covey

Prescription For Pain

You asked me to help you. To put together a plan of exercise for you. One that would help you lose weight, tone up and develop some ripped abs; simply put, to help you look good to women.

Now you tell me you can't do what I am telling you to do. Bullshit. I'm the personal trainer. I know what I am doing. I've been certified to do this – not you.

Give me ten more push-ups – now. Get going. Don't stop.

See that woman over there. Look at her. She's hot. She is in great shape and she wants a stud to be with her – not some sloppy fat pig. If you want some of that fine ass, give me 20 sit-ups – now.

Get going. Get moving.

I don't' care if you have to puke. Keep at it. But I'm not cleaning up your puke no matter what happens.

I don't care if you can't breathe. Get busy.

Don't tell me you're in pain. Pain is part of the game. No pain, no gain! Work through it! It won't kill you . . .

Table of Contents

CHAPTER 1

It was a long ride. The booster seat which Mommy had gotten for her was hard. It still felt strangely uncomfortable to Kimmy. She had been used to the comfort of a reclining car seat in which she had been placed for several years by both her father and her mother every time she rode in either of their cars. The booster seat just seemed too stiff and it didn't recline at all. However, Kimmy was a big girl now and she needed to ride in the booster seat. Her mommy had told her so and she believed everything Mommy said.

Once she and her father, Ben Lawrence, had arrived at their destination, Kimmy said, "Daddy, can I see Mommy now?" Kimmy's dad really didn't know what to say. Kimmy would see her mom, Meri Margaret Lawrence, once they went inside. The decision had been made a few days before. Everyone would see Meri and have a chance to say whatever they wished to her.

Ben let the question go unanswered as he pulled the car into the parking spot outside the old and stately brick building. He wanted to tell

Kimmy everything as if it were a story like those he or Meri had read to Kimmy nearly every night of Kimmy's young life. However, what had happened was not a fairy tale or any other make-believe fable that he could read to Kimmy before she fell asleep for the night. That just wasn't possible.

Neither Kimmy nor her younger brother, Chase, would be excluded from seeing their mother. It certainly wouldn't be fair or right to let all the others see Meri but not to allow Kimmy and Chase the chance to do so.

Chase, unlike his older sister, Kimberly Marie Lawrence– "Kimmy" for short, was clearly too young to realize what was going on. He was nearly a year old, but really could not yet communicate or understand. On the other hand, Kimmy was now six. She was certainly old enough to at least realize some of what was going on even if she was not capable of comprehending all of its full meaning.

It was May and it was beginning to warm up in Ohio. The Lawrence family had lived in Upper Arlington, near the state's capital of Columbus, Ohio for several years. Columbus was in the middle of the state, which was roughly 250 miles north to south, as well as east to west. The city was also some 150 miles away from Lake Erie – part of the Great Lakes. As a consequence, Columbus was rarely impacted by the so-called lake effect of those bodies of water which made up the Great Lakes. Those lakes made it cloudier in the summer for cities like Cleveland and Lorain but only to a much lesser extent in Columbus. Columbus had many more sunny days than those other Ohio cities.

Kimmy loved spring in Columbus because the warming weather brought forth a cornucopia of beautifully colored flowers emerging after a long winter's nap. Kimmy also liked the warmth of the sun on her face and the smell of spring flowers that their initial blossoming brought forth to the air. The smell was wonderful and something that Kimmy, Chase and Mommy had experienced together many times on their Sunday visits to the Columbus park near the river, not too far from where they lived.

Sundays were essentially just for Kimmy and Mommy. They spent time together on these special days and filled each of those days with fun, laughter and the outdoors – especially in spring.

As she reflected on those unique days, Kimmy remembered and asked her father, "Daddy, tomorrow is Sunday. Will Mommy and I be able to go to the park?"

This time Ben knew he would not be able to let the question go unanswered. But at the same time, he was not really sure what to say or how to tell Kimmy. God knows he had tried to do so, each night for the past three nights. While Kimmy was only six-years-old, she was Ben's first child, and he loved her dearly. He just didn't know what to say or even how to say it; if only he could find the right words and know how to deliver them.

"Kimmy," he finally managed to say, "Let's go inside and find Grandma and Papa. They have Chase with them. When we go in, all of us can talk about tomorrow and what we can do. Okay?"

The young girl looked at her father's face with a wide-eyed expression that only young children can seem to innocently display as they seek to gain some understanding and perspective on what was said or done. Kimmy was intent on her father's expression. As she focused her gaze on his eyes, she once again saw those eyes well up with tears and knew the weight that those tears brought to each eye. She also knew from her own experience the simple fact that the more those tears welled up, the harder it was to see. So, she decided to agree and hoped those tears would dry up and not start running down her daddy's face. She just didn't know why her daddy was so quick to cry.

"Okay," Kimmy said. "We can talk to Grandma and Papa and find out what Mommy wants to do. Chase is too little to decide. I'll vote for him."

"Alright. We can do that, Kimmy. No matter what happens when we go in, remember Mommy and I love you more than you can ever imagine. You know that. Right?"

"Of course I do, Daddy."

With that, Ben turned off the engine and opened his car door. As he swung his feet out of the car and put them on the ground, he felt as if his legs would crumble. They didn't seem to be able to support the weight of what was now squarely on his shoulders. How would he cope? What would he do? How would he do it all?

As Ben summoned up the strength and the courage to get out of the car and to walk around the car to open the back passenger door for Kimmy, he was riddled with pain and anguish. Once the door opened, Kimmy lifted the seat belt off of her waist and chest and jumped from the seat to the ground. She was excited. She had not seen Mommy for three

3

days. Even though she was with Daddy and had seen Grandma and Papa during that time, she was anxious to see Mommy and to spend some time with her now and tomorrow. She wondered what fun things they would do in the park. She was so excited. She was also worried that tomorrow might never come. Everyone around her seemed so sad and yet she was so excited. She just didn't know why everyone else seemed to be so sad. If Ben had known what Kimmy was thinking, he would not have known how to address her fears, let alone his own.

Once Kimmy was out of the car, she grasped her daddy's hand and they walked to the door of the house with Kimmy leading the way. Kimmy noticed lots of cars outside the building and wondered why there were so many cars there. She couldn't imagine so many people from so many cars living in one house, even one as big as this one.

When Ben opened the door to the house, he led Kimmy in by the hand. Once inside, Kimmy immediately smelled the fragrance of spring; of what seemed like hundreds, if not thousands of flowers, bringing forth their collective bouquet. Kimmy wondered if her mommy had something to do with all of this since they enjoyed the beauty and smells of spring and summer together.

"Daddy," said Kimmy, "do you smell the flowers? Mommy must have gotten them for me."

While Kimmy had been excited to be with her father and ride in the car to see Mommy, Ben was deep in thought. As he drove from their home to where Kimmy's mother would soon be "honored," and as he began to walk into the brick home, he was still unsure of what to tell Kimmy.

Before they arrived, Ben remembered when he had first met Meri Margaret David. At the moment of their first meeting he knew she was special and would be with him forever. He just did not then realize what forever meant.

He had met her at Ohio University during their freshman year of college. Ohio University is a state sponsored institute of higher learning located in Athens, Ohio. They had met at the student recreation center. On their first meeting, he was stunned with her beauty and her dark flashing eyes. In fact, he soon became totally infatuated with her. By the time they reached their final year at OU, as it was abbreviated, they were engaged and a date for their marriage was set.

Ben Lawrence and then Meri Margaret David were married in Canton, Ohio, some 120 miles or so north of Columbus and some 65 miles south of Cleveland. Meri's parents arranged for the vows to be delivered by a local municipal judge, Earl Miller. The wedding and reception would both take place at a beautiful country club located just outside of Canton. It had originally been a cloistered monastery which had been remodeled into a club house, reception hall, restaurant, spa and a number of very elegant hotel rooms, suites and private apartments.

Meri Margaret David was especially beautiful on her wedding day, particularly to Ben. They would have a great life together after their honeymoon in St. Lucia in the south-eastern part of the Caribbean. Ben had arranged for their week-long honeymoon stay at a beautiful all-inclusive resort there. It would be and in fact, turned out to be a wonderful start to what would surely be a more wonderful, long and perfect life together. As least that is what Ben remembered.

Once they returned from their honeymoon, both continued on with their newly started and respective careers – Ben, with the banking industry and Meri, in the world of fashion. Some years after, Kimmy was born and later, after a special trip for Ben and Meri, Chase arrived. Both of these births were happily anticipated and celebrated with a great deal of joy, particularly by Meri's parents.

As Ben reflected on those thoughts, he was forced, by Kimmy's questioning, to return to the reality of the moment. However, he was not yet ready to tell Kimmy what had happened and how it would impact their lives from that point forward - forever. The only thing Kimmy wanted to know was, "Daddy, when will I see Mommy?"

All Ben could do to reply was to utter a few pathetically delivered words, "Soon, Kimmy, soon." However, he had trouble visualizing anything in front of him through eyes laden with ever swelling tears.

Kimmy had noticed her Daddy's face and even remarked, "Don't cry, Daddy. What's wrong?" Ben was unable to articulate any response. His very essence was in turmoil and pain. He could not bear the weight and burden of what had occurred and what would continue to haunt him for the foreseeable time to come.

While Kimmy became excited in anticipation of seeing her mother and wanted to quickly enter the brick house, Ben's steps became heavier and heavier. Once they walked in though the entrance door, he was not even sure he could go up the few steps to the entryway. However, as he and Kimmy entered through the double door entrance to the home, Ben was nearly overwhelmed with the sweet scent and smell of flowers. It was as if he had run into an invisible wall. The wall impacted him with such force that his head began spinning, nearly rendering him unconscious. The smell clearly made it difficult for him to continue on.

As anticipated, Kimmy became excited on first noting the smell, but Ben could not join in. He knew what was coming. Kimmy did not.

CHAPTER 2

Tony Piccini wanted to go. He wanted to see Meri one more time . . . to finally close a chapter in both of their lives. However, for a number of reasons he could not go.

The New York corporation which owned the health club where he worked in Upper Arlington, Ohio, just outside of Columbus, had told him in no uncertain terms that he could not go to see Meri or her family. He had been told that he was not to call them or send a note, not even a card or anything in writing. He really had no choice but to do what they told him.

All the corporation had done was put out a news release. It stated:

FitAgain Corporation

News Release

Columbus, Ohio – FitAgain Corporation with offices in New York and facilities all across the United States and in three foreign venues expressed its deep regret for the recent and untimely death of one of its members in a facility it owns just outside of Columbus. Mark Trudeau, CEO for the FitAgain corporate organization, expressed his sorrow for the untimely death of Meri Margaret Lawrence who passed away at the facility yesterday. He was quoted as saying, "Apparently, a previously existing medical condition led to and caused Mrs. Lawrence's unfortunate death at our facility while she was working out in order to improve her well-being. We express and convey our deepest sympathies to her family on this unforeseeable and unpredictable occurrence." He added, "Thousands of our members safely work out in FitAgain facilities each day without any adverse effects. Our departed member, Meri Margaret Lawrence, and her family will remain in our prayers."

Tony had come to the Upper Arlington FitAgain facility just outside of Columbus some three years before he met Meri. He had been trained by staff members of the Club through the materials provided by the New York corporate office to the Club. He became certified as a personal trainer by corporate through the use of their materials within a few weeks after he started. Once he was so trained and certified, he then became a member of the corporation's recommended fitness professional organization, the USA - Personal Trainers Association (USA-PTA), which provided him with liability insurance to cover any injuries which might happen to client-members of the facility where he provided service. He paid for the insurance coverage himself, but FitAgain required the coverage if Tony was to provide any service within their facilities.

Tony liked the Upper Arlington club where he worked, as well as most of its members and almost all of his co-workers. He worked hard at selling the corporation's services and its club endorsed products. He quickly caught on to the process to serve club members and their individualized needs for attention. Those needs included exercise, weight loss, nutritional and supplement counseling, life coaching and even sometimes, more personal attention for some of the female club members who did not have all of their needs fulfilled at home.

Tony was good at keeping his female charges happy in all categories. The position he held was certainly a step up for him from a variety of waiter jobs he had previously held at a number of Columbus-area eating establishments. Since he had attended but not graduated from Kent State University in northeastern Ohio, his career opportunities otherwise were somewhat limited. However, neither a college degree nor a license was necessary to be a personal trainer. Not in Ohio. Not elsewhere. In fact, no such license was required anywhere in the United States.

Tony had liked working with Meri. She was a quick learner who really wanted to lose weight and to lose it fast. She worked hard and followed all of Tony's directions and his prescriptions for exercise activity. She also took all of the supplements and other nutritional products he recommended to her. She even listened when he told her to cut down on her physician-prescribed medications to control her elevated blood pressure. He told her that these medications were slowing her fat burning efforts and therefore hindered her weight loss.

Tony was very upset about what had happened. He did not understand how things could have gone so wrong. If only he knew more and had been provided with better training and preparation by FitAgain or for that matter anyone else, anyone at all. Any civil or criminal responsibility for what happened to Meri while she was under his care seemed almost unbelievable — even surrealistic. Certainly, Tony never intended for any of his efforts to go wrong. All he ever wanted to do was help Meri. Now all he wanted to do was say good-bye.

CHAPTER 3

As Ben and Kimmy walked into the stately brick home, Kimmy was very excited, all in anticipation of seeing her Mommy. Kimmy had not seen Mommy for three days. She missed her and didn't want to wait one minute longer.

Ben, on the other hand, could hardly walk and felt in a fog of sorts. He drifted in and out of the present to the past with a variety of thoughts and memories of the life he had previously enjoyed with Meri. It had been more than he had ever hoped for but at the same time, less than he expected to have with her. Much less.

Once inside the doors, Kimmy saw Papa holding her baby brother, Chase. Grandma was nearby talking with another woman and a man dressed in a suit. Papa was dressed up too, as was her father. Kimmy thought all of them had dressed up for Mommy. With the help of Grandma, Kimmy had picked out and put on one of her favorite sun dresses. Kimmy was sure Mommy would like it since they had originally selected it together in a small boutique shop in an area near Upper

Arlington called the Short North.

Ben too saw Meri's father and mother and his own young son, Chase, who he felt too weak to hold. As he walked in, one of the home's employees approached him and said: "Good afternoon, Mr. Lawrence. I hope you and your daughter are holding up okay. We have everything ready. Your wife is just in the next room. She looks beautiful."

With that said, Ben responded, "We are doing the best we can. Kimmy and I need to go in and see Meri Margaret now – just the two of us. Can we do that?"

Kimmy heard her father's question and instantly remarked, "Daddy, can we see Mommy now? I want to see her and know about the flowers."

As the greeter led Ben Lawrence and Kimmy into the next room, Ben's eyes again welled up and it became very difficult for him to stay focused on the present. Once the greeter opened the pocket doors to the room where Meri was located, Kimmy saw her mother apparently lying down and began questioning her father.

"Daddy, why is Mommy lying down? Isn't she glad to see us? Is she sleeping?"

"Kimmy, Mommy is sleeping but she won't be waking up. Not today. Not tomorrow. She's gone to heaven to rest. She just worked too hard here. We will miss her, but she had to go." As Ben held Kimmy's hand and they walked toward Meri, Ben said to Kimmy in a nearly inaudible whisper, "Let's say good-bye together."

CHAPTER 4

The jury was still out. Still deliberating. Maybe arguing. Tony worried that they were probably trying to place blame.

Tony remembered what had brought him to this very day, January 28, 2008. A Monday. Usually a day to start the work week, not one to end a career – even a short one, which up to this point was what Tony Piccini had hoped would not be just another job. Not another job like all the others he had done before but instead a highly rewarding profession, both financially and otherwise. Not just serving food as he had done for several years, but serving people, to help them, not hurt them.

'Hard to believe,' Tony thought. 'Here I am, sitting in Courtroom 3 of the Franklin County Court of Common Pleas in Columbus, Ohio waiting for a jury of 8 ordinary, everyday Joes (as they could be called if they faced the Pros) to return a verdict.'

A majority decision for or against Tony and the others could be returned. That verdict could include the corporation who employed him - at least the one whom he thought employed him, FitAgain – 'A Health Club For Everyone Who Wants to be FitAgain' – or so they said. 'Join our Club – Become Fit for the Rest of Your Life – It won't kill you' - or so they promised.

Tony was a personal trainer providing service to a number of clients at one of FitAgain's 300+ clubs located all across the continental United States as well as Hawaii, Aruba, Barbados, Puerto Rico and Grand Cayman.

FitAgain was his employer, at least Tony had thought so. But for the purposes of the case which just had been tried against him as well as FitAgain and the others, the jury would determine whether FitAgain, in fact, employed him. It didn't matter what Tony thought; or even what FitAgain said. The jury would decide.

That issue was a bone of contention – one very important issue – at least for Tony. The rest of the litigants were probably more concerned with the verdict, that part of the jury's decision to be expressed in dollars and cents. That part of a civil jury's decision usually matters the most to lots of folks in court.

Surely the money mattered to the parties, the so-called litigants, the plaintiffs and the defendants and of course the plaintiffs' lawyers, who were in for 40% of whatever was recovered. Not the one-third that plaintiffs' lawyers used to charge their clients – a so-called "contingency fee" – but now 40% plus expenses. With costs, expert witness fees and related expenses, such costs and the lawyers' share of a particular verdict or award would often represent nearly half or more of any settlement or verdict, depending upon what the actual costs turned out to be and, of course, the verdict or settlement granted. More could be earned in fees and expenses on any appeal.

Defense lawyers, on the other hand, were generally paid by the hour. In the Midwest, unlike the East or West coasts or places like Chicago or Dallas, where hourly rates were more, hourly rates for this kind of defense work ranged from $250 to $450 per hour.

Tony found the employment issue which was vigorously tried in his case to be ridiculous. But the jury's verdict, their determination at least once reached, would be final pending any possible contrary decision on appeal. If the jury found that FitAgain had indeed employed him, then it could be held liable for his actions, as well as his shortcomings, the latter of which were called "omissions" in legal circles. Therefore FitAgain, at least theoretically, could be held financially responsible for his actions or even his so-called omissions if a verdict was returned in favor of the plaintiffs. The plaintiffs in this case were the husband and surviving children of Meri

Margaret Lawrence. Before she died, she had been one of Tony's clients and a member of FitAgain's club in Upper Arlington.

Tony's employment or status as a so-called independent contractor was one of the arguments made in the case. The theory that Tony was not an employee was put forth by FitAgain in earnest and with a bulldog tenacity. Even though Tony considered FitAgain to be his employer, he was somewhat alone if the jury determined that issue in favor of the company. The issue was one designed completely of the company's own making in its efforts to avoid liability for what they told Tony to do, encouraged him to do and, in fact, rewarded him for doing well.

Tony had been very good at his work for FitAgain. He focused primarily on the women clients who were enticed into their clubs – to lose weight, to get fit – to look good. They even used slogans to get them started: "Join our club. Work out with us. It won't kill you!" However, as it turned out, at least for Meri Margaret Lawrence, they were wrong.

When Tony came to be associated with FitAgain, he was interviewed by a District Manager who came to Upper Arlington from Chicago searching for new club trainers. Tony agreed to the interview at the urging of one of his customers whom he had grown to know quite well and on an intimate basis. She had set up the interview for Tony with Brant Branson the District Manager from Chicago. When Tony arrived for the interview, Branson extended his right hand in a typical American greeting and introduced himself to Tony.

"Tony, I'm Brant Branson. I'm in from Chicago to interview nearly a dozen candidates who want to serve our members as personal trainers. I'm told you want to join our certified professionals in doing so – is that right?"

"Yes," replied Tony, "that's why I'm here. One of your staff members felt that I would fit in and provide some valuable services to your members."

"She may be right," responded Branson, "but we need to see. What experience do you have in the fitness industry?"

"I have worked out nearly every week since I was in seventh grade. I swam competitively in high school and have always worked out at a number of clubs and gyms. I have picked up a lot of experience during that time. I've helped a lot of people, primarily women, work through their needs and desires. I think I can do that here as well. At least I'm told that I can."

"I've heard you are good with people. Now that I've met you, I can see you are personable. However, you will need to go through our system, become certified by our trainers and then provide service to our members through a contract we will develop for you."

"I'm not sure I understand the contract concept. How much will I earn by the hour?"

"Your earning potential, if we give you the opportunity, will be limited only by your imagination. You can expect to bill upwards of $125.00 per hour. You will receive 60% of that billing amount and we will receive 40% to cover our overhead which is considerable. We do all the advertising; we supply you with the facility to provide your services; we give you the ability to be certified to provide personal training services; we give you the members to train and all we ask is that you show up on time, deliver the service and promote our concepts."

"I like what I hear."

"There's more, lots more. We give you the training you need, supply your credentials, we even give you a locker, forms and documents to use with your clients, our members. We also give you the ability to earn a 10% commission from any sales you make of our supplements, drinks, clothing, equipment or other goods and services we sell."

For good measure, Branson added, "You also get to keep all your tips and to meet a lot of new and attractive members who may like the services you have to offer. The tips could get to be more than what most people earn in salaries or wages."

"What kind of contract do I have to sign?" asked Tony.

"Don't worry," replied the District Manager. "You will be in charge of you and what you do with our members who will be your clients. It will be simple. You get your own insurance to protect you from any liability. You follow our policies but have a great deal of freedom in what you do and how you do it. Do you understand?"

"Well, I guess but I've never worked for anyone else on that basis. I'll have to learn. I'm just glad to have the opportunity to move forward."

"You now have that opportunity," said Branson. "Just sign here and here at the bold lines. Don't worry about what it says. We will treat you right. You will treat our members right and we will both make some money – more money than you have ever earned before."

With that, Tony eagerly signed on the bold lines and was more than ready to move on and start.

FitAgain and many other health and fitness facilities throughout the industry had a somewhat sordid history. Many clubs employed or contracted with poorly trained and ill prepared personal trainers or other fitness floor personnel to work with club members. Many of these "professionals" had injured, maimed or even contributed to or caused the deaths of some of their clients.

While certain segments of the industry were attempting to improve their practices and the qualifications of their personnel, effective education and real certification of service providers such as personal trainers was decidedly lacking. No state licensed personal trainers and most industry groups did not want any state to do so.

When Tony first reported for orientation, training and certification by FitAgain, he was assigned to another personal trainer who had been with FitAgain for several years, Dan Barkan, a young trainer in his late 20s.

As Tony was introduced to this trainer, Dan told him, "Tony, stick with me. Stay over my right shoulder all day as we work through the clients. Listen to what I say. Look at what I do. Think about why I do what I do and when. If I ask you to take a break, take it and leave the room where we are because I may have to provide some personal service for one of my clients."

"Okay," said Tony. "I can do that. I am here to learn. I will pay attention and do what you ask."

"Great," said Dan. "Then we will get along fine."

"Can I ask you something?" asked Tony.

"Sure, fire away," said Dan.

"I've never had a chance like this. It seems too good to be true. I help these people, they pay me, they tip me, they like me and I get paid by the company for doing what I love to do anyway. What's wrong with this picture? Where's the hook?"

"There is no hook. Do what you will be trained to do. Deliver the services, meet the clients' needs and don't worry about the rest. All of it will take care of itself."

At that moment, Felice Gibson, one of FitAgain's members approached Dan, grabbed him enthusiastically by the shoulder and kissed him on the cheek. She smiled at Tony but said to Dan, "What do we have here? Am I to be double teamed by two handsome young men today?"

"Maybe," said Dan. "Tony, here is one of our personal trainer 'trainees' and he needs to be indoctrinated about what we do here. He's going to watch today and learn how it goes. Okay?"

"Sure," said Felice. "I like to be watched."

That kind of instruction Tony thought, would not be difficult to follow. Felice was nearly 42 but had a body, from years of working out and watching everything that she consumed, which looked like that of a 25-year-old.

Tony chimed in, despite his prior instructions from Dan, and said, "I'll enjoy watching today."

Felice nearly purred at the flattery and extended her hand around Dan to Tony and said, "Hi, Tony. I'm Felice. Watch me today and if you like what you see, let me know. Perhaps you can help me more than you know."

Dan didn't appreciate the comment but knew that Felice had a mind of her own. He had served Felice's needs for the last six months or so but he knew he did not provide service on an exclusive basis. If she needed additional attention from Tony, he would not stand in the way.

"Okay, said Dan, let's get started so Tony can see what we do. Let's stretch and then warm up with some time on the treadmill. We can then move over to the exercise machines and I will see how you are coming along in your arm, leg, butt and ab development."

At that, Felice lay down on the mats next to the treadmill and began to stretch. She first lay on her back and then slowly brought her legs up to her chest, while pulling on her knees and shins. She looked at Tony as she did so to see his reaction. Tony liked what he saw. Needless to say, so did Felice. Tony was off to a good start, if with just this one potential client. So far so good he thought while he wondered where this flirtation would lead. He never thought this kind of work could ever lead to court.

CHAPTER 5

The jurors hearing the case of <u>Lawrence v. Piccini</u> - what the lawyers called a wrongful death action - would either determine that Tony helped kill another human being, one of his female customers or "clients" as those in the business liked to call them, or that he did not do so. All of this was to be addressed in the jurors' general verdict and in their answers to certain questions put to them by the lawyers with the approval of the judge. These questions or so-called "special interrogatories" as the lawyers twisted those words to make them sound more important than just questions, were always designed to make sure that the general verdict was consistent with certain issues which were important to each litigant individually. Often, however, these questions were used in attempts to create confusion, to taint a general verdict and thereby create grounds or reasons for appeal. All of this, of course, created more work and more billable hours for the lawyers.

The questions and the answers to those questions were all designed to explain a general verdict, at least in theory. The verdict could either be for Tony and the others or against them or some of them as the jurors, in their exercise of everyday wisdom and practical judgment, would determine.

If the verdict was against Tony, it would include a damage award, but only if the other side of this case, the plaintiffs (the family of Meri Margaret Lawrence, namely the husband and the two little children of that young wife and mother) prevailed on the jury with their evidence and their arguments. The children, Kimmy and Chase, were young and would need nurturing and support for some time. If a verdict was rendered in their favor, such a verdict would determine the value of Meri's young life and how the loss of that life would impact these children and Meri's husband, Ben. That verdict would be expressed in dollars and cents since there was really no other way to compensate them for such a loss.

The verdict was really at the heart of things in this case, as it is in most such cases. Justice was supposedly the ultimate issue in all these cases but one often forgotten in the shuffle and grasp for dollars and cents.

In this wrongful death case the family was asking for a lot - $42 million dollars. That was the family's "prayer" for relief. Many non-lawyers often questioned the use of the term "prayer" in legal pleadings. Some such people wondered what a quiet and solemn moment with God during prayer had to do with a legal case. To be sure, the term had caused some confusion and often some consternation when someone who was believed by many to be without any ethical underpinnings asked for legal relief in the form of a prayer. This play on words just didn't sit well with some people.

The "prayer" made in the complaint filed in Meri Margaret Lawrence's wrongful death case worried Tony. That worry stayed with him each and every day ever since the incident occurred and the lawsuit was filed. The suit was predicated upon a so-called "untoward event" as some legal commentators liked to call such mishaps. That event in this case was Meri's death, which occurred at a FitAgain facility while she was under Tony's care. She had been one of Tony's favorite clients.

Despite Tony's worry about this case, however, the other, darker side of all of this, the criminal case pending against just Tony, the one that would decide if he would go to prison for a crime, was what really worried him and kept him awake at night.

The most serious criminal charge against him was manslaughter – involuntary manslaughter to be exact. The charge had been brought by the prosecuting attorney for Franklin County, Ohio, the county in which the cities of Columbus and Upper Arlington were located.

Tony had been charged with this particular degree of homicide for his client's death because the prosecutor enticed the grand jury to indict him for that particular felony. The charge was like murder without certain elements – without an ingredient or two that would otherwise make it murder, something akin to leaving out an ingredient like sugar in the making of a cake. It was still a cake – just different.

In Tony's criminal case, however, involuntary manslaughter was the charge that the prosecuting attorney had decided to use in his efforts to prosecute Tony because Meri's death, in his view, had occurred as a proximate result of Tony's commission of another, lesser crime. In Ohio, like most other states, causing the death of a person while violating a law, even a minor one, created another more serious crime for which a prosecution like involuntary manslaughter could take place. That lesser crime in Tony's case was his unlawful practice of dietetics since Tony had no state license to so practice and yet had allegedly done so with Meri. While the unlawful practice of dietetics, a violation of Ohio Revised Code Section 4759.02, was a minor misdemeanor, causing the death of another while doing so constituted involuntary manslaughter. Involuntary manslaughter was a felony of the first degree, punishable by imprisonment for up to 5 years.

Tony had been "served" or given an indictment charging him with both involuntary manslaughter and the unlawful practice of dietetics. The indictment was delivered to him early on a Friday night by two uniformed Franklin County Sheriff's Deputies. Service of that indictment started the whole criminal process against him.

That night, the deputies drove up to his house and knocked on the front door. Tony looked to see who was at the door but once he saw who was there, he began to tremble. The trembling became worse as he answered the door and realized that the deputies were there to give him his charging papers.

"Anthony James Piccini?" asked the first deputy, dressed in a black and gray uniform seemingly held together with a large black belt. The belt was weighted down with a large and formidable looking black pistol in an even blacker and larger leather holster attached at the hip to the belt. The belt also held what appeared to be a set of handcuffs, a can of mace, two leather ammunition sleeves and other leather containers which held items not readily observable to him.

The second deputy on Tony's front porch seemed intent on staring at Tony as if to hold him in place with his fixed gaze. Tony was too scared to move or to even readily answer the first deputy's question.

"Are you Anthony James Piccini?" asked the first deputy again in a demanding tone.

"I'm sorry," stammered Tony. "I am Tony Piccini. What can I do for you?"

"Anthony James Piccini," repeated the first deputy. "You are hereby served with an indictment of involuntary manslaughter for the death of one Meri Margaret Lawrence as well as a charge for the unlawful practice of dietetics. Here is the indictment."

As soon as those words were spoken and the document was handed to Tony those words seem to strike him as though he had been fired from a gun. Tony trembled more as he reached for the charging document and began to read it while desperately trying to comprehend its meaning.

CASE NO.:   2006CR9854

INDICTMENT FOR: INVOLUNTARY
MANSLAUGHTER, 1 CT.

[R.C. 2903.04 (B)

(FELONY)

THE STATE OF OHIO, FRANKLIN COUNTY, OHIO, of the Term commencing on January 2nd in the year of our Lord two thousand six.

The Jurors of the Grand Jury of the County of Franklin and State of Ohio, then and there duly impaneled, sworn and charged to inquire of and present all offenses whatever committed within the limits of said County, on their said oaths, in the name and by the authority of the State of Ohio, do find and present:

COUNT ONE

2903.04(B) - That **ANTHONY JAMES PICCINI** late of said County on or about the 16th day of May in the year of our Lord two thousand six, at the County of Franklin, aforesaid did as a proximate result of **ANTHONY JAMES PICCINI'S** commission of the misdemeanor of the unlawful practice of Dietetics (R.C. 4759.02) cause the death of another, Meri Margaret Lawrence in violation of Section 2903.04(B) of the Ohio Revised Code, contrary to the statute in such cause made and provided and against the peace and dignity of the State of Ohio.

COUNT TWO

<u>4759.02(A)</u> – That **ANTHONY JAMES PICCINI** late of said County on or about the 16th date of May in the year of our Lord two thousand six, at the County of Franklin, aforesaid did without authorization or license to do so, issued as provided by law, unlawfully practiced dietetics in violation of Section 4759.02(A) of the Ohio Revised Code, contrary to the statutes in such cause made and provided and against the peace and dignity of the State of Ohio.

James Urban, #00846375

Prosecuting Attorney

Franklin County

A True Bill:

Jonathan J. Privacio, Foreperson, Grand Jury

THE STATE OF OHIO, FRANKLIN COUNTY, ss.

I, Emmet S. Rohnsmith, Clerk of the Court of Common Pleas, in and for said County, do hereby certify that the within and foregoing is a full, true and correct copy of the original indictment, together with the endorsements thereon, now on file in my office.

WITNESS my hand and the seal of said Court at Columbus, Ohio this 7th Day of July, 2006.

Emmet S. Rohnsmith, Clerk

By Elizabeth Carl, Deputy

Sheriff's Return:

On July 10th, 2006, I delivered personally to the within named Anthony James Piccini a true and certified copy of this indictment, with all endorsements thereon.

Robert L. Hardman, Sheriff

By: Richard Prinz, Deputy Sheriff

As he tried to read the print on the indictment, waves of emotion flooded over him, virtually rattling him to the core.

As he read, the first deputy began to talk again. "Mr. Piccini, we need to come inside?" As he stated these words, both deputies began to move through the threshold. "We need to take you into custody and to transport you for booking at the jail. You should put on some shoes and grab a shirt. I would caution you that you are now under arrest."

Tony was shocked as the following words were delivered to him by the deputy from rote memory: "You have the right to remain silent. If you give up the right to remain silent, anything you say can and will be used against you in a court of law. You have the right to an attorney. If you desire an attorney and cannot afford one, an attorney will be obtained for you before police questioning."

Once the deputy was done delivering this rote message which he had undoubtedly delivered countless times before, he asked, "Mr. Piccini, do you understand these rights?"

Tony could barely take in enough air to even respond so that anyone could hear him. He was in utter shock and disbelief. No one had prepared him for this scenario. No one probably could.

The deputy asked again, "Do you understand your rights?"

By this time the other deputy was staring even more intensely at Tony who was finally able to deliver a feeble response, "Yes, I understand."

"Good. Put on your shoes. We're leaving."

With the formalities out of the way, Tony grabbed his sneakers and sat on the couch while he laced them up with both deputies standing over him – one on his left, one on his right. Tony had trouble tying the laces, as if he were trying to do it for the first time, like a child learning to do so as a prerequisite to going to kindergarten.

The moment Tony finish with his shoes, the second deputy began his own version of rote message delivery. "Stand up. Turn around. Put your hands behind your back."

As this deputy finished his delivery, Tony complied and felt cold steel clamped on both of his wrists which were soon too tightly bound each to the other. It was to say the least, an experience Tony would later wish had been left out of his repertoire of memories.

Once the handcuffs were on, the deputy grabbed Tony's left arm and began escorting him out of the house and to the patrol car.

"Wait," said Tony. "I need to lock up."

"We will lock up when we leave," said the second deputy.

"But," stammered Tony, "I don't have my keys."

"Too bad. You should have thought of that before you put your shoes on," replied the same deputy. "It's not my job to help you. I'm, here just to arrest you, secure you, take you in and have you booked."

"Wait a minute. I won't be able to get back in," said Tony, now regaining some of his pre-arrest composure. "I want to call a lawyer before we leave."

"Save it for later," said the first deputy now entering this part of the exchange for the first time. "You can ask the booking agent for the change to use a phone to call a lawyer. Good luck with that, by the way. Not sure how many decent criminal defense lawyers you can reach in any of their offices on a Friday night."

Both deputies then exchanged a knowing look and laughed. They knew Tony would reach no one on a Friday night. He would spend at least the weekend in jail before he could get a lawyer, face an arraignment on the charges against him, have bail set for his release and be released pending trial.

Tony would soon learn what these two deputies already knew. The criminal process was now under way and the timing of the service of the indictment on him was by design as it was for many others facing criminal charges. Service of many such indictments by deputies was often completed on a Friday night. The timing was set to ensure that the weekend would not be wasted on a recipient defendant who needed to sit in a jail cell for a while to contemplate the process and to reflect on what had happened but most importantly – to consider what would happen to them in the future.

That process would lead to the trial of the criminal case which Tony would face before the civil trial even began. Both cases were based on essentially the same facts and circumstances. However, one case was about money and the other was about potential punishment and to send a

DAVID L. HERBERT

message to others engaged in the same practices as Tony.

The unsettled nature of the criminal case pending against him was still Tony's major concern. That side of all of this legal entanglement was what kept Tony up at night. The decision in that aspect of all this litigation might well result in him being locked up in a cage like some animal with God knows who else and for who knows how long. If convicted and imprisoned, he would, of course, be set free someday. However, that would be preceded by the completion of another courtroom laden drama with the same basic cast of characters and with the same grief stricken husband and two young children who were now without their mother. That proceeding would lay the foundation for the rest of Tony's life. It was not just about money; it was really about his entire life, not only the past and the present, but what would become of him in the future.

The trial of Tony's criminal case resulted in a hung jury, one which resulted because the panel of jurors in that proceeding could not agree on a unanimous verdict as required in such a case. Unlike what was required in a civil trial, when a so-called "majority" decision was sufficient to render a verdict – 6 out of 8 jurors – really a seventy-five percent standard, a criminal case required all jurors – 12 in number - to agree on a verdict. Absent such a complete agreement, the jury would be considered "hung" or in other words unable to reach a verdict. When such a situation arises, no final disposition of a case occurs. As a result, a prosecutor, with the permission of a judge after a jury is unable to reach a verdict, may dismiss the charges or accept a plea bargain to a lesser charge or even retry the case.

The fact that Tony's criminal trial had resulted in a hung jury had been, at least in some respects, a relief to Tony. But the Prosecuting Attorney for Franklin County, James Urban, declared within the first few hours of that jury's discharge that Tony's criminal case would be retried. Tony had watched the prosecutor's expressed decision to retry him unfold during a news conference held in Columbus and televised on the Fox network the very night his criminal court jury was discharged. The press conference was orchestrated by Urban and held within hours of the jury's exit from the old Franklin County Courthouse, some 10 blocks south of the state capitol building in downtown Columbus.

The news conference had started with what Tony considered a cheap shot by the prosecutor, who some said could be Ohio's next Attorney General or even Governor of that great state. During the news conference, Urban spoke to the assembled press on the courthouse steps in what he considered the most earnest of tones.

Urban began with these words: "It is with serious and steadfast determination that I have decided to re-prosecute Anthony J. Piccini for the needless and untimely death of Meri Margaret Lawrence, a young and vibrant wife and mother of two small children whose life was tragically cut short by this defendant.

"Piccini was an unqualified and ill-prepared personal trainer whose lack of skill and judgment tragically led to and caused her death. His actions in counseling this young mother to ingest a variety of unproven and dangerous nutritional substances while pushing her to engage in ill-prescribed and ever demanding physical training caused her death. His recommendations to her to decrease and then stop taking the prescription medications provided to her by her physician in that doctor's efforts to control her high blood pressure were criminal in nature and need to be so found by a jury properly informed of all the facts and circumstances. Once that is done, this defendant needs to be removed from society before he can harm anyone else through his ill-conceived recipes for death.

"The jury, which was just discharged by Judge Smythe after they could not reach a unanimous verdict, was not given a complete picture of what happened. It is clear to me that Meri's death was directly and proximately caused by the actions of the defendant. These actions were permitted and allowed to occur because the fitness industry has refused and neglected to adequately regulate itself to ensure that trainers like Piccini provide competent and safe services to their clients.

"In conjunction with my announced decision today to again prosecute Mr. Piccini for his reprehensible and criminally negligent acts, I am asking the Ohio Senate Committee on Professions and Occupations to introduce legislation to establish mandatory licensing laws for all personal trainers practicing in this state. In my view, the industry needs to establish proper educational programs for these trainers and then the great state of Ohio needs to test and license them so that other needless injuries and deaths like this one might be avoided in the future.

"When we again prosecute Mr. Piccini for these acts, we intend to offer new testimony and to present additional experts from around Ohio and from across this nation to support that prosecution. I have no intention of allowing any segment of the fitness industry to circumvent our effort. While this great state licenses barbers, massage therapists, manicurists and even dog and cat groomers, we have no regulation of any kind for personal trainers or fitness service providers or, for that matter, any system in place to protect the public from the kind of devastating harm which took place in this case.

"We will move to have Mr. Piccini's retrial set for prosecution in the next 90 days. This time, for the re-prosecution, I intend to personally present the case to a new jury. I will not take any questions today but plan to meet with my trial staff to review the evidence available for this re-prosecution and to prepare to retry this case.

I hope no other Ohio family will have to see a newspaper obituary for their wife, husband, son or daughter whose death was caused by a so-called fitness professional. I hope the Lawrence family will be the last such family to go through such needless pain and grief, at least in this state. Good day."

A chill went through Tony's spine as he heard these words and saw the determination on the prosecutor's face. He could not believe the charges against him were to be retried. He didn't mean to harm Meri. She was his client, one of his friends. He was trying to help, not hurt her! How did all of this happen? Where did he go wrong? Why does this all engender such strong emotion – such seeming hatred for him and for what he did? He tried to help, not to hurt anyone.

However, every day, in nearly every newspaper, in essentially every city in America, death notices and obituaries are included and published in each such newspaper. Pictures of those who passed are almost always accompanied by typeset notes highlighting that person's life, family, friends and achievements. If the reader knows one of those listed within those pages, such accounts of a life lived can be very sad to read. What may be even sadder is that once these notices are so carefully written, the composition of which is agonized over and over by family members and then published, there will be more such notices printed in every newspaper, in every such city the next day and every day thereafter. It is never-ending. Most people hope that the hereafter will be the same - never-ending. Tony, of course, did not know.

CHAPTER 6

Despite the prosecutor's announcement to again prosecute Tony for Meri's death, Tony necessarily began to refocus on the civil case. That case had been set for trial to occur shortly after the initial criminal case was over.

The hope of essentially everyone involved in the civil case, except of course for Tony and his lawyers, had been that a guilty verdict would assist in getting the civil case settled. However, with a hung jury in the criminal prosecution, Tony and all the other parties in the civil case and their lawyers were forced to go forward.

In the criminal proceeding, Tony had been faced with the testimony provided by a number of experts and public employees called to testify by the State of Ohio. These experts included the police officer who arrived at FitAgain just in advance of the EMS unit; the EMS responders who arrived at FitAgain some minutes after Meri's collapse; the triage nurse who gathered Meri's vitals, or in this case, the lack thereof, when Meri arrived at the local emergency department at Columbus General Hospital; the physician who attempted to treat and revive her before he was forced to declare the inevitable; the coroner who had conducted the post-mortem autopsy on Meri; an exercise physiologist who was a professor at Kent State University; a representative of the Ohio Department of Dietetics; a personal trainer from Michigan who had founded the American Society of Professionally Certified Personal Trainers; and, Meri's personal physician.

Tony had sat at his assigned table and listened over the course of three days while an Assistant Prosecuting Attorney for Franklin County, Ohio introduced the testimony from these experts. All of it was presented in an effort to establish that Tony killed Meri because of his lack of training and proper certification.

The exercise physiologist and personal trainer provided significant testimony in this regard. Peter Grant, a PhD in exercise physiology and a professor at Kent State University, an institution known by some principally because of the May 1970 shootings of KSU students by Ohio National Guardsmen, seemed to be particularly effective for the state.

On direct questioning, Dr. Grant was asked by Jack Liberatore, the Assistant Prosecutor assigned to Tony's case, "Doctor, can you define the discipline of exercise physiology for us?"

"Yes, I can," replied the academician. "Exercise physiology is the study of how human beings respond to and function during the stress brought on by various levels of exercise or vigorous activity. It includes, in some respects, general responses of human bodily systems such as the respiratory system, in order words, the lungs; the circulatory system, including the heart and its arteries; the muscular system, including the muscles of a person and how they respond to various levels and functions of stress; bodily fluids such as waste products arising from cellular activity; oxygen saturation, or in other words the intake of oxygen and the exhalation of carbon dioxide; the calculation of time for recovery of the body and its systems after activity or work and other similar areas, all essentially related to how and why the body responds to exercise.

"How many years did it take you to become trained in this discipline?"

"I studied biology and anatomy as an undergraduate for four years, I then went on to study for another two years to secure a Master's Degree in exercise physiology and then after another two years of study, I ultimately earned my PhD in physiology. All told, it took 8 years for me to earn my PhD. Notwithstanding the time I devoted, I am still learning various aspects of this discipline. I take continuing education each year, I do research on various areas of exercise physiology that interest me and I advise anywhere from a dozen to 20 graduate students each year as they seek graduate training."

"You are presently on the academic staff at KSU then I take it?"

"Well, yes but I also help educate and train professionals who provide various fitness services to health and fitness facility members in the State of Ohio."

"Do you study particular areas of exercise physiology in your research activities?"

"Yes, I study maximum or near maximum workload or in other words exercise activity in humans, the impact of various breathing techniques or modalities on the human body during exercise, the impact of various drugs and other substances when taken during periods of exercise activity, weight loss and its impact on the human body during activity and certain other areas of interest."

Then the Assistant Prosecutor began to relate the professor's expertise to the case at hand.

"Do you know the Defendant Anthony Piccini?"

"No."

"Have you ever trained him or know of anyone who has?"

"No."

"Have you had an opportunity to review the statements from Mr. Piccini that were taken after Meri Margaret Lawrence collapsed at the FitAgain facility in Upper Arlington on May 16, 2006?"

"Yes, I have."

"And did you also review the records of the EMS responders who went to FitAgain after her collapse on that date?"

"Yes."

"And what else did you review about Meri's collapse on that date?"

"I was provided with the records from Columbus General Hospital as to the status of Mrs. Lawrence once she was transported to their facility.

I received the coroner's autopsy report. I looked at the records of FitAgain dealing with Mr. Piccini's provision of service to Mrs. Lawrence. I looked at some of Mr. Piccini's records at FitAgain, his employment application, his training while there, his evaluations by FitAgain's supervisors, his commission records, the time records associated with his provision of service. I also looked at his records from Kent State while he was a student there for a brief time."

"Anything else?"

"Not that I can think of."

"Based upon your education, training and expertise and based upon a reasonable degree of certainty existing within your profession as an exercise physiologist, did you have an opportunity to develop any conclusions related to Mr. Piccini's provision of personal training services to Mrs. Lawrence prior to her collapse and death?"

"Objection," said Walt Manos, Tony Piccini's criminal defense lawyer, as he rose to his feet to address Judge Smythe. "May we approach the bench?"

"Yes," responded Judge Smythe, who knew what was coming next. "Come on up."

On that request and invitation, Mr. Manos and Assistant Prosecuting Attorney Liberatore both approached the bench.

"Your Honor," began Manos, "this gentleman is certainly qualified to teach at one of Ohio's public institutions of higher learning, but he is not a personal trainer, he is not a physician, he is not a coroner and he is not a pharmacist. Based on the discovery documents which the prosecutor's office provided, it appears he is about to testify as to matters covering all of these areas. I can't simply sit here and allow some unqualified so called "super expert" to testify in all these areas especially when he has no expertise in those areas."

Turning to Mr. Liberatore, Judge Smythe said simply, "Just respond."

"Well, your Honor, this witness is not going to testify as to cause of death. The coroner will do that. This witness teaches personal trainers and as such, he is intimately familiar with what they do, their appropriate and permissible scope of practice and on the other hand, what personal trainers are not to do. He has been doing so for many years. He knows the interrelationship of various nutritional supplements and medications and their effect on the human body and how exercise, particularly strenuous exercise, can be impacted by such substances. He is eminently qualified to testify on those topics."

"Mr. Manos," said Judge Smythe, "I have heard this witness' qualifications and his testimony about the research he does. I won't allow him to testify as to anything in this case which should be reserved for medical testimony alone. But in my view, he appears to be eminently qualified to provide the testimony Mr. Liberatore is talking about. I will allow you a continuing objection to his testimony and exceptions so you don't need to continue making objections during the witness' testimony unless you feel that is necessary, given what Mr. Liberatore may ask of the witness. Is that satisfactory for you?"

"Well Judge, it's not what I had in mind, but I don't want to alienate the jury by constant objections which you will overrule. That will make me seem like I am either not competent because I don't know the law or that I'm just trying to hide evidence. As a consequence, unless you will reconsider that issue, I will take you up on the continuing objection."

"Well that's where we are gentlemen" said Judge Smythe. "Let's move forward."

As Manos turned to walk back to the defense table, he looked at Tony who seemed to be oblivious to what was happening. Time would tell if he would ever really get it.

As Liberatore returned to his questioning, he continued with Dr. Grant, "Doctor, do you remember my last question?"

"It would be helpful if you repeated it."

"Based upon your education, training and expertise and based upon a reasonable degree of certainty existing within your profession as an exercise physiologist, did you have an opportunity to develop any conclusions related to Mr. Piccini's provision of personal training services to Mrs. Lawrence prior to her collapse and death?"

"Yes, I did." replied Dr. Grant.

"Let's turn to the first issue, Mr. Piccini's training and certification as a personal trainer. I'm going to ask you a series of questions as the law requires me to do about various matters. I want you to base all your responses on your background, training, education and expertise and provide all your answers to a degree of certainty in your profession without me repeating all of that each time I ask you a question – can you do that?"

"Yes."

"Given that statement and agreement, do you have an opinion as to the quality of Mr. Piccini's training and certification as a personal trainer."

"Yes, I do."

"What is that opinion?"

"Mr. Piccini was allegedly trained by FitAgain through its in-house program. It lasted only a few hours. It contained no training on screening of participants to make sure they did not need to be examined or seen by a physician before engaging in an exercise program or at any time during the program."

Dr. Grant continued, "It contained no training on exercise prescription – the selection of what exercise would be appropriate for the client, given the client's medical and physical condition. It contained no training in the implementation, instruction or supervision of client exercises. It contained no training in breathing techniques. It contained no training in the client's prescription of exercise stress or when a client gets into trouble during activity. It contained no instruction in the appropriate levels of exercise intensity or length of activity. It did not provide training in emergency response or automated external defibrillator use, nor did it even provide instruction in how to carry out an emergency response plan. Lastly, it contained no instruction as to the effects of medication or nutritional supplements on exercise or performance.

Dr. Grant continued, "Based upon these facts, it is my opinion to a reasonable degree of certainty existing in my profession that Mr. Piccini was not properly trained and not properly certified as a personal trainer. He was certainly not competent to provide service in this area of human activity."

"Do you have an opinion as to Mr. Piccini's adherence to the standard of care for a personal trainer providing such service in the State of Ohio and in the United States?

"Yes, I do."

"What is that opinion?"

"Mr. Piccini clearly did not adhere to the required standard of care for the provision of personal training services to Mrs. Lawrence."

"In what respects?" asked Liberatore.

"First, given her pre-activity physical condition, her weight, her blood pressure, her use of tobacco and alcohol and her overall history, she should have been referred to and been examined by a physician for the establishment of the parameters within which defined exercise activity could be safely carried out.

Dr. Grant continued, "Secondly, she should not have been pushed as hard as Mr. Piccini pushed her to lose weight through exercise activity and through his recommendations to her to reduce her blood pressure control medication while recommending that she ingest ephedra laced supplements to allegedly speed up her metabolism. In fact, those recommendations led to an increase in her blood pressure and ultimately led to the stroke she suffered during the strenuous exercise activity imposed upon her at Mr. Piccini's insistence and under his guidance.

Thirdly, Mr. Piccini's failure to instruct Mrs. Lawrence in proper breathing techniques during her lifting activities was substandard. It appears she held her breath during those activities as she lifted weights. The failure to control her breathing, to perform what is called the Valsalva Maneuver, placed further pressure on her respiratory system which also contributed to a further spike in her blood pressure which led to the stroke which she suffered."

"What, Dr., is the Valsalva Maneuver?" asked the Assistant Prosecutor.

"In any lifting activity, particularly any lifting activity of the arms and legs against significant weight, there is a tendency of most all folks to hold their breath while pushing against the weight. This leads to a temporary increase in blood pressure during the lift as the body responds to the stress. The Valsalva Maneuver is a breathing technique that all personal trainers absolutely must learn where they teach their clients to breathe during the lifting phase of the activity. If the technique is applied and applied correctly, there will be no corresponding increase in blood pressure during lifting. However, that is not what happened with Mrs. Lawrence. Mr. Piccini's lack of instruction in the proper breathing technique, coupled with the decrease in her blood pressure medication as recommended and directed by Mr. Piccini to her as well as her ingestion of ephedra laced supplements which spiked her blood pressure, proximately lead to her death."

With that last statement, Tony's lawyer, Walt Manos, was on his feet and barking an objection to the testimony provided by Dr. Grant, which Manos considered to be beyond Grant's expertise.

"Mr. Manos," replied Judge Smythe, "I understand your objection but given the prior ruling and the stated qualifications of this witness, I will allow the testimony to remain unless the coroner should contradict anything just said during the coroner's testimony."

Having done what was required, Manos simply said, "Note my exceptions for the record." And sat down. Tony's fate was moving in the wrong direction at least at the moment. While Manos hoped Dr. Grant's testimony was over, Liberatore continued.

"Doctor, what can you opine about the certification received by Mr. Piccini from FitAgain based upon the same standard we have previously established for your answers?"

"Frankly, Mr. Liberatore, the certification received by Mr. Piccini was a joke. Since there is no State of Ohio requirement that personal trainers in this state be licensed or even regulated, the only thing that anyone who uses personal training services can assume that he or she is receiving qualified services through the trainer's formal education and/or proper accredited certification provided by an agency that is recognized by a governmental agency such as the United States Department of Education. The so-called certification received by Mr. Piccini from the FitAgain Corporation was grossly inadequate and inappropriate."

"Dr. Grant, are you being paid to be an expert here today - paid to provide testimony on behalf of the State of Ohio?"

"I am here voluntarily and without charge. I volunteered to provide this testimony because of the facts and circumstances of this case. No charge and no bias for either party. I'm here to testify on the facts of this case as those facts are presented."

While Grant's statement was true in part, he was testifying so he could make a name for himself as an expert witness. Once that was done, he was hoping the money would roll in. As any litigator knows, all it takes to secure the services of an expert witness on any side of virtually any topic is money.

Based upon Grant's rehearsed response, Liberatore turned, looked to Walt Manos and clearly stated, "I think that's enough from this witness. The defense may examine."

Liberatore felt very good about this testimony from Dr. Grant. It had flowed well and without the need to pry or cajole the testimony out of him. Liberatore was sure he would stand up to any rigorous questioning from Manos.

Manos of course thought differently.

Walt Manos stood up slowly, walked to the podium but faced the jury while he asked the academician the final questions: "Should I address you as doctor even though you don't have a medical degree or a license, or as a pharmacist even though you don't have a degree or a license to practice as such, or even as a personal trainer since you don't have a license or even a certification to do so?"

Dr. Grant, frustrated with this attack, worked hard to suppress his anger and desire to fight back, and verbally retaliate against his questioner. Grant responded as a matter-of-factly as he could and said "However you wish to address me is fine with me. Any title you give me or delete for me won't impact what I say or the degrees I have earned."

"All right" responded Manos, "I will call you Professor Grant, since you teach what others actually do in the real world – perhaps that's best."

Manos continued, "Am I to understand Professor Grant that you teach undergraduate students at KSU but you are not a full professor there at this time, is that correct?"

"Not yet, I haven't been there long enough."

"Well Professor Grant, is it your testimony that there is some sort of a specific number of years in an academic setting before you become a full professor?"

"There is no hard and fast rule on that issue."

"You have been at Kent for four years have you not?"

"I have" quickly replied Grant.

"During that time how many times have you tried to become a full professor?" asked Manos.

"Twice" replied Grant.

"Is it like baseball where you get three strikes and you're out?"

"I'm not certain about that since I have five years to achieve a full professorship at Kent."

"So" questioned Manos, "You have one more strike to go before you either make it or not, is that right?"

"I suppose you could say that."

Moving on to another question, Manos asked, "Do you actually engage in hands-on teaching of trainers at Kent, where you show them what to do and actually evaluate their performances while they engage in leadership activities with their clients?"

"There is no need to do so since we use computer simulated evaluations."

Manos then said "So it's your testimony that you use only computers to judge student performance in real life exercise activities with clients?"

"It is what we do."

Sensing the need to close the door on the issue, Manos, while looking directly at Juror Number 8, a martial arts instructor by trade, asked, "Is that a little like a driver's education teacher teaching a student how to drive through computer simulation, or teaching an athlete how to tackle in football by drawing on a blackboard, or teaching a physician how to perform surgery by watching a film?"

"No" replied Professor Grant, "it's not the same."

"I guess we will let the jury decide that issue," replied Manos.

Upon that comment, Liberatore was on his feet, "I object, that's not even a question."

Manos immediately replied, "No problem, I will withdraw the question."

Manos then moved on.

"Professor Grant, did you ever have the chance to actually watch

Tony attempt to help Meri Margaret Lawrence lose weight, exercise or become fitter?"

"No, as you know, I never did."

"So then, you only are judging what Tony did by what others said about him and what they said about his services, is that correct?"

"I never saw him provide services to the decedent."

"Did you then ever talk to Mrs. Lawrence about Tony's services?"

"No, I never did."

"So your testimony is at best based upon second, third or even fourth hand information, correct?"

"It is based upon what the various reports showed."

"How do you know Professor, if what was reported is accurate and true?"

"I am assuming it was true, after all, the police completed that information."

"And Professor, are you testifying that the police are always right?" As Manos asked that question, he looked directly at Juror No. 3, an investigator who worked primarily for criminal defense attorneys in a county adjacent to Franklin County but who lived in Columbus. Obviously, Manos reasoned, he would know how often police stretched the truth or even fabricated what was needed to make a case.

Professor Grant replied, "I am assuming so here in this case."

"So if I am asked about your testimony, you never talked to my client, never watched him provide service to Mrs. Lawrence, or for that matter anyone else and you are basing your testimony only on what others, mainly the police, are telling you, is that correct Professor?"

"I am basing my testimony on the information I was given."

"I need to correct myself for a minute Professor Grant, I should really be calling you Assistant Professor Grant, should I not, because that is your current title?"

"It is."

"If that is correct Assistant Professor Grant, who do you assist?"

"I assist my students," replied Grant, "It's only a title."

"Are there any full professors in your department?"

"Yes there are."

"Are they of a higher rank than you?"

"Yes."

"Did any of them review your work or testimony in this case?"

"No."

"If no one reviewed what you say here like you reviewed what others said to form your own opinions, how do we know anything you say is correct?"

Liberatore was on his feet again objecting: "Mr. Manos is arguing with the witness."

Manos replied, "I'll withdraw the question, it appears that that last question will ultimately be answered."

Upon that note Manos stopped his questioning and said to the judge "I've had enough of this witness your honor."

Manos hoped he had succeeded in raising issues of doubt with at least two jurors, No. 3 and No. 8, both of whom should view Assistant Professor Grant's testimony from a perspective where his testimony would be much less than absolute.

While a host of other lay witnesses and experts testified against Tony, Manos was content to chip away at various segments of their testimony. The trial lasted four days and with each witness the ebb and flow of the testimony went both ways. Some weighed in favor of the prosecution, others in favor of the defense.

Since the vast majority of all civil and criminal cases are resolved in settlements or plea bargains, perhaps those that are tried represent the type where the facts are more divided than the others that are resolved without trial.

Liberatore was sure he had made major points for the State of

Ohio. Manos was equally sure he had cast more than reasonable doubt in favor of Tony's acquittal. The process however was not scientific. While a unanimous jury verdict was required for a conviction or an acquittal, a lone juror could cause a hung jury and a mistrial. What would happen in Tony's case remained to be seen.

Ultimately, the criminal case against Tony resulted in a hung jury since the jurors could not agree upon a unanimous outcome. That meant the civil case would proceed against Tony and the other defendants without the criminal case verdict having any impact on the civil case at all.

Once the civil case moved forward and the evidence concluded, Tony waited for the verdict. He reflected on what had transpired during this part of his courtroom experience, at least in part. While the lawyer for Meri's family, Frank LaPorte, had told the jury during his closing argument in the wrongful death case that the life Tony had helped extinguish could not be measured in any dollar and cents award, he suggested that the jury award $42 million to the family. That figure was fully and meticulously supported by the economist LaPorte brought in to testify on the subject of Meri Margaret Lawrence's value as a fashion executive and perhaps most importantly, as a wife and mother. The figure so suggested was supposedly based upon the so-called earning ability and capacity of Tony's now dead client. All of this had been outlined to the jurors – the "Joes" – by LaPorte with elegant verbiage and intonation.

Tony believed that none of the jurors had ever even thought of such numbers in their everyday lives, except in some of their weekly dreams of winning the state lottery, a chance of one in millions. It seemed certain, at least to Tony, that the chances of a jury awarding a verdict nearing or matching the number suggested by LaPorte and his economist was far better for Meri's family than for any of the individual juror's chances of winning the state lottery.

It was Tony's hope that the dollars awarded, if any, against him would be covered by insurance. The insurance company which insured Tony' professional activities disputed the applicability of the insurance coverage available to Tony based upon the circumstances surrounding Meri's death. Notwithstanding that issue, the first million dollars of any potential award against Tony, at least theoretically, could be paid by the insurance Tony had secured and paid for each year while he was a personal trainer. However, the amount sought by Meri's family was so large and Tony's assets so small that Tony's insurance coverage really didn't matter since it was not enough by itself to resolve the case. Much more money would be needed and Tony didn't have any more. The other defendants did have more insurance coverage, but all of them were pointing fingers of blame at Tony and away from each other. The unsettled nature of the criminal case pending against him was still Tony's major concern.

During the civil trial, Tony's thoughts wandered. He sat at one of the long tables placed in the courtroom in front of the judge. Tony was restricted by courtroom custom to sitting at the "defense table." The defense table was the farthest table in distance from the jury. The jury was also placed in a particular spot in the courtroom. Again set by custom and tradition, that spot was the so-called jury box.

As to his placement in the courtroom, Tony could not believe he should be the one most distant from the jury and the jury box – from those who would determine his fate. He also had the same position during the trial in his criminal case since he was placed the farthest from those whose verdict would set in motion a judge's sentencing decision that would either imprison him or set him free.

Tony's lawyer explained to him that the "order" of things in the courtroom was how it had always been. The party who went first in either proceeding – the one who also had the so-called burden of proof – was the closest in physical distance to the jurors.

Tony's lawyer told him, "The plaintiff in a civil case, as well as the prosecutor in a criminal case, sat at the table closest to the jury box since each such party had the burden of proof."

All Tony could say is, "Bullshit. This is all set up to disfavor me." It seemed to Tony, however, that he should be the one closest to those who would judge him since he had the most to lose.

Tony thought the jurors in both cases should get to see him up close and personal. If he was given a chance, a real chance, they would surely like him as all of his clients, Meri included, had always liked him – especially the women on the jury.

He thought that if the jurors could see him in that way, he would have a better chance at a favorable verdict in both cases. Surely they would understand that he was a decent human being, someone who was trying to help his clients, not to hurt them. Perhaps the women jurors would also find him attractive as most women did. Surely such a feeling would help him along the process as it had always done before.

Women had always liked Tony. When he was in high school, he was on the gymnastics and swim teams and always prided himself on his appearance both with and without his swimsuit or gymnastics shorts on.

Tony loved the attention he got and worked hard at developing his return of certain looks he always got from his female admirers. Those looks came not only from the girls in his class but also from their mothers, his female teachers and even from the women in the stands who attended his athletic events.

One particular woman he came to know during his last semester of high school had begun to share a quest for his attention with her daughter, Sheri, who was then Tony's girlfriend. Much to the disappointment of Tony's father, Tony would often go across town to see the girl as well as her mother as it later turned out. When Tony began to realize that he could have the undivided attention of an experienced and very well endowed woman as opposed to an inexperienced, not yet as well-endowed and still somewhat awkward teenager, his choice of a partner seemed rather clear.

Tony went over one day after school to see the girl – or at least he was prepared to say so. As he knocked on her door, Sheri's mother, Suzanne, a relatively recent divorcee, answered the knock on the door and greeted Tony with an affectionate smile and with what he perceived as a hungry smirk.

Suzanne said, "Tony, Sheri's not here. She went shopping with some of her friends at the last minute. I think they will be out until sometime after dinner. They were supposed to have a bite to eat and then go see a show."

Tony had known what Sheri had planned but acted as though he did not.

"It's okay; I just stopped by to say hello." Tony stopped and gazed at Suzanne and said, "Looks like you're working out." As he made the statement, he admired her supple and attractive body clothed in a tight and sheer aerobics outfit. His gaze lingered for a second or two on her full and voluptuous breasts.

Obviously, Tony thought, she was in the midst of working out since she not only looked the part but he also heard the aerobics music on the television's sound system in the background, still humming with a distinctive Latin beat. The sight of her, the sound of the music and the overall setting stirred something within him and encouraged him to act.

Suzanne had indeed been working out and was gleaming and glistening with a hint of perspiration which merged with a distracting and alluring blend of perfume. The brand was Mon Cher, Tony thought. She smiled when she noticed Tony's gaze and asked him to come in.

"I need someone to watch me – to tell me if what I am doing is working. Would you mind? Come on in and see what I can do," she said with a smile.

Tony hesitated for a moment – but just for effect. Any thought of leaving the presence of this beautiful woman was out of the question.

"I can help. I've probably done routines like this before myself. I've certainly seen others do them. Maybe I can give you some pointers."

What he was really looking for was pointers from Sheri's mother in the timeless sport of carnal knowledge. He was hoping he would show her what he could do for her while she showed him the ropes!

Tony walked past her outstretched arm pointing the way through the door and in toward the music. As he did so, his left bicep slightly, ever so slightly, brushed across Suzanne's protruding right breast. He perceived, or at least thought he perceived, an outreaching and erect right nipple, which at the same moment he touched it caused an immediate and responsive reaction in him. As he moved next to her and through the door, he wondered what he could possibly teach her.

That first encounter with someone who sought his athletic attributes in an environment different from that offered by high school sports or even by the young girls who watched him as classmates, stimulated and tantalized him. He looked forward to later passing on to others what he learned from Suzanne.

He was a quick learn for Suzanne. Perhaps too quick. But he stayed with her and enjoyed her company as well as that of her daughter, Sheri, long enough to become a devoted subject of Suzanne's instruction. He was able in fact to even pass on some of what he learned from Suzanne to Sheri.

Tony looked forward to being on both sides of this kind of teacher-pupil experience and the reaping of repeated rewards from his efforts. That feeling would stay with him for many years, while he worked with dozens and dozens of different clients. Help and be rewarded. Learn and teach. Offer attention and enthusiasm and receive benefits. Smile and wink – be appreciated. Give attention and reap the enthusiastic joys of life often from those in need of attention themselves. Give compliments and receive stimulation and release. Give and get. In the work setting, the feeling changed somewhat and became money for pleasure. Cents for sensations. Tips for tantalization. On and on. It was a great life for Tony while it lasted. At least he thought so.

Tony's thoughts returned to his litigation. In the trial of his civil case, he trusted his fate to the defense lawyer provided to him by his insurance company or he thought in retrospect, the one provided to him through the insurance company which really had been selected by his employer. The FIT PROS Insurance Company of North America had in fact been selected by the CEO of the financial holding company of FitAgain, namely the FitAgain Corporation of the United States. FitAgain in turn owned the facility where Tony was formally designated as a certified personal trainer. He was not classified by FitAgain as an employee of FitAgain, as they repeatedly said during the court trial – but as an independent contractor.

In reality, Tony was selected, not just hired, because he was good with the girls. He was also one who could show some biceps, pecs and glutes and one who could conjure up some smiles and giggles along with client signatures on personal training contracts for 20 sessions at $150 per hour every few weeks. The rates could change to a potentially lower hourly amount if the client referred other budding women to his personal, but so-called independent services at the club.

Tony always used the club's facilities and their equipment, forms, contracts and methods of operation to service those in his charge. He was good at the service and at providing attention to his clients. He believed he was very good at his own form of fitness leadership and in providing certain "other" services, all designed to meet the needs of those in his care. He looked and acted the part and knew what to say and what to do – all while promoting his own well-being and that of the club. He never let his clients go unsatisfied in any respect nor in the provision of any service, personal or otherwise.

Tony's independent contractor agreement with FitAgain was said by all of FitAgain's trainers to be "ironclad." In fact, he had been told that once he signed his name, Anthony Piccini, to the bottom line of their agreement it would enable him to earn $2,000 per week – more than $100,000 per year – all the time while he was dealing with wealthy, sometimes young but often middle-aged women in need of his personal attention, one-on-one. That's why they called it personal. Personal in time. Personal in service.

Tony provided personal instruction in technique, exercise methods and even touch. What to eat, when to eat it, what to take in the form of supplements, even how to breathe or at least he thought so.

Tony knew that more money could be made on top of his set hourly rates as established by FitAgain for his services. Those additional earnings would come from tips graciously and repeatedly provided by his clients and through commissions earned on the sale of related services and products. These latter items included vitamins, supplements, energy drinks and special waters not to mention clothing, exercise balls, video tapes and a host of other products. All of those products now on the shelves or soon to be placed there were on the horizon at both FitAgain and elsewhere.

Within a little less than ten years of work and a few well-earned tips, together with the company provided commissions to be earned from a network of health care product lines, masseuses, clothing designers and others, he would earn a nice living. If only for the potential downside that he now faced . . .

CHAPTER 7

In New York City, some 485 miles north and east of Columbus, Ohio, Mark Trudeau, the CEO of the holding corporation which owned FitAgain, emerged from a meeting. Along with Tony Piccini, FitAgain was also a target defendant in the Columbus, Ohio <u>Lawrence v. Piccini</u> civil litigation. Trudeau had been in conference with his marketing gurus, two of the company's lawyers and their paralegals, as well as his personal assistant and secretary, Kathy Casey.

He had been at it all morning and was ready to workout at a nearby hotel with a vibrant and vivacious young lady named Belinda Ross. Belinda had sold him on a liability insurance plan offered by her company, the Fit Pros Insurance Company of North America. FitAgain marketed and provided the plan and its insurance coverage to its so-called independent contractor personal fitness trainers.

It was a lucrative arrangement for Trudeau. The trainers got the liability insurance "opportunity" as part of their membership benefit in the USA - Personal Trainers Association, the USA-PTA. The USA-PTA was a non-profit organization Trudeau formed for fitness professionals like Tony Piccini and many others. It was managed by a Board of Trustees, all of whom were selected by Trudeau and each of whom received an honorarium for serving on the Board. Moreover, each of them had all of their related corporate expenses paid for by that entity. Those expenses included a variety of perks including travel, entertainment, per diems, meeting fees, insurance and a host of other benefits.

The USA-PTA was a 501(C)(3) organization established under the United States Tax Code as administered by the Internal Revenue Service. As such a non-profit organization, it paid no income tax to the federal government. Moreover, donations made to the organization were tax deductible by donors. In addition to donations, its membership dues and the fees generated from the educational offerings provided to individual trainers sustained the organization. Trudeau and a few others in the group received six-figure salaries and a host of benefits from the USA-PTA, even more than the other Trustees. Trudeau was paid $340,200 per year for his service to the organization. He also received a $40,000 expense account and a $50,000 contribution to his 401k. Not bad for minimal work especially from a non-profit.

Another of Trudeau's companies, a for profit corporation, "trained and certified" personal trainers. It was named the World Personal Training Academy or the WPTA for short. Once personal trainers enrolled and were prepared by the WPTA, they then took a written and practical examination to become certified and thus "eligible" for membership in the USA-PTA. After they were so trained and certified, these trainers were also then "allowed" to purchase Belinda's liability insurance products. However, some trainers like Tony who worked in FitAgain's clubs could also be "trained" and "certified" internally by FitAgain. It was less costly for FitAgain to do so and the process also benefited Trudeau by keeping costs down at FitAgain. Once the FitAgain internal training and certification process was completed, the trainers then also became eligible for USA-PTA membership and its liability insurance coverage.

Belinda had worked a steady 14 months to get the USA-PTA's endorsement for her liability insurance products. In turn, she arranged an indirect "payback" to the USA-PTA of a portion of the insurance premium proceeds received by her company from insured trainers. Those payments were to be used to further the education, as well as the social and professional endeavors of its members. She also arranged for a number of educational grants to be paid by her company to Trudeau's for-profit entity, the WPTA. After deducting its administrative and other "handling" costs, a portion of those grants were used to provide scholarships to WPTA standouts. It was a nice arrangement for all concerned.

All of this effort was done under the banner of getting an ever growing segment of the American population to get off their fat duffs and engage in exercise activity. The movement was admirable in some respects and designed to get the populace to take some responsibility for their increasing susceptibility to various disease processes brought on by their inactivity and related obesity. Inactivity and obesity often brought about what some physicians liked to call the "metabolic syndrome." This syndrome included obesity, high blood pressure, high total cholesterol, especially high LDL levels ("bad" cholesterol) and low HDL numbers ("good" cholesterol), high triglycerides and frequently, Diabetes Type II, also called adult onset diabetes.

One of Mark Trudeau's favorite sayings to characterize this growing metabolic syndrome which so many Americans frequently brought onto themselves was "diabesity." The characterization represented one of the ways he could use to promote FitAgain services and to get people into his clubs to buy the products and services he sold in those facilities. FitAgain's personal training services like those offered in Upper Arlington, Ohio and in other similar facilities all across the United States and elsewhere, were one of the most profitable centers of all of FitAgain's client services.

Trudeau had also obtained personal benefit from Belinda's efforts and not just in bed. Not in the form of insurance premium sharing or direct kick-back payments for the placement of the insurance business which the law clearly forbade, but by way of donations and other financial incentives provided to the USA-PTA which he enjoyed individually through the USA-PTA. Her efforts also benefited his growing health club facility business and the training academy – the WPTA – from which he and his holding company clearly benefited.

The donations to the USA-PTA and the scholarships, loans and outright grants provided to those students seeking training and certification through the Academy were one of the life bloods of the WPTA as well as the USA-PTA. FitAgain and Trudeau obviously benefited from what could otherwise be termed altruistic actions. However those personal benefits were overshadowed by the corporate structures which he had developed to protect himself from "too much" personal exposure and potential examination by regulators, the media and the IRS.

Trudeau's personal benefits from all of these affiliations also came to him through increases in the value of the stock he held in FitAgain's holding company and in the WPTA. But he also received perks and benefits from all of the companies. These benefits included stock options in the profit corporations, retirement programs and non-qualified retirement benefits in all the companies, travel allowances, consulting and speaking fees and a plethora of other perks which only those "in the know" get to enjoy personally. His enjoyment of Belinda's physical charms and attributes in a variety of venues was merely icing on the cake.

Mark Trudeau's thoughts of an afternoon of delight, as well as his continuing vision of personal and financial satisfaction brought forth by this young insurance executive were soon interrupted as he stepped out of his Manhattan conference room. At that moment, one of his staff members, Kathy Casey, stopped him. Trudeau had assigned her to watch the Tony Piccini civil trial in which Mark's company, FitAgain, was named as a defendant. Unlike the insurance company defense provided to Tony, FitAgain was insured and its defense was provided by the American Standard Fitness Insurance Company.

All FitAgain had in coverage was $10 million - $5 million from the primary insurance provided by American Standard and $5 million for the excess coverage. This "extra" insurance coverage went into play to cover any lawsuit seeking in excess of $5 million dollars and which resulted in a judgment or settlement over that amount. The extra or excess insurance was provided by the company's excess liability insurance carrier, the Fitness Insurance Company of North America. That excess insurance coverage could be exposed to cover any potential verdict in excess of $5 million but under $10 million because the Lawrence wrongful death case sought to recover $42 million in its prayer for damages made in the case. If the truth were known, FitAgain's exposure from what could happen in the Lawrence v. Piccini case was for much more than either its base or excess insurance coverages.

"Mr. Trudeau," Kathy, his trusted personal assistant said as he emerged from his conference room, "the jury on Tony Piccini's case is still out. As you know, this is their third day without a verdict. The judge, his Honor Charles Davis, has our lawyer and all the other attorneys in his chambers. The judge is trying to beat a settlement agreement out of them. I thought you should know."

"What the hell does he keep pressing us for? Doesn't he know that Piccini was off on his own with that young lady who was his client, not ours. That we knew nothing of what he was doing. She was a member of our club. That's it. She got her services from Piccini, not from us."

Trudeau said it loud enough so the others could hear but then whispered to Kathy, "What do you think will come of Davis' efforts? Didn't we squarely put the blame on Piccini?"

She responded, "I'm not sure what's going on, sir. This latest round of pressure was brought on by the jurors' most recent question to the judge. They asked him if they could find against some of the defendants but not all of them. They gave no indication as to which defendants they were considering to be responsible. I'm not sure what to make of it all. But it's 4 o'clock there – just like here – and the judge needs to answer this question soon or make the parties settle the case."

Trudeau contemplated Kathy's statement and in turn wished Piccini's criminal trial had proceeded with more dispatch and had not resulted in a hung jury. If Piccini had been convicted, evidence of that conviction could have been introduced in the civil case to help place the blame on Piccini and Piccini alone. If that blame had been placed just on Piccini, then FitAgain would be out of any potential liability. Too bad for FitAgain and Trudeau.

Six months earlier, Tony Piccini had sat in another courtroom in Columbus, Ohio. On that occasion, he was in the Franklin County Court of Common Pleas Criminal Courtroom 6A. He was then extremely worried about his fate and what had led him into Judge Lee Smythe's criminal courtroom facing a potential manslaughter conviction, as well as an unauthorized practice of dietetics charge after the death of his young client. Meri Margaret Lawrence had died while in his "personal" care. However, the backdrop to both the civil and the criminal case had been written long before he sat in criminal courtroom 6A waiting for a verdict.

CHAPTER 8

By early January, 2006, Meri Margaret Lawrence had decided that she had enough – enough of the stares and enough of the whispers she overheard in bits and pieces. She was sick of all the comments made behind her back. Despite their subdued nature, she clearly heard some of these remarks and hated all of them.

She had by then delivered her second child, a beautiful little boy with fair skin, curly blond hair, blue eyes and a smile that would sway the sternest of onlookers. This child, Chase Andrew Lawrence or "CAL," as she and others would come to call him, had been born near Christmas in the year 2005. He was born after a pregnancy which had been highlighted by Meri's frequent binges on pizza, chocolate chip cookies, ice cream and more.

Her pregnancy fueled a variety of never-ending cravings which were all duly fulfilled with chocolate covered peanut butter cups, thick wedges of carrot cake and slice after slice of pound cake. Those slices of pound cake were supercharged by Meri. She dropped each slice into a toaster to slightly brown the outsides of each piece before she coated them with gobs of butter. Once so prepared she wolfed them down each morning while she rubbed her ever expanding abdomen filled, she envisioned, with pure love and joy.

On most of these mornings, Meri purposefully forgot to look into the full-length mirror in her bedroom to view the look that those coming upon her from behind would see. Instead, she enjoyed her favorite pregnant pastime – eating. As her mid-section grew with young Chase's life, so did her behind which would need considerable attention if she were ever again to pour it into a size 3, 2 or, God willing, a size 1 outfit.

When Chase was born, she vowed to Ben, her husband of six years, that she would workout with a vengeance to trim her pound cake thighs and butt to beat both of them back into shape. She promised him that her work as a fashion consultant to one of the country's foremost women's stores, "Flair," based almost unbelievably in the middle of Ohio, would take second fiddle to her desire, her utter need, to get back into shape.

She pledged to Ben, during her ten hours of Chase delivery time, "Ben, I will do whatever it takes to get back into my clothes." And to remind Ben of his enabling activity during her pregnancy she told him in between her contractions and pants, "If you ever bring another piece of pound cake into our house I will kill you for sure."

She also told him if Kimmy, her first-born, needed any sweets as a treat, "You can take Kimmy out and give them to her before I get home from work or after you pick her up from daycare but before you bring her home." She realized she had to do something to return to her pre-Chase clothes size. She also knew she had to return to the stature of the office she held at "Flair" before her pregnancy. She knew she had to do something drastic to avert the ugly stares at her own expanded derriere as well as the whispers behind her back.

Meri's prior years of high school cheerleading and gymnastics would prepare her for the effort and the workouts she needed as soon as Chase was ready for her to go back to work. In the meantime, she would enjoy Chase's frequent smiles and the precious post-birth time she would share with him.

Those smiles from this beautiful little boy would also be shared with a host of waiting friends and most importantly, Chase's grandparents, who as to this latter foursome, were enjoying their first grandson. They had eagerly awaited the birth of Ben and Meri's first child, Kimmy, but Chase would be the first male grandchild for this group, and his arrival was much anticipated.

Meri knew she would do what needed to be done to get back into shape and soon. However, she did not know nor anticipate the accompanying rise in her blood pressure that Chase's birth had put on her circulatory system and heart. While a certain susceptibility to some adverse cardiovascular conditions ran in her family, she didn't think it would ever impact her, even after she had taken up cigarette smoking some years before. Even though Meri quit smoking before Kimmy's birth, she fell back into the habit after Kimmy was born. While she had taken up the habit again she quit once she became pregnant with Chase. Little did she consider the addicting nature of the nicotine and the host of other chemicals emanating from the smoke of cigarettes – all to ease the tension from the fourteen hour days she logged in at work in the design and marketing of women's clothing and related retail sales. Smoking was not good for her or her blood pressure. The adverse impact of the smoking could creep up on her, worsen her pre-existing susceptibility to hypertension and surely could contribute to what might later affect her well-being.

Ben had been supportive of Meri's personal and work-related needs both during and after Chase's birth. He recognized the stress she was under and her need to release it. But his own character and upbringing didn't allow room for his participation in some of Meri's bad habits.

Once Meri had initially kicked the cigarette habit, he had been pleased, very pleased indeed, even taking her on an early Spring 2005 trip to Paris, France. Chase had been conceived there in a night highlighted by their joint frenzy over a nineteen-year-old bottle of French merlot, fine escargot and decadently delicate pastries. All of this was enjoyed by them atop a 600 thread count Egyptian sheet overlaid with an identical top sheet folded neatly upon a custom bed, just inside double glass doors overlooking the Eiffel Tower. The Tower had been illuminated that night just as it had been on countless other nights by hundreds of lights oriented upward from inside the Tower, illuminating it internally – in to out. That trip and that night in particular provided an event to remember in more ways than one for both of them.

CAL would someday be told of the enchantment of that night and of Ben's love for and devotion to Meri. However, it would then be told in a subdued way because of what would later happen. Ben's sole recollection of that night would not offer truly joyous memories for him or others because he would remember it alone, without Meri. He would be forced to reminisce about that time without her presence and without her joining in with a similar but slightly different perspective than just his own.

CAL was born one day near Christmas in 2005. Meri thought that she would easily and readily shed the 42 pounds she had added during her pregnancy with him like some unwanted baggage to be discarded from her body. The first 7 to 10 pounds would easily come off after CAL was born and became disentangled physically from Meri. The rest to be lost, however, would take some considerable work and effort. Certainly some hard after birth gym time would be necessary for Meri as she eased back into her post-CAL work along with the related long hours and the ever-present stress.

CHAPTER 9

While Mark Trudeau was trying to decide which of Belinda Ross' many physical charms he would like to enjoy the most, across Manhattan, some blocks uptown, another considerably more powerful and financially well off executive was trying to figure out a way to stop the government and media attacks on his company's weight loss products. This executive, Mitchell Malloy, believed the efficacy and viability of these products was proven and above reproach. He had worked too long and too hard and had put forth way too much of his personal time and resources to establish and market these products just to lose them to some governmental regulations brought on by media criticism and pressure. He had repeatedly acted to convince a bunch of Washington politicians to in turn cajole a host of Food & Drug Administration (FDA) bureaucrats to deregulate a complete line of his diet and nutritional products. He could not lose what he had worked so hard to gain.

While these products contained a Chinese herb, Ma Huang, an ephedrine alkaloid used to promote weight loss, it was a natural substance that had been used for a variety of purposes over a time period encompassing literally thousands of years. For example, Ma Huang had been used for centuries in years past to energize and mobilize Asian fighting forces, sometimes short during battle on energy from readily available food sources. Ma Huang was thus used as a hunger suppressant and energizer to spur on warriors in need of a fast acting stimulant to summon up enough bravery and courage to in turn fuel each day's combat.

The use of substances like Ma Huang in ancient times to drive combatants to fight on during conflict, to more aggressively fight or even to make it easier for them to kill was nothing unique nor limited to just ancient warfare. In more recent wars, rum, ale or whiskey was often furnished to off-duty troops to help appease them after a day's combat. The Nazis and even the U.S. Army used amphetamines to fuel their respective troops in France during WWII. The United States military also did so for their troops in Vietnam during that conflict.

Of late, in more recent U.S. combat engagements in Iraq and Afghanistan, antidepressants such as Fluoxetime and Sertaline, were frequently prescribed by American Army doctors to help eliminate a combat related condition demonstrated in some troops, commonly known as post-traumatic stress disorder or PTSD. The use of chemical or natural substances before, during or after combat was longstanding, effective and some would say, necessary. Certainly the use of these items was acceptable in war.

Anything was permissible in combat to further the objective, to attain the goal, to give an edge. Such actions in the venues of war were always acceptable. Why not in fitness venues as well? Surely these efforts won't kill anyone! The so-called metabolic syndrome and the propensity of many toward obesity as experienced by perhaps millions of Americans was wide-spread and affecting perhaps more than 60% of the U.S. population. Even a significant number of American armed forces personnel and especially recruits were adversely impacted by weight gains. Many young Americans desiring to enter the military could not even qualify to do so because of such conditions. Something had to be done.

Malloy's company, SlimLine Products, Inc., had been dragged into the litigation brought forth by Meri Margaret Lawrence's family because its products allegedly had been recommended by Piccini to Meri during their personal trainer-client relationship. The contention was that the products were dangerous, particularly so for Meri given her medical conditions and post Chase delivery status.

When "Mitch," as his close friends called him, heard that the judge in the Piccini case had called all the lawyers into his chambers to try and beat a settlement out of them, he buzzed his own personal assistant, Mary Stone on his phone's intercom and said, "Mary, get Hatfield on the line – call him on his cell phone, the one I told him to keep with him at all times in that hick town courthouse – even during the trial. He can take a break if the jury is still in front of him. I want to know what's going on."

Dutifully, Mary completed the Hatfield call. On the third ring, Jason Hatfield answered. She said, "Mr. Hatfield, Mitchell Malloy is on the line and needs to talk with you at this moment."

Before Hatfield could say anything, however, and as Mary started to put the call on hold, she heard a very frustrated male voice bellow, "Mr. Hatfield, I have told you repeatedly, no cell calls during the trial – not out there in the courtroom– not in here, not now, not ever, not in my courtroom, not in my chambers, not in my presence - period. . ." As that voice droned on, Mary put the call on hold and transferred the call to Mitchell Malloy.

By the time Malloy got on the phone and said, "Hatfield! What's going on down there? Why isn't this case over yet?" All Mitchell Malloy could hear was the echo of his own voice and utter silence from Columbus . . . The call had been ended by order of the Honorable Judge Charles Davis of the Franklin County Court of Common Pleas.

CHAPTER 10

At the moment Jason Hatfield's cell phone rang a second time during the attempted call from Mitchell Malloy, Judge Charles Davis was then completing his third, six-year term on the Franklin County Court of Common Pleas. That kind of trial court was located in each county in Ohio, all 88 of them. The court was established to conduct all serious state, as opposed to federal, civil and criminal trials in Ohio. It had jurisdiction to receive and consider civil cases involving damages over $15,000 and for criminal cases constituting felonies as opposed to misdemeanors.

When Hatfield's cell phone rang, Judge Davis began by staring intently at Jason Hatfield. The Judge reiterated his distaste for and prohibition of all cell phones in his courtroom proceedings and during the meetings which took place in his chambers.

Once he stopped the call to Hatfield, Davis looked at Hatfield and said directly to him and in no uncertain terms: "Give me that cell phone! In fact, someone call my bailiff in here – NOW!" He then threw out the few remaining hard candies from the candy dish which he always had on his desk and held it up reaching across his desk toward the lawyers in his chambers.

"All of you put your cell phones in this bowl." Bill Morris, his bailiff for nearly 18 years on the bench, then came in. Davis told him, "Collect all of the lawyers' cell phones and put them in this bowl, take it to your desk, and turn all of them off. Keep them there till I tell you otherwise."

Bill did as he was instructed. But as the bowl was passed from lawyer to lawyer, all of whom were neatly seated in the judge's chambers, and as the last of the phones was put into the bowl by each of them, Bill was not certain how to turn each of the phones off or how to at least disable their sound so as not to disturb the proceedings. Each was different and some were obviously more complex than the others. He would do the best he could. At the very least, he would keep them out of the judge's presence.

As the bailiff left the judge's chambers with the candy bowl assortment of cell phones, he wondered what the judge would do without the readily available supply of hard candy he had kept on his desk in that bowl for the last five years. The judge used the candy to satisfy his cravings for a sweet nectar of a different vintage and manufacture that he had enjoyed for many years before and both during and after court, including at lunch or during any court recess as the case might be. The judge had been known in years past to even imbibe in his chambers during trial recesses and sometimes was known to lose track of evidence, and even, in a general sense, to lose track of what was transpiring in his courtroom during trials. It had gotten so bad on some occasions in the past that lawyers and jurors in his courtroom could not even understand what he was attempting to communicate to them because his words were so slurred. In any case, as Bill left the judge's chambers, he could hear the mood in Davis' chambers grow foul.

The inner sanctum of Judge Davis' courtroom chambers was full with all of the lawyers who had entered an appearance or, in other words, had been hired by the parties, in the case of <u>Lawrence, et al. v. Piccini, et al.</u>, Franklin County, Common Pleas Case No. 2007 CV 00239. The jury in this case had heard all of the evidence from both sides of the conflict and had been sent by Judge Davis to deliberate and determine the facts of the case and then to reach a verdict. Their deliberations however, had been interrupted with a question they posed to the judge.

While the question was simple and straightforward, it was also potentially troubling. They wanted to know if they could hold some of the Defendants responsible for Mrs. Lawrence's death – but not all of them.

In attempting to address the jurors' question with the lawyers in his chambers, now without their cell phones, Judge Davis said, "Mr. Hatfield that should solve the cell phone problem and allow you to focus your attention, in fact all of your attentions, on this jury and the question they have posed to me." Jason Hatfield was not unfamiliar with jury questions since he had tried dozens of cases in this and other courtrooms across Ohio and the Midwest. He had tried cases in Pennsylvania and across the middle of the country from Ohio to Illinois, east to west, and from Ohio to Virginia, north to south.

Hatfield knew that all jury questions were important and needed to be answered promptly and correctly by the court but only after consultation and discussion among the lawyers involved in the case. Discussion by the court with an individual juror or the entire jury without the presence of all counsel on a case was not permitted. Such "ex parte" communications could result in a mistrial and even misconduct charges or more serious allegations against a judge. That kind of conduct could lead to sanctions, removal from judicial office, disbarment – even criminal prosecution.

Hatfield also knew that judges hated to deal with their questions and often suggested – even demanded – ways to resolve cases rather than risk hung juries, errors on appeal or misunderstandings arising out of the answers provided to their questions. Problems in the answers provided could lead to an examination of a judge's competence, his or her ridicule in the media or even reprimands by higher courts.

Seven lawyers in total filled Davis' chambers. All of them sat in chairs neatly arranged before the judge's mahogany desk. Jason Hatfield was there of course, sitting in the first row. He was the latest victim of Judge Davis' attention or rage as some would call it. However, Hatfield was a lawyer of considerable experience. He was one of the best litigators in the Columbus, Franklin County law firm of Smith and Dewey. He had been retained for this case by the liability insurance carrier for SlimLine International, the nutritional supplement manufacturing company for which Mitchell Malloy was CEO and its foremost promoter.

Hatfield was generally well respected in the legal community, the "bar," as it was called – not because drinks were served, but because that is what an entire group of lawyers was called – whether located in a particular city, county, state or nationwide. Hatfield was thus part of the Columbus, Franklin County, Ohio bar.

Jason Hatfield was rated in the number 1 category by the oldest lawyer rating service in the United States which published their lawyer ratings each year in a series of thick books. The publisher's volumes of these books on rated lawyers seemed to grow each year. A full set of their books cost over $2,800 per year. In addition, each listed law firm was charged $1,000 for five lines of very small print provided by the publisher for lawyers to demonstrate their biographical sketches in these books. These sketches could then be viewed by various companies, insurance carriers and other lawyers in their efforts to find and retain qualified lawyers to represent clients and insureds. If more space was needed for one of these firm or individual lawyer sketches, space could be purchased at the rate of about $5,000 per page.

Lawyers employed with large firms were very often satisfactorily rated through this service assuming they kept their lawyer noses clean and to the grindstone. Lawyers in smaller firms and so-called "solo-practitioners" often did not fare so well, at least from this rating source. Lately however, this old and esteemed source of all lawyer rating services was starting to charge each lawyer an individual fee just to be listed in its publication – a charge merely for the publication of a lawyer's name and nothing else.

That charge alone could add millions to the coffers of this rating service whose profits may have been down of late due to the relatively recent practice of many lawyers to rely more heavily on computer based, World Wide Web resources for their generation of legal business. These resources were readily available through a host of Internet service providers. Such resources represented an attractive alternative to buying space in heavy, multiple volume sets of expensive books upon books, all of which seemed to be going by the wayside due to the advent of other resources, including so-called "open" or totally online, computer generated publications.

Jason Hatfield was also rated by an insurance industry rating service called the American Insurance Lawyers' Group, AILG. The Group charged a listing fee for each insurance defense lawyer of each law firm listed in its several volume publication. These firm bios included a listing of those insurance companies which retained and thus implicitly recommended such listed insurance counsel.

This list could only be published upon verification of industry source materials for each lawyer and each firm. Inclusion in this publication was limited to insurance industry lawyers who, some contended, despite ethical commentaries to the contrary, owed their allegiance to the insurance companies that retained them, not to the insureds for whom they provided service. The argument was that if insurance companies paid the lawyers' bills, the lawyers' allegiance would be to the companies and not to the companies' customers – the insureds.

Jason Hatfield had also recently been classified as one of the "Foremost Lawyers in America" by a relatively new lawyer rating service which published the names of selected lawyers in various magazines and periodicals in which these "Foremost Lawyers" were named. Those so named were sometimes highlighted in magazine stories about them which appeared in these publications. Some of these magazines also carried advertisements from these same lawyers or their firms who often paid hefty advertising fees to those magazines for those ads. Perhaps they were truly Foremost Lawyers, but perhaps not.

Jason Hatfield was not entirely sure what would come of his "Foremost" designation, but he liked it. The senior partner at Smith and Dewey liked it, and Hatfield's wife, Susan, an up-and-coming socialite in Columbus, Ohio, also liked it. She used it to further her own movement up the Columbus society food chain which had always been in existence there and elsewhere for some status-seeking women involved and participating in various social and service organizations.

Aside from Hatfield, who had been retained by the Midwest Insurance Company under a reservation of rights letter to defend Malloy's Company, SlimLine Products, he was assisted by SlimLine's own corporate counsel Matthew Reuger. Reuger was licensed as a lawyer in the state of New York where SlimLine's corporate officers were located. He appeared as one of the lawyers in this Ohio case on behalf of his company through what was called a pro hac vice application. Pursuant to this application, Hatfield, an Ohio lawyer, vouched for Reuger's qualifications, standing and good work so as to permit the trial judge to allow Reuger to appear in Davis' Ohio courtroom for the purpose of helping in the Lawrence case.

When the application was filed for Reuger by Hatfield, Judge Davis had commented to Hatfield, "Do we really need some New York lawyer here trying to tell me how to run my courtroom or try this case?" While Hatfield had no real answer for Davis' question, the process was generally rote and almost always completed with an approval. Indeed, Davis approved the pro hac vice application for Reuger who was thereby authorized to enter an appearance in the case but only after Davis declared: "Hatfield, you keep this New York lawyer in line. No smart talk, no offensive remarks or tactics. I won't stand for it. Got it?" Hatfield dutifully acknowledged the concern and promised Davis he would do so.

As for the other lawyers in the Piccini case, they were a diverse and eclectic bunch. While Reuger was strictly a corporate lawyer, familiar with shareholder meetings, directors' and officers' actions and similar issues, as well as the handling of various matters before the Federal Trade Commission (FTC), there were others with varying and diverse backgrounds in Davis' Chambers.

Hatfield and Reuger were also assisted in the case by a younger corporate lawyer, Vince Harper, who had been with SlimLine for just 16 months. Harper had been brought on board at SlimLine from a nutritional supplement trade association group at about the same time Meri and Ben had visited Paris and started the chain of events that would lead them some 3,000 miles back to their home town of Columbus, Ohio.

Columbus was also the home of "The" Ohio State University and its respected and revered football team, the "Buckeyes." Harper had played for the Buckeyes some years before and with considerable distinction. He was good enough to be "All Big Ten", the athletic conference in which Ohio State chose to participate, but not quite good enough for "All American" status or for the pros primarily due to a persistent knee injury sustained during his junior year which lingered on and plagued him thereafter. He was also bothered by intense headaches brought on by a number of head knocks – small concussions received during his participation in high school and college ball. Often referred to as having one's 'bell ringed', such occurrences were common in football but were overlooked for many years by sports medicine physicians and athletic trainers.

Harper's knee injury had been treated by a well-known and respected sports medicine doctor, Dr. Ted Adams, who was Chief of Orthopedic Surgery at Riverfront Hospital in Columbus. He, like Harper, was also an Ohio State football grad but the good doctor had played pro ball before completing medical school, his internship and residency in orthopedic surgery.

Dr. Adams had been a great Ohio State University linebacker and a Detroit Lion for many years. He also became an avid Ohio State football fan after he completed medical school and ultimately appointed to be one of the sports medicine physicians for The Ohio State football team.

Once Adams began to treat Harper, he concentrated on keeping him in the game as Harper had requested. That scenario consisted of weekly left knee fluid drainages with a huge needle attached to a vial equivalent in dimension to a family-sized tube of toothpaste.

The "treatment" to remove what some would call "water on the knee" was performed under a local anesthetic or with none at all. The procedure would often require Dr. Adams to insert the drainage needle and then to manually squeeze Harper's knee to force additional blood and fluid out of the joint and into the vial. If there was too much blood and fluid to be suitably contained within the needle vial, Dr. Adams would remove the top of the vial, leave the needle in the knee and squeeze the bloody fluid into a pan as Harper watched.

Harper didn't always "make it" through these treatments; he sometimes passed out when the bloody fluid was squeezed out of his joint. On these occasions, he would be awakened with Dr. Adams holding his head in Adams' hands, looking closely into his face and calling out his name.

"Harp," as Adams called him, "You're okay – toughen up – you play for Ohio State."

Harper never forgot Doc Adams' hands despite their use for a time on patients while Adams was still performing surgery. Adams' hands were gnarled and twisted from past football injuries and eventually were of little use in the operating room due to the early onset of arthritis into the bones and joints of his hands.

Dr. Adams' treatments allowed Harper to play football through the end of the season during Harper's junior year. However, once the season ended and his knee was operated on by Adams, the damage had been intensified by the delayed surgery and continued play. Even after months of post-surgery rehab, Harper was never able to return to the field or to his own days of gridiron glory with the same effectiveness he had enjoyed in the years before. His desire to play, to stay on the field, to work toward his goals, while assisted by Dr. Adams, as well as his own choices furthered Harper's immediate desires and goals; but in the long run the decisions which were made by Harper and Adams cost Harper his last year of effective college football and his own shot at the pros. He was somewhat bitter at the loss and always wanted to get even in some way – not against Dr. Adams necessarily, but against someone. Return to play as soon as possible after injury was almost always the mentality of most athletes. Harper just happened to be one of them.

On the other hand, Harper's series of high school and college football practice and game concussions were never adequately diagnosed or treated by anyone. Like most other football players, he was almost always returned to practice or play after these events by a trainer or one of his coaches who were often unaware of the seriousness of the condition. While Harper never lost complete consciousness for any significant amount of time, the headaches he suffered from these incidents were debilitating and almost threatened his law school education and his subsequent practice of law. Recent research findings indicated more potential problems in the years ahead for him and other similarly situated football players with similar conditions. Memory disturbances, dementia, and even potentially, Alzheimer's were all possibilities for him and many others. Time would tell what would befall all of them or at least some of them in this regard.

Davis, Hatfield, Harper and even Ben Lawrence, Meri Lawrence's surviving spouse, were all Ohio State football fans. Except for Harper, once he went to work for SlimLine in New York, few of them ever missed a game in the Buckeye's famed Horseshoe stadium in Columbus.

For many years, Meri Lawrence had also claimed that Columbus, in addition to its Buckeye football fame, its well-known Horseshoe stadium and even its renowned marching band, was also what she called the "Women's Fashion Capital of the Midwest." If Columbus really was what she hyped, she helped make it so. Ben, for one, later hoped that someone would remember her – not just for her boastful claim but also for her real contribution to that hype aside from her more personal role as a wife and mother. Time would tell about this as well. Ben hoped she would not merely be remembered for her status as a victim of some ill-trained and poorly prepared personal trainer. He thought that legacy would be the worst of all for his beloved.

CHAPTER 11

Tony Piccini was defended in the <u>Lawrence</u> wrongful death lawsuit by Alan Finestein, who had been selected by Piccini's insurance carrier, through the USA-PTA group which had "sold" the insurance to him through his membership in that association. However, Piccini's defense in the civil case was undertaken under a reservation of rights notice. When Tony received word from the USA-PTA insurance company that Finestein would represent him but under a reservation of rights, something smelled sour to Tony. He was uncertain about how far the group would go to protect him and defend his interests, particularly if he was convicted of the criminal charges which he also faced and which arose out of the same facts.

As of the time that the <u>Lawrence v. Piccini</u> case was filed, Ohio, like some other states, had just recently updated the ethical rules applicable to all Ohio licensed lawyers. These rules which were developed and published through the Supreme Court of Ohio, required lawyers like Hatfield, and, in fact, all the lawyers who had been retained by liability insurance carriers in the <u>Lawrence v Piccini</u> case, to send written notices to their named clients, the insureds of the carriers at the start of each case. These notices were designed to advise the insureds that even though the lawyers were retained by an insurance carrier, the lawyers ultimately represented the insureds whose interests the lawyers would serve to protect at all costs and under all circumstances, despite the fact that the insurance companies would be paying those lawyers' bills.

Under these new ethical rules, when insurance carriers determined to defend a case under a so-called reservation of rights, which a number of the insurance carriers in the Lawrence v. Piccini case had determined to do, they were required to send formal letters to the insureds explaining the company's decision in that regard. The idea of all this was to make the companies and the lawyers more accountable to the insureds; however, those carriers still paid the bill. Financial clout was still clout no matter what the rule.

Reservation of rights letters are written statements from an insurance carrier to an insured stating that while the company may defend and pay for the defense of a particular litigation filed against an insured, it may not pay any judgment against an insured if one was rendered. Often these letters are sent because of uncertainties related to the insurance coverage, or due to some of the allegations made in a particular case. If there is an allegation of particular facts, which, for example, might not be covered by the insurance policy in question due to so-called "exclusions" from coverage, then the letter served to protect the insurance company's right not to pay if there was a judgment rendered in the case.

Tony also worried what would happen to himself if a big verdict was awarded against him. Moreover, Tony was specifically told that the company would not defend him in the criminal case although as it turned out, they would readily throw in their views about that case whenever they saw fit.

Walt Manos, Tony's criminal case defense lawyer, was in his 30s. He worked for a big Cleveland, Ohio law firm and was considered someone who would soon be a top rated lawyer, someone who would surely be a "Foremost Lawyer in America" just like Hatfield. Perhaps the Lawrence case outcome would catapult him into that vaulted position. Time again would tell.

Unlike how Tony felt about Manos, he was concerned about Finestein and who he really worked for. Tony learned that insurance company retained lawyers generally based their billings upon an hourly rate. Lawyer time spent on insurance company cases was always closely watched, monitored and controlled by those companies. Pressure was frequently put on these insurance oriented lawyers to keep their billings competitive – in other words, to the bone. In reality, insurance companies consistently beat down their lawyers' billings so as to improve their bottom lines. Some contend that these billing practices, lawyer to company, really cause these lawyers to owe their allegiances to the insurance companies rather than to the insureds, even though the insureds are supposed to be the real clients whose interests these lawyers are sworn to represent and protect.

At least one insurance company – a medical malpractice insurance carrier – actually tried to test the concept of who was really the lawyer's client in an Ohio court. That company filed its own lawsuit against a medical malpractice defense lawyer and his firm over the lawyer's representation of one of its insured physicians in a medical malpractice case. When the carrier didn't like the trial result which occurred once the underlying medical malpractice case was tried and they were left with a large verdict against their insured – which, by the way, the lawyer tried to avoid when he repeatedly recommended a settlement which the company refused to complete – they sued the lawyer and his firm for legal malpractice.

The lawyer and his firm defended the suit on several grounds including one based upon the proposition that the lawyer in question represented the physician who was the client, not the insurance carrier that selected the lawyer to do so. These lawyers therefore argued that they owed no duty to the insurance company since their duty was owed to the insured and the insured was more than satisfied – happy in fact – with the legal service. As a consequence, according to this "no breach of duty" argument, no malpractice could have occurred since no duty was owed by the lawyer to the insurance company in the first place.

The trial court, the appellate court and finally the Ohio Supreme Court all agreed with this proposition and held that the lawyer and his firm owed their duty and allegiance to the physician who was the real client, not the company which had to foot the bill for the defense and then the judgment. The lawyers in that case and many other defense attorneys all across the state then breathed individual and collective sighs of relief due to this ruling. However, the precedent which came out of this case seemed to remind all such lawyers about whom they really represented.

Despite the ruling in this case and as a practical matter, control of the purse strings also gives those in control a lot of weight to throw around. Insurance carriers often participate in deciding critical issues in litigation – defense tactics, witness selection and the questions asked of them, the identification and retention of experts, and a whole host of other litigation decisions which they almost always know more about than the clients. The knowledge and ability of insurance carriers to monitor defense lawyer payments by dictating the work to be done, or not to be done, often gives them considerable power over what is done in the defense of cases filed against their insureds. Tony hoped for the best from Finestein because he really had no other alternative.

While Finestein had been assisted in the <u>Lawrence</u> case by a number of paralegals, each of whom were charged out at about one-third of his own rate of $300 per hour, and all of whom had helped work up the case for trial, Finestein would try the case by himself without the benefit of a second chair.

A second chair is one filled by another lawyer to assist the principal lawyer with the defense or prosecution of a case and to help mold the outcome of the trial and thus hopefully the case. The idea simply put is that two heads are better than one. It is also used as a means to train the other lawyer, the one to sit in the second chair, at the client's cost and expense. Perhaps more important to the firm and its revenue-sharing partners is the fact that the presence of a second chair lawyer increases firm billings, total firm revenues and the size of profits to be distributed to individual partners at each year's end.

The other lawyers in the case represented the other named defendants. FitAgain was represented by a locally well-known female lawyer, Joan Childs, a member of an old and well established Columbus firm with offices in that city as well as Cleveland, Cincinnati, Akron and West Palm Beach, Florida. She was definitely a "Foremost Lawyer." In fact, she was a "legend in her own mind" as some would say, making a mockery through these twisted words of the time tested phrase, "a legend in her own time."

A number of other lawyers represented the other defendants. Those defendants consisted of a retail food store known as The Natural Food Store and a pharmacy, Pharmette, both of whom had allegedly sold various SlimLine products to Meri Margaret Lawrence upon the asserted recommendation and advice of Piccini. According to the allegations of the suit, Piccini actually had taken Meri to both places to oversee her purchase of the products he recommended. It was also alleged that Tony got a cut from all such sales.

Mrs. Lawrence's physician, Alice Janowitz, DO, was also named as a defendant due to her claimed failure to advise Meri of the problems associated with the adverse interactions of various supplement products with the medications she had prescribed for Meri. It was also alleged that she should have advised Meri what would happen to her if these prescriptions were discontinued.

A pharmacist, Bill Peters, was also a named defendant. It was alleged that he failed to counsel and advise Meri about the same such matters. The company which employed the pharmacist, Pharmaceutical Professionals, LLC, and provided him, as well as other pharmacists to Pharmette, was also a named defendant.

Each of these parties was represented by other lawyers who were selected by their insurance carriers and/or their respective companies. These were as follows: Jacklyn Osbourne who represented The Natural Food Store, David Taylor who represented Dr. Janowitz, Dennis Devit who represented Pharmette, and Henry Spirles who represented the pharmacist and the company which employed him. While Dr. Janowitz was covered by a medical care provider's professional liability insurance company – a medical malpractice insurance carrier, the pharmacist and his employer were insured by a so-called risk retention group. Such a group was something like an insurance company but one which had not really achieved state recognized status as an insurance carrier subject to more extensive state regulations and required monetary reserves from which payments were made to satisfy settlements and claims that reached the verdict stage. Insurance companies, on the other hand, were subject to considerable regulation in the various states where they were authorized to provide insurance products and insurance policies. The State of Ohio, through the Ohio Department of Insurance – whose commissioner was appointed by the governor of the state – comprehensively regulated insurance companies but not as thoroughly for risk retention groups.

Since the claims made in the <u>Lawrence</u> case included allegations of willful, intentional and even criminal conduct, such conduct, if proven, would not permit insurance companies to use insurance provided resources to pay out settlements or judgments based upon such conduct because to do so would be against the public policy of the State of Ohio. This rule was established because the State of Ohio through its court system, like essentially all other states in the United States, did not believe it was appropriate for individuals or companies to insure against this kind of conduct because to do so would in essence encourage such conduct. Moreover, since the claim was made at least against Piccini in the Lawrence civil case that he had engaged in the unauthorized practice of dietetics, in essence, nutritional counseling, he ran the risk of having no coverage. The practice of dietetics was subject to statutory regulation in Ohio requiring providers of such services to be licensed by the state. Since Tony had no such license, he had no real insurance coverage for violating state law in providing those services. If the jury determined that he could not provide such services because he was not a licensed physician nor a licensed dietitian, the insurance policy he received would not cover such conduct.

Alan Finestein, Anthony Piccini's lawyer, knew that he had a tough way to go to defend Piccini in the civil case particularly due to the criminal charges which Piccini also faced. When Alan first met Tony, they talked in earnest about the pending litigation. Finestein told him: "Tony, if I might call you that, we have a very tough situation here. We are dealing with a young mother whose family is alleging that you treated her like a physician would treat a patient or a dietitian would treat his or her patient and that you did so in a grossly neglectful way, in fact in a criminal way; that you prescribed various nutritional supplements made by SlimLine, one of which was made available to her at FitAgain and some of which were sold to her on your recommendation by the Natural Food Store and/or Pharmette."

Finestein continued as Tony began to grow angry, "They allege that you took her to buy these products, all of which her family claims led to and proximately caused her death. They allege you made recommendations to her to lose weight despite her high blood pressure, under circumstances where you were neither qualified nor licensed to tell her anything. On top of all of that, the allegation is that you told her to stop taking her blood pressure medications, lisinopril and diltiazem. They say that you told her these medications slowed down her metabolism and thus slowed down the effect of the supplements you suggested to her and that all of this decreased and slowed her weight loss. However, those recommendations, they contend, also failed to lower her blood pressure which when coupled with the elevation in her blood pressure caused by the Ma Huang – the ephedra in the supplements you recommended – together with your prescribed heavy workouts and lack of appropriate direction about proper breathing techniques used during activity served as the basis for your killing her.

"The principal allegation here is that the ephedra in the SlimLine products led to her death at 32 years of age. She left a husband and two children behind, not to mention her substantial employment as a fashion consultant earning in excess of $150,000 per year plus perks. Since her life expectancy was over 45 years while her work life expectancy was in excess of 33 years, her projected lifetime earnings compounded at 6% per year, exceeded $14 million. Even when this sum is discounted to the present value of that sum, we are looking at a potential verdict of over $10 million – possibly over $20 million even without factoring in pain and suffering, child care costs, loss of services for the husband, funeral expenses, etc. Once you figure all of that, her medical care costs, the funeral expenses, and the income she and her family lost, not to mention the potential – if not the probable assessment of punitive damages – we are looking at a potential award of perhaps $30 million, maybe more. All you have in potential insurance coverage is $1 million, and you are still facing criminal charges."

Finestein continued, "You could well be stripped of all of you have and all you ever will have, as well as your freedom. You could take bankruptcy, except you already did that just a couple of years ago and can't do it again for approximately seven years from the time you previously did so and even if you could, it won't make the criminal case go away. You could not escape any award for punitive damages due to such conduct through bankruptcy."

Tony squirmed but Alan continued, "You're in a bad spot, between a rock and a hard place with nowhere to go. I can't settle your case even if the company would let me because you don't have enough insurance money to do so and it won't resolve the criminal case. The others at this point aren't budging and everyone is pointing a finger of blame at you. What do you expect me to do?"

"Listen," Tony said to Finestein, "energy bars, drinks, nutritional supplements, even vitamins are big business, and they work. People take them all the time. I take them. Have for years. They never hurt me."

"But," Finestein interrupted, "you don't have high blood pressure, you are not on medication to treat it, you didn't just have a baby and you are not forty pounds overweight."

Tony listened but became incensed: "That's why folks come to me in the first place. They want to lose weight, to get fit, to get buff, to look good and to feel good. That's why Meri came to me, and that's why the club had me on her case. They knew I got my clients to lose weight and fast. I got results. They knew what I did. I did what my clients and, God forbid, my employer wanted me to do. This business about me being an independent contractor and not an employee is bullshit. That crap is all designed to save the club money and exposure in cases like this one."

"That may be," said Finestein, "but they have disavowed any knowledge of what you were doing or recommending to her. They have said that they had no knowledge of your recommendation of supplements, not to mention those containing ephedra ingredients, to her or anyone else."

"That's not so," retorted Tony, "They knew all along. They knew exactly what I was doing. They told me to get results. That's the name of the game."

"However," responded Finestein, "they had no right to tell you anything. They say you were an independent contractor operating in their facility on a contractual basis. That they had no right to tell you how to perform your service and if they had known what you were doing, they would have stopped you by terminating your contract."

"That's crap! My supervisor, the club manager, the regional vice president and even Mark Trudeau and his group all knew what I was doing and encouraged me to do it. I was never really a contractor; this is all legal mumbo-jumbo! All they were trying to do was avoid paying withholding taxes or making contributions to a 401k or pension plan for me. They made me get my own liability insurance, they required me to join USA-PTA to get USA-PTA's recommended insurance, and they required me to pay for it and provide them with proof of it every year. This is all just bullshit. They even took a big percentage of my fees – 40% of everything I earned from my clients. I kept my tips but otherwise they were in my pocket all the time."

Finestein tried to interrupt, "But . . . "

Tony in turn stopped him, not letting go of his own thoughts, "But, Bullshit! They even told me when I could work, where I could work in their club, where I should go with clients and for how long. They required me to use their contract documents so my clients wouldn't sue them or at least think they couldn't do so. What about that? They made me have these clients sign waivers of liability. They also got waivers of liability when the clients joined their clubs. Don't these waivers protect me and them against this suit?"

Finestein listened, gathered his thoughts and began responding as lawyers respond sometimes rotely to their clients' legal questions: "Waivers are generally effective against clients who want to sue personal trainers and facilities for ordinary negligence. Ohio recognizes these waivers in most cases. The problem here is that they are suing you and the club for gross negligence and the unauthorized practice of dietetics which they allege are akin to criminal law violations. Moreover, the family is contending that the releases don't bar the husband's separate suit against you for interference with the marital relationship he had with his wife because they say you killed her. They also say that the family's suit for wrongful death is a separate suit. It is the family's suit, and they are exercising their right to sue you – something which they say Meri could not waive or give up for them ahead of time. You know the court has ruled in their favor on these issues. Absent some ruling on any appeal, that's the law of this case. For now, we have to live with it."

More bullshit, thought Tony. "You just don't get it do you?" Tony finally asked. "This company put me here, they told me what to do, how to do it, when to do it, and they are really trying to pin this whole thing on me."

Tony continued, "The only one who ever trained me was this company. And now, I am being sued here for among other things, not being certified by some independent group. The USA-PTA through WPTA didn't even start certifying personal fitness trainers in the way they do now – so-called PFTs – until after this lawsuit was filed. Why aren't we in turn suing these companies, including FitAgain, and getting into Trudeau's pocket? Can't we claim that they all improperly trained me, negligently certified me and that they caused all of this?"

Finestein responded: "If what you did amounted to a crime, they don't have to pay." Tony's frustration was obvious and the response Finestein gave, any response he could give, would not be adequate.

Finestein continued, "I'm here because your liability insurance carrier hired me to defend you, not to sue FitAgain or its CEO. They won't pay for that. In fact, because of what is alleged here, they may not pay for any judgment if one is issued against you. They sent you a reservation of rights letter on that. They sent me a copy. While they are paying me and footing all the expenses of this suit, they may not pay any judgment issued against you. That's the way it works."

"Why?" Tony responded. "You know Trudeau is in bed with this insurance company and I mean that literally. He has been screwing their chief marketing executive for a long time. He's pulling the strings here – with her directly, and with you indirectly. All this crap is hurting me!"

"If you want a lawyer to sue the company in this case, you can hire another lawyer to do so," said Finestein, "but if you do, you may well seal your fate here. If the jurors see the Defendants are obviously fighting among themselves, it may well appear that all of you are responsible for Meri's death and that you should pay for her funeral and be required to feed and educate her kids, etc., etc. Don't you get it?"

"I get it," said Tony. "FitAgain may not be suing me, but every time anything comes up, they point out that they are not my employer, that they didn't tell me what to do and didn't control what I did – despite the fact that I worked in their club, with their club members, using their equipment – even their towels. They took a big chunk of my commissions. If I go to jail in the criminal case, are they going to share my cell with me like they shared my money?" With that, Tony got up, walked out and slammed the office door as he left.

As he watched Tony leave, Finestein thought he would have to figure out some way to control him during the trial of the case as well as during the time leading up to the trial. Tony, he thought, was a loose cannon it seemed, and he was ready to go off at any time.

Despite all of his frustration in the civil case, Tony was grateful that he had someone who he felt was really on his side to defend him in the criminal case. Walt Manos, the lawyer defending him from the criminal charges, was recommended to him by another trainer, Jeff Holder. Holder had been accused of rape when one of his clients, the attractive and fit Mrs. Admink, got caught with Holder by her husband while Holder and Mrs. Admink were in an act of pure and unadulterated fornication. The exact position they were in at the time was confidential, but neither Holder nor the client knew the husband had been suspicious and had been watching them. Holder's client was simply not willing to give up her considerable lifestyle with her husband despite Holder's physical charms and instead cried wolf in the face of what was at stake.

Manos had defended Holder admirably against these charges and with great effectiveness. Holder had been able to retrieve numerous pre-fornication cell phone messages from the good Mrs. Admink to Holder, not to mention the intimate and revealing emails she sent to him along with embedded photographs of herself in various yoga-like positions. Holder had suggested these activities to her and had used them to enhance what had been before that, many years of the same sex, in the same position and in the same boring way with her husband.

Stimulation separate from normal exercise routines and separate from the ordinary day-to-day boredom of oft repeated daily chores, along with increased bodily enhancement was what most female clients sought from Jeff Holder, from Tony and from many other trainers just like them. All the trainers had to do was assist them in the process of metamorphosing their lives. To change them from ordinary to extraordinary, at least in some cases; usually, however, just in their own minds.

While the criminal charges against Jeff Holder resulted in his acquittal based upon the facts of his case and the competence and effectiveness of Walt Manos, not all similar complaints against other personal trainers ended that way.

Carlos Ortega, for example, was a freelance trainer who worked out of a number of health and fitness facilities in Phoenix, Arizona. He picked up clients who watched him as he worked out and who came to believe that he knew what he was doing. He certainly looked the part.

Many of those clubs allowed Carlos to work out in their clubs on a no-cost or low-cost basis since he agreed to bring other clients into their gyms or to help keep those who were already there. Such arrangements were common in the health and fitness industry particularly with independent, non-chain health clubs. These arrangements worked well in many circumstances and increased client memberships for health clubs and thus their revenues and profits. In addition, these practices sometimes improved client retention rates and benefited personal trainers who needed an exercise floor and equipment to use to train clients and thus earn a livelihood.

These kind of symbiotic relationships – facility to trainer and trainer to facility – were generally loose, undocumented and probably more akin to a true independent contractor relationship between a facility and a trainer, rather than between someone like Tony Piccini and FitAgain. However, these relationships were frequently in place often without control by the clubs over the trainers except on a very loose, verbal basis. Fee sharing for services charged by these trainers was sometimes put into place but not close to the more formal basis which existed between Tony and FitAgain. There was also no real supervision of the actions, activities, short comings or failings of these trainers. As a consequence, adverse untoward events sometimes occurred.

Carlos was a personal trainer who had put in considerable time honing his craft with women. He targeted females in their 30s and/or entering the beginning of their 40s. He charmed them, baited them into his training routines and brought them into his fold. He encouraged them to trust him, to share their innermost confidences and desires, their problems and worries and their goals for exercise and training.

Once he gained their confidence, he used them in a variety of ways, not only to provide his livelihood through training sessions, but to satisfy his base desires, sometimes for sexual relations, sometimes for other kinds of personal satisfaction, sometimes for money or other things of value, stock tips, the use of cars and vacation homes, participation in sponsorships for his own training competitions or for similar needs.

Generally, those clients freely provided what Carlos needed. In fact, once they came under his considerable influence, they often exceeded Carlos' needs or expectations, whatever they might be at the time. Sometimes however, Carlos might find resistance, even considerable resistance from a small segment of his potential client population. On one of these occasions, Carlos' own desires overcame his better judgment and lead to his criminal prosecution and ultimately time behind bars.

One day in 2003, as Carlos worked out at a new facility in a well-to-do area outside of Phoenix, a stunning woman in her late 30s used a treadmill a few spaces from where he was assisting a client with circuit training activities designed to improve that client's core fitness.

As Carlos watched this non-client use the treadmill some 20 feet from him, he began to desire her, to want to service her, to use his charm on her in all of his areas of expertise. When he finished his session with his client, he approached the treadmill where the stunner was finishing her workout. As she did so, he introduced himself and offered his services.

"Hi, I'm Carlos Ortega, a personal fitness trainer here at this facility. I've been watching you work out and believe I can help you meet your goals, to achieve a new fitness level for you, to satisfy all of your desires."

At that moment he reached out to shake her hand, but there was no reciprocation, just a puzzled look from the stunner and some words provided politely but matter-of-factly in reply: "I've been with trainers. I have a set routine and know what I want and how to get through my own workout. Thanks for the offer but I'm fine."

Not to be defeated, Carlos replied: "No obligation. I would be honored to try and help you meet any of your needs. I just finished with another client and would be glad to spend some time with you, without obligation."

Carlos smiled with his best look at that point and hoped it would work but all he got in reply was, "Not today."

With that, the beauty before him stepped off her treadmill, walked away, out of the exercise floor area and into the women's locker room. He later observed her in the facility hot tub drinking a sports juice drink from the club's sports bar.

The beauty's routine always stayed the same. Stretching, treadmill, locker room and then a hot tub with a sports drink.

Carlos watched her from a distance for a number of weeks and gradually became intensely focused on the beauty's routine. He learned that her name was Laura Baker, she had been married but was recently separated from an older and quite wealthy husband and had a very aggressive divorce lawyer working on her post-divorce life with a vengeance. Carlos was sure she would have her way in that action. Carlos also believed he would have his way with her in his own action.

Carlos decided to begin using the hot tub just before Laura began her own use of it and when she entered the tub, he attempted to strike up a conversation with her in that venue. Little was gained from this new attempt. Despite his adoration of her beauty, his comments on her outstanding physical attributes and the display of his own physical attributes, Carlos seemingly got nowhere with his efforts. Laura's lack of admiration for his obvious attributes was most puzzling to him and not understandable given his own physical charms and his standing at the club.

Over time, Carlos became obsessed and determined to have Laura, no matter what. Eventually, on a particularly slow day, with no one else in the hot tub area but Laura and he, he slipped Ketamine, one of the date rape drugs, into her drink. Carlos knew Ketamine was a very fast acting anesthetic used mostly on animals. Carlos got it from one of his "connections" who in turn got it as part of the loot from a veterinarian's office break-in.

While she wasn't looking, Carlos poured the Ketamine liquid into Laura's drink. The rest was easy. This drug, known on the street as "K," among other names, was very fast acting and created a sense of dream-like feelings in Laura who lost all sense of time and personal identity. She became numb from the anesthetic and thought she was having dream-like, out-of-body experiences while in the hot tub.

After the K took its desired effect, Carlos deftly removed Laura's bikini bottoms and positioned her over himself while he was seated in the tub against the wall jets. He enjoyed his initial and repeated entry into Laura's somewhat limp and semi-conscious body while he explored her other physical attributes. This singular pleasure for Carlos continued until he finished. He then replaced and re-adjusted Laura's suit bottoms on her body. He was certain that no one else had been present and no one else had seen them together.

When he arranged Laura's suit back to its original position, he moved her out from the tub and to a lounge chair near the spa. He left her there to regain consciousness and most importantly for him, to believe she had fallen asleep after her workout and subsequent relaxation in the hot tub.

What Carlos did not expect was that all of the activity which had taken place was recorded on a ceiling installed video camera. He did not know the cameras had been put in place by the owners of the clubs who wanted to have at least some ability to monitor their facility. Once Laura regained consciousness and felt something was wrong, she complained to management. One thing led to another until someone decided to review the videotape. Once done, they called the police.

The residue of the date drug in Laura's system coupled with the evidence provided by the videotape and a DNA test on the remainder of Carlos' semen in Laura's body was more than enough to charge and ultimately convict Carlos for his supposed surreptitious activity. Despite Carlos' lack of formal connection to the facility, the facility was also named along with Carlos in a successful civil lawsuit brought by Laura which sought and secured, among other things, substantial punitive damages. Since Carlos had very little of his own assets and no insurance which would cover the punitive damage aspect of the case, the jury's award was enough to put the club out of business, while Carlos spent the next 7 to 10 years in prison.

Charges related to alleged sexual crimes by personal trainers or other lurid conduct were not limited to just the use of date rape drugs or even false claims like those which had been put forth by the good Mrs. Admink against Jeff Holder. Charges against personal trainers had included allegations of sexual acts against minor clients which, despite the fact that the victims were willing, were criminal nonetheless because the victims were underage and therefore incapable of granting lawful consent. Other criminal charges against personal fitness trainers included assault, battery, gross sexual imposition and other forms of impermissible sexual activity not to mention other types of "smaller" crimes including theft, unlawful videotaping or eavesdropping and even blackmail.

Blackmail type charges were not uncommon, however. Clients often confided in their personal trainers, expecting them to preserve and protect their innermost secrets which they often confided to their trainers. Due to the close, one-on-one relationships developed between clients and trainers, clients sometimes provided very detailed glimpses into their private lives. Since no regulation of any kind applied to personal trainers, there were no statutes, laws or ethical rules which were governmentally imposed upon these trainers to control any breaches of confidential communications made by trainers to third parties. In fact, gossip columnists clearly knew that trainers were often an available and ready source for securing sometimes scandalous information about celebrity clients.

Such rumor mongers often chased and hounded personal trainers for inside information about celebrity clients. Aside from secrets about who was sleeping with whom, much was to be learned about celebrity's substance abuse, financial problems, recent trips, and you name it. Personal fitness trainers were as good a source for such information as hairdressers, nannies, personal valets, attendants and other similar non-regulated persons. Often, however, once trainers stepped over the line, they needed a good lawyer, usually a criminal defense lawyer, to help them through their troubles.

Criminal defense lawyers were a different breed. Often loaners, many were solo practitioners or members of small firms. They were very frequently individualists in their decision making and in their own life activities. Some of these lawyers eventually turned to alcohol and/or drugs in efforts to cope with their personal and professional pursuits. Walt Manos had not yet gotten to that point. Good thing for Tony Piccini.

DAVID L. HERBERT

CHAPTER 12

In response to a FitAgain advertising blitz, Meri Margaret Lawrence showed up one day at the FitAgain facility in Upper Arlington, Ohio. The facility was the one where Tony Piccini worked either as an employee or an independent contractor. The answer to that question depended totally on one's perspective about that relationship.

Upper Arlington or UA as some called it, was a wealthy, affluent and trendy neighborhood just outside Columbus, yet near "The" Ohio State University. It was a good area with very nice, sometimes even elegant homes, valued in the upper six figures and some even in the seven figure category.

There was money in Upper Arlington, both old and new. Many of the streets were lined with established shade trees which often formed a kind of natural arch over most residential streets in this suburb of Columbus. Most streets were outlined with grassy green strips separating the streets from sidewalks and front lawns, commonly known as tree lawns or "Devil Strips."

Properties along the thoroughfares in UA were often lined with river rocks carefully stacked and placed along such roadways, usually without mortar, to create beautiful stone fences which added a distinctive charm to the area. In the springtime, flowering dogwoods and very beautiful, blooming crabapple trees often added bursts of color and fragrance to the landscape. The purple hues of some of these trees were particularly striking.

Affluence in UA was obvious, not only from looking at the residences located in the area but also from looking at the cars parked in the garages and driveways to those homes: Mercedes, BMWs, Audis, Acuras, Cadillacs and even a Rolls Royce or two. Ohio State's legendary football coach, Judson Trapp, reportedly lived in Upper Arlington in a very nice section of that Midwest city, in an area reserved for the very affluent or the best known people among its residents. No one was supposed to know where he resided, but many knew where he lived or at least thought they did.

Two private jet companies served the greater Columbus area along with more than half a dozen national airlines and regional carriers with readily available connections out of Atlanta or New York. Area residents were thus afforded the opportunity to travel the world with relative ease. Columbus and UA had much to offer, not only in easy travel but in educational opportunities, research facilities, law, medicine, entertainment, fine dining and much more.

Meri was drawn into FitAgain, like many clients, by the intense and extremely well planned advertising campaign put on each New Year, which in this case, was the year 2006. The ad campaign promised results and effectively told Meri and every other like-minded consumer, "clients" as FitAgain liked to call them: "FitAgain can make you over, burn off your fat, trim your flab and your cellulite and make you whatever you care to become. We can make you fit again." FitAgain advertised one particularly poignant message: "Work out with us. It won't kill you!" The message took several forms, but its meaning was clear. FitAgain promised effective, personal treatment and attention by "certified personal trainers."

"Certified" sounded good to Meri and most other clients. It made the trainers appear to be qualified. However, no state licensed or even regulated personal trainers or for that matter, any fitness professional. Louisiana was the single exception, where one legislator changed that after he had benefited from an exercise program in a cardiac rehabilitation facility. Following quadruple heart bypass surgery, this state Senator liked his post-surgery exercise physiologist so much that he caused that state's legislature to adopt a new enactment bestowing licensure and thus government-issued credibility upon clinical exercise physiologists who provided service in that state. The Louisiana Association of Cardiac Rehabilitation/Clinical Exercise Physiology (LA-CEP) was thrilled with that legislator's attention and hoped what he did for them would serve as a model for similar efforts in other states.

The LA-CEP even asked the American Clinical Exercise Physiology Association (ACEPA) to lead this effort to push for licensure in other states. As a result, the ACEPA then asked the Louisiana State Senator in question, Orpheus Ray, to help. While Ray was very powerful in his own state, he had little regional or national influence. As a result, the effort to secure licensure for any category of fitness professional lagged on as it had for many years in other states including California, Nevada, Maryland, Massachusetts, New Jersey and even the District of Columbia. No one was jumping on the bandwagon to license any type of fitness professional – not exercise physiologists and certainly not personal trainers. "No need," many authorities said. "Too costly," asserted industry trade associations. "Why bother," was the frequent response of others. "Fitness personnel aren't rocket scientists. They don't perform brain surgery. They don't hurt anyone. They certainly don't kill. No reason to regulate," said still others.

Industry trade groups like the USA-PTA opposed such legislation. The North American Association of Health Clubs, the NAAHC, did likewise and preached self-regulation as the cure for any shortcomings of the profession. Self-regulation they said would better protect the clients they served.

These stated positions were plain and simple. No case had been put forth by anyone to really convince any state to license or regulate fitness professionals. Moreover no one could justify the expenditure of state tax dollars to regulate any particular fitness professional or any other segment of the fitness industry. It didn't matter that barbers, beauticians, manicurists, masseuses, and even dog and cat groomers were subject to licensure or regulation in many, if not most, states. Without a clear case demonstrating the need for governmental intervention into the area or the effort becoming someone's pet project as happened in Louisiana, no licensure or regulation of fitness professionals or personal trainers in particular would happen. Even though personal trainers could cripple, make lame or kill one or more of their clients, no one believed that they could really do so. Until such a case was clearly demonstrated or until some major consumer interest was put forth or serious dollars were at jeopardy, no regulation would come to pass. Media attention to the problem, if there really was such an issue, was sporadic at best.

While there were cases of client injury and even death at the hands of fitness professionals, no one seemed to adequately quantify the problem even if there was one. Moreover, no one had raised enough media attention to cause either the public or state legislators to do something to address the issue. At least not before Tony began to train Meri in a FitAgain facility.

CHAPTER 13

When Meri first arrived at the FitAgain facility in UA, she was greeted by a very fit young woman in her twenties who obviously – at least to Meri – had never had children. She was tan and blonde, with impeccable poise and perfect makeup. Meri wondered if she actually could sweat or merely glow during activity. She was dressed in a black leotard with a wide red belt to which a pager and a cell phone were clipped. Her legs appeared to be perfectly toned and so long that they seemed to never stop. She gave Meri a short pep talk, determined and analyzed Meri's wishes and goals, and provided her with a guided tour of the facility, its equipment and amenities.

On the tour, she pointed out to Meri several young personal trainers working with clients. One of them was Tony Piccini whom she referred to as one of FitAgain's up and coming training stars, one she guaranteed could whip Meri "back into shape or die trying." This little FitAgain jingle was one which they would later regret having ever coined for the market.

This joyous greeter, Lindsey, as her name badge read, promised:

"Meri, you will have the best of care. Our personal trainers like Tony are certified and able to develop a personalized prescription plan of activity, exercise, nutritional assessment and meal planning as well as lifestyle modification to help you achieve your personal goals. The program is only staffed with the best people, utilizing time and result-proven activities to work you over and to return you to the place where you want and need to be." She continued, "You can trust me Meri; you can trust all of us. We will get you where you want to be or, as we promise, 'die trying.'"

Meri was impressed. Tony and the others were good looking, obviously fit and seemed to know what they were doing. She remembered that her college gymnastics coach was certified. He had been wonderful to her and helped her to get at least a place at the Mid-American gymnastics championship when she attended Ohio University, not "The" Ohio State University but OU as it was called. OU was a school in Athens, Ohio with a reputation some said as a "party school."

Certifications for personal trainers had to be important, Meri thought. It surely had to mean something. Her gymnastics coach was certified, and he was great! Tony and the others must be too.

"When can I start?" Meri blurted out. "I can't wait to get going. I'm busy but I've got to make time for this. I'm available between 5:30 and 6:30 each morning. Who do you have to work with me at that time, every day or at least five days a week, to get me back into shape?"

Lindsey smiled and began to review her list of early morning available trainers. Tony Piccini worked that time slot and Lindsey thought he would be perfect for her. "Tony Piccini, one of our very best, is available to work with you four or five mornings a week. You just saw him. He will be perfect for you."

Lindsey forgot to mention that Tony's "perfection" did not stem from his education, training, or certification. Lindsey had personal experience with Tony and considered him to be one of the very best, especially at fulfilling her base, carnal desires. Tony would give Lindsey a referral fee for Meri in addition to some long overdue personal attention that Lindsey hoped to enjoy very soon, perhaps early one morning before Meri's assigned time slot or even late one night on any day of Tony's choosing.

When Meri was referred to Tony by Lindsey he was 26. He had taken care of himself physically and utilized his charm and personal attributes time and time again to get himself ahead of the game and out of jam after jam. It was of little consequence that he didn't get beyond the second semester of college at Kent State University, another Ohio institute of higher learning or that he had not been able to define a clear career path. He was young and had all his wits and good looks about him.

He had worked several jobs once he flunked out of Kent or, as he would say, "matriculated" out of Kent reversing the meaning of the word. His experiences as a waiter at several Columbus area eating establishments, including Lucita's Steak House in the downtown section, exposed him to a lot of well-to-do folks. Many of these folks offered advice, great tips and as to the ladies, and even some men, an occasional personal note with phone numbers, dates, times and addresses. Tony had often flirted with his female customers, giving them a longing look, a cute smile, a wide grin or some other hint of what might come as he served them with some culinary delight. However, the provision of earthly delights was often his real goal with many of these customers.

While in one of these server positions, he even met one of the client closers from FitAgain, Nanett Nelson, who ultimately convinced Tony to try to use his charms, obvious fitness and physical attributes at one of FitAgain's facilities. She was sure he would be appreciated by one and all. She worked on Tony over several months, till she used her tipping power and various appetites for other kinds of culinary-like delights to convince Tony to leave his job at Lucita's and to go on a quest for life with those in need of all his services. Nanett convinced him to give it a try and promised, "It won't kill you." The promise was often used in various contexts at FitAgain to promote lots of things to help clients and even trainers focus on their own needs and wants. The phrase was not to be contradicted, not in real life. After all, it was just a phrase, one Tony would often use with his clients in efforts to help them move ahead, to overcome, to meet and achieve goals, to improve their lives. Not to prove the phrase wrong.

Meri was ready to sign the contract papers and to start the next day on FitAgain's program which was really designed by FitAgain to be carried out for an internally established period of two years. She was eager to join in. She believed what she had heard. The effort wouldn't kill her.

Unfortunately, she was wrong.

Meri was ready to sign all the contract documents necessary to start the FitAgain program the very next day. Once Meri was primed and ready, Lindsey passed her on to Nanett Nelson to close the deal as Nanett had done so many times before.

Nanett was just like one of those paper pushers in car dealerships, the ones who had customers sign all the necessary documents evidencing their commitment to pay more than they should, for more car than they needed. It was all part of the American dream.

Meri reviewed the forms in a cursory fashion, not really reading all that she signed. While Nanett handed over one form after another for Meri to sign, Nanett quickly summarized several pages of contract language legalese printed in small-point type into a few sentences: "This is your contract form, sign here. This is a release form, put your signature here; it's not worth the paper it's written on, but it's required, so sign here. This is a health questionnaire, I've filled it out for you, but don't worry about the details. I've checked all the right answers. If you ever have a problem or a health concern, tell your trainer, Tony. He will know what to do. You wouldn't be here at all if you couldn't do this. No worries. Sign here."

Meri really knew better than to just sign these documents. Her dad was a lawyer. He always told her to read carefully what she signed and to understand what she signed; or he would say, "Walk out and call me." Meri overlooked that advice in her quest to regain some quality of life. She was in a hurry since she was to start the next day. She thought, "How important could these papers be? These folks aren't doctors and this isn't surgery. After all they won't kill me."

CHAPTER 14

Meri Margaret's dad began his legal career as an assistant prosecuting attorney, also known as an assistant district attorney or assistant PA or DA. He had focused on the prosecution of career criminals and organized crime members. He had even served on an Ohio Governor's organized crime task force having been elected to that position by a large assembly of law enforcement personnel participating in a week long seminar designed to stop the infiltration of the mob into legitimate businesses.

He had successfully prosecuted some big cases involving major local drug dealers, organized gambling members and even some prostitution ring leaders. Initially he approached his assigned efforts with vigor and enthusiasm but soon realized that an Assistant PA pay would not sustain a growing family and his ultimate responsibilities to them. He quickly appreciated the need to plan to earn a higher income for when his children were ready to start college, become engaged and then married or to have careers of their own. While public service in a prosecuting or district attorney's role could lead to higher office or even a judgeship, Meri's dad chose to enter the private practice of law and focus on business and transactional law as well as civil litigation.

John Allen David began the part time civil practice of law while he phased out of his ever demanding prosecutional duties. It took three years to complete the transition, but he did so gradually and in pre-defined steps over that period. The transition was not easy. However, a number of other lawyers and public officials from whom he had earned respect, assisted him with cases and clients. Some ten years into that process, his future and that of his family was assured, not completely as with any entrepreneurial venture, but John Allen David was confident that the decisions he made were the right ones for him and his family. In most respects, he was right.

His sons participated in football and wrestling. They had significant success and performed admirably. They won varsity letters from their school and accolades from the local press. His older son even earned a college scholarship for his athletic abilities.

Meri, however, was a constant achiever in a variety of endeavors. At an early age, she began dance classes, then tumbling and then gymnastics. Youth cheerleading followed and then high school cheerleading and competitive team and individual cheer activities. She traveled far and wide across the continental United States to various competitions and soon began to excel as no David child had done before. In the off-season, she took up gymnastics and placed at the state level her last two years of high school. She was driven and not content with just doing her best but really being the best. That determination made a significant difference in her life, and it would permeate all Meri ever did.

John David was extremely proud of Meri's activities and appreciated the dedication and perseverance she displayed in all of her endeavors. She ultimately won several college scholarships for her cheerleading and gymnastics activities and then a place at the Mid-America Conference Gymnastics Championships – Third Place All Around and Second Place on the floor routine. Her performance didn't get her to the national tournament though, and she therefore failed to fulfill her own goals. Her dad, however, never ceased bragging about her accomplishments. She had a special place in his heart. All who knew him came to know of Meri's accomplishments as well.

CHAPTER 15

Meri had been introduced to Tony as a client who was a young and energetic fashion executive, a former college gymnast and cheerleader, and a mother who had just had her second baby. He was told that she wanted and needed to lose some baby-related weight that hung on after the delivery. She had been described to Tony by Lindsey as a "workaholic" who needed not only fitness training, instruction and motivation but also weight and nutritional counseling, meal planning, stress relief, muscle toning and flexibility routines in a six-week plan, one hour a day, four or five days a week to be repeated one six-week plan after another over a two-year period.

The plan was really a cake walk. Routine service and near guaranteed results – at least in the short term, where quick weight loss of a few pounds always happened in the first couple of weeks. Tony would also try to get her to quit smoking which he noticed when he met her. Despite the wonderful smell of her perfume, he detected a lingering but somewhat permeating smell of nicotine on her which the perfume she wore did not completely mask.

When Tony was introduced to Meri as her own "certified" personal trainer, Tony smiled as he always did when he met new clients. He told Meri the plan he would develop for her would be perfect.

"We will work great together," Tony stated. "I will work you HARD, but it won't kill you. I promise." Little did either realize the hollow ring of those words.

Meri almost didn't notice the comment. She replied however and told Tony, "I have a short time to lose 35 pounds and to tone up. I'm persistent. I will be here early and I will follow what you tell me to do. We need to get going."

Three months later when Meri was indeed making progress but had only lost 15 pounds she became somewhat discouraged. Tony had worked her legs, arms, core and more and had developed meal plans, off premise fitness activities and even individualized daily exercise prescriptions and plans. However, Meri was at a stalemate between her incredible willpower and Tony's need to carry her over the next hurdle which was to lose more weight, to tone and to shine. He would have to do more to push her further, to add an edge.

As Meri and Tony became acquainted and their near daily routine began to gain hold, Meri revealed many personal and private details of her life to Tony. She told him of her burning desire to lose weight after Chase's birth but she also told him of Paris and the night of Chase's conception and Ben's support of her needs for many of the past years.

She told Tony of her college days and of her achievements at OU as well as her sorority and school activities. She even revealed the circumstances of her first lovers to Tony and her experiences with some of them as she then began to learn of and appreciate the joys of life.

Meri also told Tony about her formative years and told him of her experiences with her parents, siblings and friends. She also recounted the successes she had experienced in her fashion career but also of the incredible pressures brought to bear upon her employment nearly every day during that career. She added information about her children and told Tony of the activities she enjoyed with them and with Ben in the few spare moments she seemed to have with both her children and her husband while away from the hammering pace of her career.

Over this period, Meri began to trust Tony. She even began to rely upon him for emotional support. It was the kind of relationship that Tony had enjoyed many times before and with almost all of his clients. Tony was a good listener and paid attention to verbal, as well as non-verbal cues to determine all that his clients really needed and desired. While he thought he read Meri correctly and perceived in her a need to get closer to him physically, his overtures in that regard were always rebuffed. Such a reaction was not unheard of for Tony with his clients. It just didn't happen too often. However, he learned to live with it in his relationship with Meri.

DAVID L. HERBERT

CHAPTER 16

Tony had seen things happen at FitAgain and had heard of numerous incidents of client injuries and even some deaths at the hands of personal trainers. However, all of these untoward events occurred at other facilities and with other trainers. Whatever happened, happened only at other clubs and with other clients.

One of Tony's college buddies, a personal trainer named Carl Snyder, had a client who lost a finger when the client put it under a stack of weights to adjust the load on an older weight machine while he was working out. All the client was trying to do was adjust the stack, but in doing so, he let go of the weight bar and the weight stack came down with 155 pounds of force which crushed most of his index finger. It could not be repaired. The top half of the finger had to be amputated above the knuckle.

Carl had been sued by the client who also named the facility, the equipment manufacturer and the equipment maintenance company as defendants. The client contended that they failed to properly instruct him in the use of the machine, that they failed to warn him of the potential dangers associated with the activity, that they failed to properly maintain and keep the machine in good condition, and that all of the defendants failed to properly word and post adequate instructions and warning labels on or at least near the machine.

The case was settled for an undisclosed sum by FitAgain's insurance company when they rolled out the release/waiver the client had signed one year before. They used the release, like the one Meri Lawrence had signed, to beat down the injured client's settlement expectations and demands. It worked in that case like many others, even when client waivers were misrepresented by facility personnel, or were ill-described, hidden in the fine print of long contract documents or often not even read. This latter failure to read could not really be used as a successful legal defense because the law requires legal responsibility for contract documents which are signed even when not read.

When Carl was first sued he called Tony. "Tony," he said during the call, "I have a client who lost a finger on one of the weight machines. I just can't believe he didn't pay more attention to what was going on. I'm not sure why I'm being sued."

Tony considered his comments and replied, "Hey, this kind of thing happens on occasion. We can't be expected to be responsible for every bad thing that happens. Shit happens. It's a fact. Don't worry too much about it. Your club will back you."

Carl considered Tony's comments but replied, "I don't know Tony. I'm not sure the club will back me up. If the truth were known, the machine should have been taken out of service long ago and replaced with a machine that had a proper safety guard in place to protect against this kind of thing from happening. However, the club manager is claiming that I should have provided more cautionary instructions to the client in the use of the machine. That's just crap."

Tony could not believe Carl would be hung out to dry and encouraged him to hang in there. "Carl, consider the source. No one can really believe you were responsible for a dated and outmoded piece of equipment. Didn't this client sign a release?"

Carl quickly replied, "Yes he did and if that piece of paper has any validity, I should be home free."

Tony thought and then said, "I hope FitAgain never tries to pull that bullshit on me. I won't stand for it." Such a mental and then verbal response gave Tony a degree of confidence even if provided just in his own words during a conversation with a fellow trainer. He really didn't know what FitAgain would do with him if one of his clients and one of their members were hurt while under his care and during his watch. 'Hope I never have to find out,' thought Tony.

Other more serious personal trainer incidents, however, had also occurred. In another Columbus area facility across town from the one Tony worked in, a personal trainer's client had died when he suffered a sudden cardiac arrest or SCA, as the term is abbreviated by those in the medical profession. While the facility had staff on site who were trained in CPR, no one allegedly responded in a proper way to the stricken client which led to that middle age client's death. He left a widow and a daughter, a near-to-graduation high school senior. His spouse, daughter and estate filed suit against the facility and everyone else they could think of, including every CPR trained staff member and personal trainer on site that day who did not come to the client's aid or did so in a feeble way.

The attorney for the plaintiffs also alleged that the facility should have had and used an AED – an automated external defibrillator which, according to the estate's expert, would have in all probability shocked the client's heart back into proper rhythm if used right away with the first sign of SCA. However, there was no AED on-site. One had been on order, but not yet received. Even if it had been on-site no one in the facility was trained in using such a device at the time the incident occurred.

The client, according to the estate's expert, died as a result some 11 to 14 months after the incident. Prior to expiring, the client had slipped into a sustained coma because his blood supply and the oxygen to his brain was compromised by his sporadically beating heart which could have – and according to the experts – should have been shocked with an AED back into regular rhythm within a short time of the incident at the club. It seems that the client's brain was deprived of oxygen for too long while he waited for defibrillation to shock his heart back into a proper and stable rhythm in order to properly pump oxygen enriched blood to his brain. No defibrillation was provided to him until the paramedics arrived and used their own AED. Unfortunately, by that time a total of 9 minutes had passed from the time he went down until the time an adequate emergency response was provided – too long a period of time for an effective response but apparently too short a period to cause imminent and certain death.

It also seemed that no one started proper CPR until the EMS paramedics arrived some minutes after the onset of the SCA. By then, the client had been without oxygen for too long since his heart had only fluttered out of normal rhythm and could not effectively pump oxygenated blood to his brain. He did start breathing again once a defibrillator shocked his heart back into some semblance of normal rhythm, but that was about a minute after the EMS unit arrived and some 10 minutes after the onset of the SCA. The client never came out of his coma and never spoke to his family again.

Ultimately the client's heart followed his impaired brain function and simply quit beating some months after the untoward event took place. Once suit was filed, the facility and its insurance carrier brought in several industry experts to counter the testimony supplied by the plaintiffs' experts. The plaintiffs' experts contended that the facility's inactions, the lack of an AED and the failure to have even a written emergency plan all led to the client's death.

The experts for both sides were all eminently well-qualified. During the later filed litigation, a cardiologist, a cardiac rehabilitation physician, a neurologist and an emergency/critical care doctor testified for the plaintiffs. Another cardiologist, an exercise physiologist and an emergency care expert, testified for the fitness facility and all of the defendants. The critical testimony in the case centered on the industry's evolving standards as published by the National Center for Fitness and Medicine (NCFM) and the American Network of Health Clubs (ANHC), both of whom had previously issued position statements before the incident occurred recommending the presence and use of AEDs in fitness facilities. In the case of NCFM, that group actually stated in its standards statement that facilities were required to have an AED present and available for use as part of its so-called standard of care information which it had previously developed and published. Too bad Tony thought, for the decedent client and his family in that case, since the facility in question did not implement the recommendations provided in that standard.

Tony had learned of the standard quite by accident from a client who had read about it in the local newspaper. The client asked Tony, "Does FitAgain have AEDs available here in the event of need?"

Not knowing what to say in response to such a direct question, Tony said, "I am sure that FitAgain has developed the necessary planning and policies to deal with those incidents. I'm a certified personal trainer here but I'm not responsible for policy implementation or for the selection and purchase of equipment. You should ask the floor manager or the receptionist." While he provided what sounded like a good and plausible response, Tony simply passed the buck.

The adoption of one or the other of these standards statements dealing with AEDs – two sets of standards and guidelines, as the lawyers liked to call them – had not been an easy task for the industry. Some members of the ANHC had vigorously opposed any statement on the subject and had fought tooth and nail to keep out any requirement for the presence of AEDs in health clubs. The group was very much concerned with its member's bottom lines, and it believed the cost of the devices (then currently about $2,000 to $3,000 each, with the price dropping each year) coupled with the additional upkeep and maintenance costs for the devices as well as staff training and certification costs were simply too great a price to pay for any such effort.

While the development of an AED requirement for health and fitness facilities was advocated by some, the final standards requirement was considerably tempered and watered down from what many believed was necessary. That weak standard was developed even though the group knew from previous incidents in its member clubs that the occurrence of SCA in all health and fitness facilities was high enough to warrant affirmative and substantial action for facilities to be properly prepared for the occurrence of these untoward events.

The ANHC had learned of these matters from a survey it conducted of its member clubs. While the survey results were shared with some ANHC members, the results were not published for just anyone's perusal and certainly not made available for public consumption. In fact, the ANHC had tried to hide its findings not only from the press but from a number of plaintiffs and their lawyers in other cases – even from some of its own members as well. The survey concluded that instances of SCA and sometimes death occurred with predictable and regular frequency in health and fitness facilities during member exercise activities. Because of that finding, it was important for facilities to anticipate and plan for such events which were clearly "foreseeable," as lawyers liked to argue, when attempting to hold others to blame for their clients' injuries. Such concepts helped those lawyers secure compensation/damages for the victims of the "if something bad happened to me it must be someone else's fault" syndrome.

The plaintiffs' lawyers in the case Tony remembered had heard about the survey findings. They also knew that the survey results had been intentionally suppressed from public view and examination. When the plaintiffs sought and secured the results of the survey through an order of the trial court in their litigation, the facility was "encouraged" by the ANHC to promptly settle the case and seek a confidential settlement agreement to keep the survey results out of the files of other plaintiff attorneys who had similar cases pending in other areas and other states on the same issues.

When it became clear that the court would not unilaterally order the survey results held in confidence, the facility and its insurance carrier had no choice but to settle the case and secure a confidential settlement agreement from the plaintiffs. Once the settlement money was on the table and a confidentiality agreement reached, the plaintiffs and their lawyers were required to maintain the secrecy of the survey results. The agreement provided that they would never reveal the contents of the survey or its findings. The threat in that pact was that if they ever did so, they would breach the agreement. If such a breach of agreement was later proven, monetary penalties would then be imposed upon them. Moreover, since the court had ordered the parties to comply with the settlement agreement, any disclosure of the survey results which was prohibited by the agreement could also result in potential, if not probable, contempt of court findings.

While Tony knew there had been numerous claims, suits and even some settlements in the health and fitness industry due to the alleged negligence of facilities and fitness service providers, including personal trainers, claims and litigation in the industry, some suggested, were mounting. This increase in claims and suits might be due to a variety of problems: lack of proper training or real certification of fitness personnel, including personal trainers, poor equipment selection, improper assembly, maintenance and even negligent instruction in the use of equipment by clients, improper supervision of activity, lack of recognition of client exercise stress or fatigue, inappropriate exercise prescriptions, over-training, pushing clients too hard or too fast, lack of timely emergency response, even the recommendation to clients to take nutritional and other potentially harmful substances containing substances like Ma Huang. This substance alone caused an increase in metabolism for those taking it but also frequently caused a corresponding increase in blood pressure, heart rate and respiration which could become very dangerous to some. Tony for one, just didn't know nor appreciate the potential damage that could readily flow out of such matters. He hoped he would never find out.

CHAPTER 17

As Tony and the other defendants in the civil wrongful death lawsuit of Lawrence v Piccini waited for the jury's verdict, and as Judge Charles Davis reveled in the meeting with counsel in his chambers, some distance across the country, in the District of Columbia, a courier walked into the United States Patent Office. The courier was there to file a request with full documentation for a patent on a new boon to all of mankind. The application was a request to the Patent Office to issue U.S. Patent #7,863,894NS. The product for which the application was made was simply described as citra-aid, made from the rinds of oranges and from a previously unknown substance first isolated and then extracted out of the leaves of a certain green tea. According to recently published studies funded by the nutritional supplement industry, the mystery substance, when taken in proper dosages and frequencies, resulted in substantial weight loss for those taking it while also increasing their capacities for work and/or exercise.

The combined substance had been tested first on very lethargic and overfed rats. Once these rats ingested the product, they demonstrated a significant and substantial increase in their aerobic capacities after only two weeks on the substance. As a complete surprise to the investigators, however, the mice also lost 5% of their body weights in that same time. Researchers were astonished to observe this finding. The dramatic weight loss properties of the substance were accidentally "discovered" in the first place as the investigators contemplated doing research on how to make assembly line workers in third world countries endure longer shifts and be more productive while doing so. The rat's reaction to the substance could well become important to humans.

A five percent weight loss in rats translated to humans in a loss of nearly 10 pounds in a two-week period for a 200 pound man. Apparently the benefits were twofold: increased capacity for work or exercise and fast weight loss, both of which were readily demonstrated in the study. As a consequence, the principal investigator of the study, the one who isolated and then combined the substances, a young and very bright assistant professor at the Florida Institute of Nutrition and Human Performance, part of the Florida University system, was about to become famous and surely very, very rich.

This researcher, Roger Barnet, Ph.D., had received his undergraduate degree in biology from Harvard University, his masters in molecular biology from Princeton and his doctorate in human nutrition and exercise physiology from VIT. His credentials, professional training and background were impeccable. He had published in all the right peer-reviewed journals and had sat on his university's institutional review board, or IRB as it was called, which had the responsibility of following federal guidelines related to research performed with and on human subjects. The idea was to insure no overreaching or undue influence on those subjects during the course of their volunteering to participate in research studies while also not exposing them to inappropriate and unreasonable risks. IRB protocols and requirements were based upon federal law and regulations developed after World War II during which bizarre, cruel and sadistic medical experiments had been carried on against unwilling concentration camp prisoners by Nazi physicians.

While peer-reviewed journals like those which carried Dr. Barnet's findings were designed to give a degree of credibility to articles and research findings published in those journals, some contended that peer-reviews for these publications were little more than colleague provided rubber stamps for the articles submitted for publication. The belief was that these approvals would someday result in similar favors provided by those whose work was being reviewed to those acting as reviewers. Normally, every reviewer involved in academic publications or research studies also had their own articles and studies reviewed at some time by other "colleagues" from these journals. It was a kind of buddy system – you review and approve mine now, and I will review and approve yours later. Those involved would swear otherwise, but in reality, it was just another form of the "good ol' boy network." However, this one was occupied by so-called academicians living and working in ivory towers.

Dr. Barnet had completed and filed all the proper documents with the university system about his research study protocols on citra-aid. He did so initially in his grant application submission to the university system's oversight committee and later when progress reports were due. In his original application, Dr. Barnet seemed to have provided a certain rather considerable degree of financial disclosure and information, but he would soon be accused of failing to report his receipt of nearly one million dollars of sponsor payments provided to him from among others, SlimLine, Mitch Malloy's company, for what should have been designated at the very best as consulting work. These payments had made Dr. Barnet's life quite enjoyable and allowed his wife and children to accompany him to various professional meetings each year in a number of desirable vacation destinations – San Diego, California; Orlando, Florida; Las Vegas, Nevada and cities like New York, Chicago and Los Angeles. These payments also helped to insure his and their respective futures. While he might have to suffer an investigation into alleged conflicts of interest by the university as well as the state and federal governments, his interest in the proprietary rights to citra-aid seemed to be well assured.

In the face of considerable criticism about the payments he received, including those put forth by jealous colleagues who had not fared as well as Dr. Barnet with their own research related projects and benefits, and with the threat of multiple investigations looming against him, Dr. Barnet issued a press statement which provided:

> For the past five years, I have worked diligently with the aid of grants provided to the university, not to me, to seek ways to better the lives of all overweight Americans. I have isolated and enhanced a natural substance made from a simple citrus fruit and combined it with another, previously unidentified substance from green tea which will greatly aid in adult weight loss efforts, exercise capacities and the opportunity for many Americans – in fact everyone – to live longer and better lives. There have been overwhelming beneficial results reported in our studies of these substances when regularly taken by human subjects. The drawbacks have been very, very minor. The side effects of taking citra-aid are essentially insignificant and amount to a potentially negative outcome in only 1 in nearly 100,000 subjects. It will not cure disease, but it will be of great benefit to all Americans and all of mankind.

What he forgot to relate was how the development of the product and the further prospects of the product would be a financial benefit to himself and his family. He also forgot to mention that he had also received substantial indirect "consulting" payments from SlimLine for, among other things, product development. He also never mentioned his expectation that the anticipated profits from this product might make the financial holdings of many Wall Street bankers seem "slim" indeed.

Some people considered it strange, perhaps even funny, as to how researchers always referred to those who participated in their studies as "subjects." What about just calling them people, ordinary, everyday folks, not subjects. Calling these folks subjects seemed far too distant. Too detached. Perhaps that was what was intended. Keep the label on them impersonal and detached. No wonder a percentage of subjects were almost always hurt in some of these studies. One in 100,000 doesn't seem like such bad odds unless some real person is the one! According to this impersonal view, calling a person a subject, not a person helps in dehumanizing adverse research issues and findings. Such matters go over better if something bad happens to a "subject" rather than if that same individual is referred to as a "person."

If Mitch Malloy could somehow get the focus off the <u>Piccini</u> case, he eagerly anticipated the riches that Barnet's find would create for SlimLine, Barnet and even himself. While some would question how the money to come from the product would go to Barnet and not the University where he worked, this kind of scenario seemed to occur all the time.

University professors, including those working at state supported institutions of higher learning, were always involved in research from which real products, applications or patents were frequently developed. These products or applications were taken to market by entrepreneurial "sponsors" from whom the principal researchers benefited, sometimes with very lucrative profits. No matter that tax dollars provided the facilities, supplies, computers, graduate students and other personnel with the opportunity for a professor to develop findings or applications which led to the creation of products. Those who developed the findings should profit, even if they worked all the while on the college or university payroll and thus on taxpayers' dollars.

Colleges and universities rarely question no less attack the diversion of profits related to product or application discoveries from their coffers to those of the professors on their payrolls and whose laboratories, graduate students, supplies and resources are paid for with taxpayer and student funds. In private industry no such practices would ever be condoned.

At least one university out West had actually challenged the practice. When one of the institution's researchers, a tenured professor, refused to turn over a fair share of the profits from his on-school time and premises-related product discovery, the university filed a 20-page civil complaint against him. The action was one for a declaratory judgment which alleged that the university was "the lawful and proper owner of the inventions, patents and patent applications developed, conceived and reduced to a product as those were so conceived and developed on university premises, using university buildings and facilities, fixtures and supplies during the scope and course of the defendant's employment with the university." The university sought a court declaration that the processes, applications, patents and patent applications for the product were legally the school's property and further sought an injunction to stop the marketing process as well as an order requiring the defendant professor to provide a list of all of his discoveries and products derived therefrom, applications available and patents and patent applications made which were related to this effort. The school also sought an accounting of all monies received by him as well as a judgment against him for all the damages and sums due the university.

The university prevailed in the suit, but a counterclaim filed by the professor in question also sought all or at least a large percentage of the profits derived from his research findings. Due to the fact that a good bit of the research had been performed, at least according to the professor, on his own time during summer recesses, he received an award of 25% of the profits, which in the first year following commencement of the suit amounted to over $600,000 with much more expected. Perhaps university employment was not so bad after all, even if a professor gets sued.

If products like Ma Huang were successfully attacked and thereafter removed from the market place, time and good old market based ingenuity, not to mention the greed factor, would always lead to efforts to replace those products with something else. Some such products would be used in wars, and some would be used in everyday life. Some would help. Some would be abused, and some would lead to pain, injury and even death. That's the way it always is, for good or for bad.

CHAPTER 18

Following college graduation, Meri went to a prestigious institution of higher learning for fashion studies known as the American Fashion Institute of Technology (American FIT) in New York City. She was a top student and worked diligently to complete all of her assignments and projects with vigor, enthusiasm and excellence. Following graduation from American FIT, she interned with several giants in the clothing industry, including one in women's wear and two other clothing retailers. She ultimately decided to go with one of the women's wear companies, simply called "Flair," as a management trainee with an emphasis on the petite line of women's wear. All of Flair's clothing was designed in-house but manufactured elsewhere in third world countries, returned to the United States and then retailed in Flair's own stores.

Meri started in the Tampa, Florida store but was soon promoted to the Atlanta area. She worked out of a Dunwoody, Georgia location just outside Atlanta, as the petite wear buyer for four states in the Southeast: Georgia, North Carolina, South Carolina, and Alabama. She spent nearly two years in that capacity and was thereafter promoted to the Columbus, Ohio headquarters of Flair after she managed to increase the sales of petite wear products in her stores by 80% in her two years in Atlanta.

While in the Columbus headquarters of Flair, she was given considerable responsibility for the entire Southeast Region of the country including the states of Florida, Georgia, North and South Carolina, Tennessee, Kentucky, Alabama, Mississippi, and Virginia. She worked even more hours in Columbus than she had when she started in Tampa or even in Atlanta and regularly worked over 70 hours a week. The stress was incredible and the nights were often long when she attended various meetings with local store managers, buyers, marketing personnel and designers. She put her mark on new clothing designs as well as their initial fabrication, production, advertising, sale and shipping. She even addressed store window displays with each store merchandiser and had a particular penchant for this task.

Meri liked this end of the business and it was in her blood. Her grandmother had been a visual merchandiser and fashion display designer long before her grandmother's position with what was then generally known as Sears, Roebuck and Company actually fit into that label or name. "Honey" as her grandmother was affectionately called by all who knew her, had a real talent for fashion, color, clothing construction and visual merchandising. She was a master at point-of-purchase display work and got along with her numerous co-workers, supervisors and customers in all of the stores where she worked. Meri had some of the same qualities as her grandmother and could usually create something out of nothing in the same artistic way Honey had done many years before.

Meri's day typically began at 6:00 or 6:30 a.m. and often continued until 9:00, 10:00 or even 11:00 at night more than 5 days a week. These hours often included working dinners which unfortunately got Meri into the habit of eating too much and too late in the evening. She generally skipped breakfast and sustained herself each morning on strong coffeehouse brews.

Sleep was often short, and Meri's body was often deprived of proper rest and rejuvenation for extended periods. Depravation of sleep, as some researchers had come to know, was a significant adverse factor contributing to weight gain, perhaps even to a greater extent than overeating. So, was skipping breakfast which actually caused her body to preserve the available caloric fuel left in her body's fat cells from the night before. Skipping this meal slowed her weight loss process down considerably.

The foods at some of Meri's dinner functions were loaded with unnecessary and "unworthy" calories and were generally preceded by "dirty" vodka martinis accompanied by bleu cheese stuffed olives, often followed with a select chardonnay or an old merlot to wash down dinner. Once she took up cigarette smoking – slowly, ever so slowly, not for the desire to do so but simply to fit in and relieve the stress of the day – she began a downward spiral from where she had been in high school and college as an elite athlete excelling in gymnastics and cheerleading. Indulgence in bad habits was not her real style, but it helped her get through the stress, the long hours of work and sometimes even brash or far out dinner company.

Her first real contact with this kind of lifestyle occurred at corporate when she learned what was expected of her and how she would fit in. Her immediate supervisor in Columbus was Margo Robbins, a long time Flair employee who worked her way up the ranks, through many stores and regions. Margo had been through a number of sexual escapades with several male executives at the company, each of whom helped pave the way to her position as one of the Vice Presidents of Flair.

On Meri's first day in Columbus, Meri was summoned to Margo's office to be indoctrinated with corporate expectations. "Hello Meri," Margo began. "Welcome to Columbus. I have reviewed your resume, your prior store and company positions and your very solid performance. Your increase in petite sales in Tampa was most impressive and your results in the Southeastern Region were exemplary. But in this business, at this company, and in this industry, it's not what you did before, it's not what you did in your prior job or even who you previously gave head to in efforts to get ahead. Here it is what you do today that matters, how you perform now and who you can trust to get ahead."

Meri was somewhat taken aback by some of Margo's comments but was not shocked as she would have been some years before. Meri replied, "Margo, if I might call you Margo . . ."

Margo nodded affirmatively, and said, "You may. I've sure been called a lot of other things, but Margo will work."

Meri continued, "I'm here because I have performed in the past and am doing so at the present. I didn't get here through favors, sexual or otherwise, but through hard work. Except for my father, a lawyer up north of here in Canton, I have outworked everyone in my family, all of my friends in high school and every teammate on my college gymnastics team and cheerleading squad, essentially every one of my so-called peers."

Meri continued, "While with this company, I have worked 70 hours or more per week every week for 3 years. In my opinion, I deserve to be here. I have performed in the past, I am doing so now, and I will perform in the future. I hope together we can be a team that will let me make both of us look good without having to get on my knees to do so."

Margo smiled. She immediately liked Meri's response; then and there she determined to help Meri work her way through the Flair corporate maze and to see to it that she succeeded.

"Well Meri, I like what you say. I hope you can live up to your potential as well as my expectations.

She continued, "We can start now with a meeting of the fashion design team and some buyers. Recently, many of them have been in all of our competitors' stores, checking out new designs, styles, colors, prices and the like. Two have just returned from a meeting in New York. Two more have just flown back from Paris. And one just got back from Milan. All of them picked up some great new trends and ideas. It appears to me at least for the upcoming fashion season that what was shall be again. I'm sure you already know that. Let's go. Afterwards I'll take you to dinner with a few of the women here so you can meet the team that really runs this company."

That session with Margo and the others that very night set the stage for Meri's plunge into Flair's corporate complex. More work, more stress, more food and more drink than was good for her. She would pay a price for her success, more than she had ever dreamed of – or some would later say, feared. The problem was that Meri was fearless.

CHAPTER 19

Meri showed up early for her first one-hour session with Tony at the UA FitAgain facility. Tony was late by 6 minutes, and Meri made note of it.

"Tony," she began, "At these prices I need you to be on time and to tell me what to do. If I get here early, or at least before you, tell me what I can do to get started or at least to warm up."

Tony smiled at Meri as she talked. He took in and digested what he saw: a five-foot, four-inch, 30-something-year-old young woman, about 35 pounds overweight, dressed in shorts over leg tights and a baggy tee-shirt covering too much of Meri's body underneath the fabric. Tony would help her and work her hard to get rid of her excess. After all, it won't kill her.

Tony had heard it before, countless times in fact. Despite the number of times he was so indoctrinated, he liked what he heard. Regular exercise, especially with the help of a personal trainer in a clean, modern and up-to-date facility, reduced the risks of heart disease, high blood pressure, high cholesterol, increased triglycerides, diabetes, bone loss, anxiety, depression and a host of other physical and psychological ailments including cancer, allergies, dementia and more.

The byline was - get fit and stay youthful, exercise regularly and prolong life, fit into your clothes, get in shape and pick up some good looking guys or girls, body build, look good in a tuxedo or a swim suit or on a nude beach in Saint Martin or on the French Riviera.

Tony believed that the benefits from exercise and fitness were really endless. All it took was some tutelage from a good trainer and a willingness to work. Exercise is tantamount to well-being; it's a prescription for a long and good life. But as it turned out, at least for Meri, exercise was a benefit only if it were properly dispensed and only when taken in the appropriate dosage through a prescription for exercise provided by a truly professional personal trainer.

Tony responded to Meri: "Today I will more than make up for the few minutes I was delayed in getting ready to help you. We start today to change your life."

While Tony knew the benefits of exercise were many and diverse, more accolades were on the horizon about the benefits of exercise from many sources.

In fact, but unknown to Tony, exercise in a pill was coming. More literally, the benefits of exercise in a pill were being developed. This product promised ever more benefits and profits than that which Dr. Barnet had discovered. Other researchers had already isolated a compound that would increase the aerobic capacity and training ability of laboratory mice which were given the compound when compared to sedentary and overweight mice. Given the benefits of the drug, it was only a matter of time before it would make its way up the food chain to humans just like Dr. Barnet's weight loss discovery.

However, in anticipation of what was certain to come, various athletic organizations, including the International Olympic Committee, were already working on a test to analyze blood samples to detect the exercise pill substance, which had already been placed on a list of prohibited agents in competitive athletics. Even though the "exercise pill" was yet to be refined and then developed and designed to supplant real exercise and training, the substance was sure to be used by athletes to gain an advantage, an edge over their competitors, a small fraction of whom almost unbelievably stayed within the rules.

The exercise pill would be another substance to be added to a long schedule of prohibited chemical agents used by those athletes who hoped to win while violating the rules of fair play. As it had been, so shall it be whether in fashion or in athletics. However, back room chemists operating in clandestine laboratories were sure to be working on a way to mask or avoid detection of the "exercise pill" by any banned substance testing procedure. Time would tell if their efforts would be successful.

CHAPTER 20

Even though Tony wasn't always late for his early morning training sessions with Meri, he sometimes showed up as much as 10 or 11 minutes after their appointment was scheduled to start. Given the early hour for Meri's sessions, perhaps that tardiness was to be expected. However, as determined as Meri was to get her excess baggage off her body, she didn't particularly like to wait on Tony.

Meri never wasted time; she always arrived early. She often said to Tony, "It is just as easy to be early as it is to be late."

When Tony was late as occurred more often than not, she began her preparation for that day's training activity by stretching and warming up. She had always engaged in these activities during her previous athletic career, so these activities were nothing new to her.

If Tony was late, she stretched out and then got on a treadmill set at 2.7 mph to start her aerobic activity. She tried to work up to 3.5 mph or sometimes faster. On rare occasions, she set the treadmill on an incline.

Usually by the time she got going, Tony would arrive in a fanfare and a flurry of activity, stop her, sometimes abruptly and then get her into his prescribed cross training activities.

Tony would always start the session with the same kind of instructions: "Come on, Meri, let's get going. Give me 25 sit-ups and then 10 push-ups. It won't kill you. Let's move."

Then he would put her on a number of exercise machines to work her abs, her core, her glutes, legs, biceps and shoulders. Then they would move on to heavy leg lifts, more sit ups and push-ups, followed by a faster treadmill pace than she had tried herself before he arrived.

"Meri, get going, it won't kill you," was his frequent statement.

On a regular basis, Tony would set the treadmill for Meri's use at 4.5 to 5.0 mph. It could be a grueling 30 minutes to nearly an hour of treadmill exercise depending on Tony's original arrival time and Meri's paid session. The speed required Meri to do more than just jog but to run.

Sometimes Meri objected to the pace at which Tony would cajole and push her to move her from one activity to another. No breaks. No chance to decrease her heart rate or to recover.

Tony pushed Meri because he thought that's what he should do. After all FitAgain had certified him to engage in personal training. He knew what he was doing. All those years in the gym had prepared him well. He looked good, therefore he must be good at exercise prescription and personal training. No doubt.

Tony's training to become certified by FitAgain had consisted of classroom sessions one hour a week for 12 weeks in a number of disciplines deemed important for personal training activities by FitAgain. The training sessions included the topics of psychological motivation, interpersonal sales techniques, personal speaking and one-on-one communications, building client trust and rapport, getting client referrals and recommendations, and the very basic information about the fundamentals of exercise. Additional "on-the-record" topics were sometimes thrown in and promoted by FitAgain. These special topics included contracts, waivers, other legal documents, exercise equipment cleaning and maintenance techniques as well as perceived exertion levels.

No testing or written exams were required of Tony or any other FitAgain certified personal trainer. No practical demonstration of actual exercise prescription, supervision or leadership skills were required of the soon to be certified trainers. No training in exercise testing, prescription or supervision was on any FitAgain agenda for people like Tony. No training in cardiopulmonary resuscitation (CPR) was mandated, not to mention any other emergency response technique including any instruction in the operation of an automated external defibrillator (AED), even after the cross town litigation over that issue which had occurred some years previously.

No personal trainer candidate for certification by FitAgain ever failed to achieve that designation. Their pass rate was 100%. While some candidates dropped out and moved on to other jobs, no candidate flunked out. In some respects, this was a totally new experience for Tony given his previous and short educational efforts at Kent.

Whatever else Tony really knew about fitness and personal training he picked up from other "trainers" operating in a number of FitAgain's facilities or in the gyms that he had previously been in prior to coming to FitAgain. Certification in FitAgain's personal training system had little to do with fitness, safe exercise prescription or leadership but more to do with the business of training.

Sessions that FitAgain trainers were required to attend were also presented on other topics but not recorded or logged in by FitAgain in any official document or record. It seems that they didn't want unnecessary attention to be directed to what they were doing, especially from the Ohio Board of Dietetics.

That Board had previously prohibited fitness personnel like Tony from engaging in the unlawful practice of dietetics. If they had known what he and FitAgain were doing, they would have certainly stopped it as they had done with other fitness organizations and professionals in Ohio on many separate occasions.

If ever questioned, FitAgain would have only vague recollections of any such training or educational sessions. They would disavow any knowledge if caught and probably throw to the wind any personal trainer called on the carpet. Some training personnel might even forget about these sessions. They certainly never told Tony or any of the other trainers to keep notes.

These non-recorded training sessions included informational presentations on nutritional counseling, weight loss, vitamins, energy drinks, other similar products as well as nutritional supplements. Information was provided about those substances which would work best with certain other substances and which products, even medicines, would slow down the effectiveness of those products. Weight loss to be achieved through some of these products when administered along with personal training was stressed and promoted.

In these sessions, Tony learned that many prescriptions for ailments such as high blood pressure, diabetes or other conditions often slowed down weight loss and interfered with a number of fat burning agents and weight loss products like those made with Ma Huang. Tony mentally filed this information away for later use but it was a lot to remember. He learned that sales of some of these nutritional products were the key to success for FitAgain, himself and his clients – in that order. He sometimes wondered about who would look after the rest. However, he knew it was important for him to meet FitAgain's advertising quotas and client expectations. Weight loss was deemed to be paramount to overall client health. After all, if client expectations were not met or at least addressed, no repeat services would be necessary or provided. Most importantly, the lack of repeat business would equate with a lack of revenue for Tony and FitAgain. He didn't want to see that happen – no matter what.

CHAPTER 21

Back in the Honorable Charles Davis' chambers, the judge was enjoying his second piece of hard candy as well as the undivided attention of his captive audience, the lawyers in the <u>Lawrence v. Piccini</u> matter. They were all local except, of course, for the one New York lawyer in the bunch, an out-of-towner, the one that Davis really didn't like very much. Davis had put up with him during the trial. He had admonished the New York prima donna twice in front of the jury. He probably didn't need to do it at all, but he did so to let that lawyer and all the other lawyers know their place in Davis' court. Davis was in charge; he was in command in that courtroom and in his chambers. He wanted all of them to know it.

In his chambers, Davis liked to line up rows of chairs in front of his desk and to beckon the lawyers to sit in them while directing their individual and collective attention solely on him. His ego demanded that fixation. He would stand for nothing less. Whether in his chambers, at his desk or in his courtroom, he was the star actor, and the lawyers were bit players.

For the <u>Lawrence v Piccini</u> case, the judge placed the plaintiffs' lawyer to his left and all of the defendants' lawyers to his right. Once all of these players were in his chambers, he first focused on the plaintiffs' lawyer, Frank LaPorte. "Frank," he said, referring back to the jury's question given to him on the third day of their deliberations. "You read the jurors' question. It may mean that they have decided to hold one or more of the defendants liable, but which one we don't know. It may be Piccini. If it is, he doesn't have a pot to pee in. Maybe, from what Mr. Finestein has said to us, he may have no insurance to pay and satisfy any verdict. If they pick him, solely him to blame, your clients will be out of luck."

"Judge," LaPorte began, "the jurors' question may also mean that they may let the pharmacist out of this or perhaps his employer. It may be the supplement store, or perhaps others, or perhaps no one. But somebody here will be responsible for Meri's death. Somebody will pay. I expect it to be most of the defendants, if not all of them, despite the question. Maybe the question is in the abstract. Surely they will hold Piccini, FitAgain as his employer and SlimLine to the wall. This crap about FitAgain not being responsible for Meri's death because Piccini was an independent contractor is just that; it's bullshit."

"Well, I object to these poisonous comments to the Judge," said Joan Childs referring to LaPorte's comments. "FitAgain didn't employ Piccini and had nothing to do with his shortcomings there. Piccini killed Mrs. Lawrence. We had nothing to do with it. We intend to have the Judge dismiss us from this case no matter what the jury may say, because the evidence is incontrovertible that FitAgain was not his employer."

"I've had just about all I can take of this crap," said LaPorte. "FitAgain knew everything Piccini did and encouraged it. I can tell you ... "

"Stop," said Davis. "I've had enough of this; don't tell me Ms. Childs what I will do here."

Just then Davis' eye caught one of the lawyers, Vince Harper, sitting to the judge's right, leaning over in his chair, but ever so slightly, looking to the side of Davis' office and at a picture of the Judge with the former Governor of Ohio, now Vice-President of the United States, Samuel L. Wilson. When Wilson was Governor of the state, he had appointed Davis to his first judgeship. The two appeared in a number of photographs together since the day Davis was sworn in, including the one on Davis' wall. Davis still maintained contact with Wilson even during Davis' drinking days. However, Davis wanted Harper's attention focused on him.

"Mr. Harper," Davis admonished, "pay attention to me and what's going on here, not the photograph. You won't learn a damn thing by looking over there. What you need to know is in front of your nose, not next to your ear."

"Yes, Sir," replied Harper. "Just curious."

"Curiosity killed the cat and the lawyer who didn't pay attention," said His Honor Charles Davis. "Sit up." Harper did so but was embarrassed. He was only looking at the photo. What was the harm? He felt the blood rush to his neck and his face turn hot and surely red. The color spread to his cheeks and ears. He hoped no one would notice.

He would be able to properly respond to the egotistical Judge Davis someday. Davis was only a lawyer who moved up to become a judge. He wasn't God. Harper didn't like what had needlessly been done to him in front of the others. He thought he would someday make Davis pay for this embarrassment.

With that, Davis reached for his intercom and summoned his Bailiff, Bill Morris into his chambers, "Bill, get in here and get these lawyers out of my office while I take a break to figure out what to do." With that, Davis told them all to get up and get out for at least 30 minutes.

Once Morris escorted them out, Davis had the bailiff come back into his chambers. "Bill," he said, "what can you hear the jury saying through the door to the jury room?"

Bill replied, "Judge, it's hard to know. There's been a lot of arguing, some of the women have been crying. I can hear it. Some don't understand how such a 'nice boy' as Piccini could have done all this without someone else's knowledge and approval."

Bill continued, "It seems to me that they just don't know exactly who to blame for Mrs. Lawrence's death. But certainly they will return a verdict for the family, especially to benefit those kids."

"Have you gone through the wastebasket in there to see if any of them threw away any notes or straw vote ballots?" asked Davis.

"Not yet," said Bill. "I can look during the jury's next break."

Davis replied, "Let's give them one and see what they are thinking. Tell the lawyers we will give the jury an early dinner break. Then, once everyone is out, go through the wastebasket in there and tell me what you find."

      Bill knew what to do. He had done it before. He wasn't supposed to do so; Davis wasn't supposed to do so either. It was a violation of both Davis' and Morris' oaths of office as well as the laws of the State of Ohio to mess with a jury. If anyone found out, they could both be removed from office or face criminal charges and prosecution. Davis would be disbarred. But if Davis told him to do it, he would do as he was told and as he had done before without question. Davis was his boss and Davis was a judge. That was all Bill needed to know.

CHAPTER 22

His Honor Charles Davis had not always been a judge. He started his career fresh out of the prestigious Michigan Law School and had joined an equally prestigious Midwest law firm, Smith, Oglebee and Badger. "SOB," as it was known in various legal circles, had ties all over the Midwest as well as the East Coast. More importantly, it had very strong political ties to many politicians and bureaucrats in the District of Columbia, "the" political center of the United States.

SOB served as a hot bed for many aspiring lawyers who also desired to pursue political careers. In many cases, after their political careers were over, those lawyers would return to the private sector to use and benefit from their public service. SOB also had a reputation for being comprised of a bunch of lawyers who thought they were better than everyone else. They let their reputation go to their heads, and the SOB label stuck with them for many reasons with a good many other lawyers and law firms.

Entry into politics by some SOB lawyers was nothing new. Other lawyers did it and so did military personnel, business people and defense contractors. The policy, in this regard, was always first into government service of some type and then a return to the private arena to appear before those same public sector agencies to use the knowledge and influence previously acquired by them during public service. Those doing so could make serious money and spread influence. The application of power for the benefit of clients and themselves was paramount. A number of these lawyers, in fact, had used such positions many times before in back and forth, ping-pong type play to maximize their value and then to reap the rewards from such a process. Some had done so effectively and with great benefit to themselves, their families, their colleagues and their clients.

One of Davis' cohorts, who had joined SOB with Davis, had become a virtual master at the game. This associate, Sam Wilson, or Sammy, as he became known among all the young associates who began at SOB in 1980, eventually left SOB for the U.S. Department of Justice, worked his way up the chain in that Department and then returned to SOB in the late 1980s. He handled a number of high profile antitrust cases for the Department while he was there and upon his return to SOB, he became co-chair of SOB's corporate department. In that position, he made frequent contact with his old cronies at Justice and handled a variety of matters for SOB's top corporate clients with his prior employer.

Wilson ultimately returned to the government sector where he became an aid to an Ohio Senator and then succeeded that Senator in the U.S. Senate in 1992. Sammy held that position for a number of years until he ran for and was elected Governor of the Great State of Ohio. He continued to be a sought-after rising politician and ultimately was asked to be on the national Republican ticket as Vice President. He enthusiastically joined that effort and became Vice President in 2004.

During Sammy's meteoric rise to the Vice Presidency, he continued to stay in touch with his old colleagues from SOB, including Charles Davis, or Charlie, as some of his close friends called him. Sammy helped Charlie when asked and despite a number of Charlie's shortcomings and problems, Sammy stayed in Charlie's corner for many years.

Charlie did not have the same extraordinarily good political fortunes as his friend Sammy. Charlie did, however, have some success. He stayed with SOB for six years before making the grade of junior partner. Yet a number of incidents restricted his role at SOB and what surely otherwise would have been a much faster and rising career.

Charlie had the good sense to become very well acquainted with the daughter of one of SOB's senior partners. He married her just before he became a junior partner at the firm. That effort moved him forward substantially on the SOB ladder of achievement. However, in his seventh year with the firm he began to pay far too much attention to a new and extremely attractive young secretary named Jillian.

Jillian began to work for Charlie when he became a junior partner at SOB. While Charlie no longer needed to work in excess of 70 hours per week as he had done before he became a partner, Jillian often stayed with him beyond 5:00 p.m. on many days to get his work done. Pleadings, motions, briefs, deposition summaries, case outlines, subpoenas, witness lists and on and on – the work brought them into close contact, often with the two of them enjoying evening meals in Charlie's office while reviewing the next day's work. What began as innocent flirtations during these sessions soon became something more.

Charlie would frequently start those sessions simply: "Jillian," he would say, "we are going to have to stay a while tonight; there are some loose ends on this case I want to explore and work out with you. Plan on a couple of hours to see how far we can move forward."

Jillian would get the true meaning of these invitations over time and began to be almost as excited as Charlie over the potential prospect of intimacy and reward.

"Mr. Davis," she often started, "I would love to help you get to the bottom of any matter or give you the best of what I can offer."

Charlie liked these responses and it enticed him to move forward with his advances.

Eventually the closeness of their contact, the amount of time they spent together and the need for simple release inevitably led to intimacy. One night in particular, Charlie could not wait to partake of Jillian's charms before he should have and wound up with Jillian sprawled atop his desk beneath him. While both were enjoying the benefits of consensual and highly charged intercourse, but unfortunately for Charlie, his wife's father walked into his office at the moment of Charlie's climactic performance. From that moment on, Charlie's career at SOB and his marriage to the senior partner's daughter was on very rocky ground.

Charlie's in-office, on top of his desk performance and then Jillian's termination with severance pay from SOB could not even begin to repair the damage that had been done. Charlie's pick of junior partner cases was no longer from the first tier, and he was relegated to ever diminishing responsibilities and even less interesting or important cases.

Charlie no longer could pick and choose what he wanted to do from first tier clients or their cases; he was now told what to do, not only at SOB but at home as well. His relationship with his wife became strained and then it began to poison and permeate his relationship with his children who soon were brought into the fray by his wife.

His wife's father and the senior partner at SOB had chosen to make his daughter aware of Charlie's desktop performance. From that point on, Charlie was doomed at both SOB and at home. His wife's venomous retaliations increased with time, and while her father made sure Charlie provided for her and the kids, it finally led to Charlie's very serious drinking problem and other aberrant behavior. Ultimately it led to an ever downward cascade of events that culminated in Charlie screwing up some of the less-than-major cases he was handling for SOB, his divorce from the senior partner's daughter, loss of his employment and most of his accumulated profit sharing, pension, 401(k) and similar benefits to his wife. Charlie's drinking continued to spiral, but he managed to join a very small Columbus law firm composed of some of his former law school classmates and friends. He managed to persevere through it all, despite his personal trials and tribulations.

Most of these new colleagues at the Columbus firm were drinking buddies who enjoyed Charlie's company and even his legal abilities, though Charlie was tormented by his own personal demons and downfalls. Some of these other colleagues were politically connected on a local level and helped Charlie ease into the real world of second tier legal work – no big corporations, no insurance company defense work, no big estates or substantive probate work.

High profile work for well-known businesses or corporations was nearly out of the question at this level. Rote work for local businesses, with an occasional personal injury case with the potential for six figures and some smaller estates, divorces and custody disputes were more like what could be had at this level. Specialization was also out of the question with no opportunity for concentration in small practice niches that some lawyers at firms like SOB had enjoyed.

Despite the shortcomings impacted by Charlie's relegation to second tier lawyer work, he managed to succeed at that level and utilized all of his local, state and then federal contacts to help him get ahead. Ultimately, despite years of hard drinking and a number of bad decisions, he used his friendship with Sam Wilson to rise above his self-created situation.

Sammy helped Charlie get out of the doomed spiral of alcohol addiction and even into an appointment to the Franklin County Common Pleas Court bench. Sammy's behind the scenes endorsement of Charles Davis helped immensely and led to his post-appointment election to the Common Pleas Court. However, despite Wilson's help, he could not solve all of Davis' problems.

Soon after Davis was elected to his first six-year term on the bench, he began to return to the company of his old drinking buddies and their bad habits. His drinking generally started at lunch then continued during court recesses and culminated the work day with a nip or two during afternoon court breaks. He always met his friends at the local watering holes as soon as his court recessed each day. Charlie sometimes had trouble getting home on these nights.

The local Columbus area police departments sometimes had to help Charles Davis find home on these occasions. They became aware of his identity as they often stopped Davis for some traffic infraction such as erratic driving, frequent lane changing, failure to stop at traffic control devices or to signal anticipated and then completed lane changes. On those occasions, Davis would always have the presence of mind to show his judicial credentials and ask for an escort home.

Such behavior continued for many years until it became a problem for virtually the entire Columbus bar. When Davis could no longer deliver perceptible sentences in court or give understandable jury instructions, Wilson was asked to intervene once again. He did so, but Wilson told Davis, "This is the last time."

Wilson's intervention worked, at least as of the time that Tony Piccini's case made its way into Davis' courtroom. However, by that time Davis had already adopted a significant number of shortcuts to get through his duties and responsibilities. First, he used a law clerk, generally in his or her last year of law school to research and write his decisions on various motions and matters in the cases that made their way to his bench. That same clerk developed his jury instructions and kept him informed on developments in the law.

Davis used his court reporters to compose and prepare all of his reports, correspondence and related paperwork. He used his courtroom security deputies to complete his errands and grab his lunch to avoid his old watering hole problems. He used his magistrate, another lawyer but less experienced than himself, to handle and decide a number of issues, motions and even less important trials which would otherwise come before him. Lastly, he used his bailiff as his courtroom assistant to work with, contact and manage the juries during criminal and civil cases when such individuals were summoned to decide civil litigations or criminal charges.

Jurors slowed down the process of justice, at least in Charles' mind, and had to be managed and instructed on the legal requirements to be applied to the cases that they were chosen to decide. In this regard, jurors were not predictable as to the time they required to decide the cases submitted to them or to consistently render proper decisions, so Davis often chose to intervene in some manner to either speed the process along or to direct it toward a result Davis had determined to be the "right" one.

Davis became a master at moving matters along when they were placed by him in the hands of the jurors in his courtroom. He sometimes had unauthorized meetings with individual jurors or more frequently used his bailiff, Bill Morris, in subtle ways to impermissibly communicate with jurors outside the realm of normal events in the legal system and without the permission or knowledge of lawyers handling these cases.

Through his bailiff, he encouraged jurors in his courtroom to see him individually, if need be, so he could answer and address any of their concerns. Sometimes he even used these clandestine meetings to get to know particular jurors, especially when he needed female companionship. In one case he handled shortly before he had to deal with the Piccini matter, he was required to preside over another wrongful death case involving a rather horrendous automobile accident that had claimed the life of a young father. The jury on that case included an extremely attractive woman in her mid-30s who looked somewhat like Charlie's old secretary from SOB. He was immediately drawn to her and made sure the lawyers kept her on the case.

This juror, number 642, as she was referred to during the trial, was a real looker and seemed very impressed with his Honor Charles Davis. When Davis arrived early one morning during the trial, this juror, Linda, as he learned her name, was already in the courtroom. Aside from his bailiff, Bill Morris, she was alone.

Charlie approached her, introduced himself and asked, "May I introduce myself? How about a cup of coffee?"

"Sure," Linda said, "and, I, of course, know who you are."

With that exchange of hellos, Charlie led her into his chambers. That morning's coffee then led to coffee with her each morning in his chambers before each day's testimony during the trial. When the case reached the stage when the plaintiff's case was to be rested and the defendant's evidence to begin, Davis found himself with Linda on a Friday morning before the trial was to reconvene. While in his chambers alone with her, he decided to act on his instincts.

"Linda," Davis said, "this case will be over for the week around 3:00 today. Why don't you stick around, and I'll take you to dinner over at a nice inn I know just outside of town in Spruce Hill."

Davis knew what he was doing. The Spruce Hill Inn was perfect for what he had in mind for Linda. It was far enough outside Columbus that it would be very unlikely they would be seen by anyone he or she knew and even more unlikely that they would be seen by anyone from this case. The Inn also was a very fine, very elegant eating and sleeping establishment with a great chef and a very nice table in a private room reserved just for judges and other politicians in need of an out-of-the-way place for discreet encounters. It also had a number of well-appointed rooms for overnight accommodations. It was indeed perfect for all Davis had in mind.

Linda had never been to the Inn but liked the idea of spending some more private and longer time with Davis. She played coy but indicated that his interest was appreciated.

"Why Judge, I'd love to. Should I wait for you after the recess today?"

"Yes," explained Davis, "I need to finish up some other things before I can go, but my bailiff will direct you after the recess; I'll join you shortly thereafter. We'll have a great dinner and spend some time to get much better acquainted."

"Great," said Linda. "I'll wait after the recess for your bailiff, and we'll go from there. Should I follow you in my car?"

"No," said Davis, "I'll drive."

"And of course, I'll bring you back," he added with a devious look on his face.

"Alright," added Linda. "If I can't trust you, who can I trust?"

On that note, Davis had her exit his chambers through the

backdoor to the private hall that adjoined Davis' chamber with the offices of his law clerk, magistrate and court reporter so that none of the other trial participants would see where she had come from. Davis then summoned Morris into his chambers and said, "Bill, once we get through today, take Juror number 642, Linda, down to my parking space and put her in the passenger side of my car. Make sure everyone else is out of here before you go, and then come get me and I'll join her."

"Sure," replied Morris, "A little research for the trial?"

"Yes," replied Davis, "I need to know what I can do to help Juror number 642 enjoy her experience in my judicial embrace. After all, I need all the votes I can get."

As the day wound down to the 3:00 p.m. recess, Davis could hardly control himself. He was primed and ready as 3:00 approached. He hammered down his gavel with a new vigor and a renewed energy to end that day's session. By the time Morris worked everyone out of Davis' courtroom and Juror number 642 down to Davis' car, he was really ready to go when Morris came back to his chambers to get him.

Davis threw on his coat and made his way down to his car and the beautiful Linda's presence. As he entered his car's driver's seat, he hoped it would not be the only entry he had that night. Linda's greeting made him hopeful in that regard, very hopeful indeed.

"Judge Davis," she said, "I've been keeping your car warm for you. That didn't take you long at all."

Upon that last comment, she reached over and gently touched Davis' arm. As she held and caressed it, she lingered there long enough for Davis to know the night would not be without its rewards.

"I'm glad I was able to break away and even happier that you're joining me. We'll have a great time together tonight."

"I'm sure we will, your Honor," Linda responded, lingering on the last word for emphasis.

Davis knew the night would be special. On the way, while he drove toward Spruce Hill, he got a slowly but ever growing feeling low in his core which gradually worked its way up to his heart which began to beat with increased vigor as he pulled into the Inn's valet parking area.

"Good evening sir, glad to see you again," said the young attendant who opened his door while another valet on the other side of the car helped Linda exit from the vehicle. "How are you tonight?"

"Just fine," replied the Judge. "Park it for me, will you?" Davis said as the attendant gave him a ticket for later delivery of the car, hopefully the next day. The Judge whispered with a wink, "Probably overnight," as he handed the attendant a $5.00 bill.

The attendant smiled and replied, "Thank you, sir. I hope so for your sake."

With that, Davis grabbed for Linda's elbow, put his arm around her and escorted her into the Spruce Hill Inn.

The maître'd was expecting Davis and had his table prepared in one of the one-table dining rooms off the west side of the main dining area. It had a private door, deep red colored leather chairs and a cherry table large enough for four but perfect for two. A bottle of sparkling water and a select Chilean chardonnay was chilling in a table-side ice bucket. The chardonnay was iced down and gently resting in an antique, copper lined wine cellarette from the early 1800s. It had been in the Inn for many years and was one of Davis' favorite objects there. The Inn was filled with a number of very well appointed antiques and objects of art, all of which Davis liked despite his otherwise various and somewhat base appetites.

Davis had ordered the wine for his companion but would drink only the sparkling water while Linda partook of the South American treat. As the maître'd shut the door to their private dining room, Davis poured Linda some of the vintage and then his own glass with sparkling water that came from across the ocean from Italy.

As Davis poured the chilled wine for Linda, she asked, "Aren't you joining me?"

Not wanting to let her know of his weakness, he lied and said, "I'm on criminal court duty for the weekend, and I may be called for an arrest or search warrant by the prosecutor or the police. I've got to have my wits about me, so I have to pass on the wine tonight."

Davis lied easily – in fact, very easily. It was one of many lies he had told before and one of the many he would continue to tell over the years ahead. If he were ever caught in such lies, he always had another of his influential political friends, including hopefully, Sam Wilson to call upon to get him out of any jam arising out of any such lie.

"Besides," Davis continued, "the only thing I need to enjoy is you and your company."

"Judge Davis, you are really too sweet." Linda responded as she began to taste the sweet nectar of the select Chilean chardonnay. "This is delicious. Great selection."

"I know," said Davis, "I enjoy it very much when I can. Shall we order?"

Linda looked over the menu and responded with a clear sparkle in her eye, "Why don't you pick. I like most everything except lamb. I'm sure I'll be happy with whatever choice you make."

"I have a great choice for us. You'll love what I have in mind," said Davis, with a grin.

"I'm sure I will," replied Linda, with her own wicked smile.

Davis ordered, Linda drank and eventually the meal came – a wonderful quail, crab and asparagus dish. The selection would be enjoyed with another bottle of wine, which Linda greatly appreciated. When they finished, Linda and Davis enjoyed the special dessert of the day – cherries with brandy on rich, fresh vanilla ice cream. When done, Davis stood, grabbed what was left of the second bottle of chardonnay and eased Linda's chair from the table. "Come with me while we continue to enjoy our evening."

Linda replied, "You're the Judge. I'm led to believe you're in charge."

Davis then kissed her full on the lips and enjoyed a warm, sweet and open kiss eagerly waiting for his next move. When they finished that first kiss, Davis led her from their private dining room and off to the suite he had previously reserved for them, the cardkey to which the waiter had deftly passed to him at the end of dinner along with his check. As they walked to the suite and down the hall, Linda said, "Where are you taking me, your Honor?"

"To my chambers," replied Davis. "I've got to evaluate your case."

"I hope you will show me some mercy, Charlie."

"I'm planning on giving you a stiff sentence," said Davis. He had Linda stop just outside suite 107 while Davis used the cardkey he had been handed by the waiter for access to the room. As he opened the door and gestured for Linda to go inside, she began unbuttoning her top as she looked back over her left shoulder and said with a wink, "Judge, how long a sentence do you have in mind?"

Both of them knew what would come next. Davis' current dry spell would soon be over, at least for a while.

DAVID L. HERBERT

CHAPTER 23

Despite FitAgain's approach to "qualifying" personal trainers, in Georgia a new effort to license personal fitness trainers was underway. State Senator Frank Lapri had once again introduced Senate Bill 614 into the Georgia Legislature. The same legislation had previously been proposed by him in 2005 but was never reported out of the Georgia State Senate Commerce Committee to the entire Senate for a vote. The Chair of that Committee, Louise Stanford, had stubbornly asked Senator Lapri during a Committee hearing on the bill if the legislation was really necessary.

"Senator Lapri," she began, "is there any evidence of harm that would support the need to license fitness professionals, specifically, personal trainers in this state? We have heard from several of your witnesses, all of whom supported the legislation, but none of whom cited to us to any situation where great harm or even death has resulted at the hands of or due to the negligence of any personal trainer. Can you refer us to any such situation?"

"Well, I can tell you there are those situations out there. I know of at least one such case from Ohio where a personal trainer allegedly caused the death of a young mother who was under his care."

"One undecided case from another state does not set forth sufficient justification to proceed with the cost of having yet another government regulated profession in this state," replied Chairwoman Stanford.

"But," countered Lapri, "one needless death at the hands of any trainer in any state is one too many."

"However," said Louise Stanford, "that case is still pending. Nothing there has been finally determined."

"I don't think the jury in that case has even yet reached a verdict. The criminal charges against that trainer resulted in a hung jury and the civil case is pending. This is hardly clear evidence of the need for Georgia taxpayers to foot the bill for licensure protections in this state if there is only one undecided case in one other state."

Senator Lapri could do little to respond to such concerns since Chairwoman Stanford had allocated but one short legislative session to consider the proposed legislation. Without some clear examples of why legislation was needed, there was really little point in attempting to do more in this session. As a consequence, the Senator's proposal was not reported out of Committee to the entire floor of the Georgia Senate for a vote. Senator Lapri would reintroduce the legislation in the next session and at that time would be ready to proceed and answer Stanford's inquiries.

For the next four months of 2006 and into 2007, Senator Lapri scoured the media for any news reports of personal fitness trainer mishaps with clients. He also used the lawyers in the Georgia Legislative Service Office to research the past fifteen years of actual reported case filings involving criminal conduct of personal trainers as well as personal injury and wrongful death cases asserted against such fitness professionals in any state in the United States.

While Frank Lapri knew there was evidence of the need to license personal trainers, once he had all the research findings, he was shocked at the breadth and diversity of cases filed and determined against trainers. The list of personal trainer misdeeds and mishaps was seemingly endless and represented a broad group of untoward events as well as both criminal and civil cases.

For example, he found a situation in New York where a personal trainer providing service to a Broadway and Hollywood star had been approached by a number of gossip columnists in their attempts to secure tidbits of information about his client. With certain financial inducements, the trainer had remembered and then communicated to these folks a number of very private matters which the client had communicated to the trainer – all under the assumption that what was communicated was private. While the trainer had been certified by a nationally-based fitness training organization and had agreed to its Ethical Code of Conduct specifying that no certified trainer would reveal client confidences to third parties without specific client authorization, the Code did not have the force of law. Several thousand dollars in financial incentives caused the trainer to reveal that the star was really "gay" and had contracted a sexually transmitted disease, both of which facts had been previously undisclosed to the public.

The trainer's release of what otherwise was clearly confidential information caused the celebrity considerable unwanted publicity and public scorn. She could not sue the media outlets for libel since, if any such suits were filed, discovery in the case would only confirm what was printed. After all, truth is a complete defense to a libel or slander lawsuit. Instead she had to endure the considerable public spotlight and in some cases, scorn brought forth by the articles.

Her subsequent suicide was directly attributable to the trainer's indiscretion, but since no law forbade his disclosure of what otherwise was very private and confidential information, no criminal nor civil law had been violated.

Senator Lapri also learned, aside from the pending criminal and civil proceedings against Tony Piccini, that a 72-year-old woman in Ohio was gravely injured while under the care of a personal trainer as a result of a fall off an unsupervised treadmill. It seemed that she had previously suffered a broken hip, which led to hospitalization, surgery, and then physical therapy. Once her insurance coverage ran out to cover the costs of that therapy, she was referred to a personal trainer. The trainer put her on a treadmill set at 2.70 mph and walked away to serve other clients.

When the trainer returned to see how the "patient" was doing, he found his unattended client slumped against a wall behind the treadmill with the treadmill still running. The device had been placed within 2 feet of a back wall, and when the client could not keep up with the treadmill pace, she lost her balance and was thrown violently against the wall behind the treadmill.

According to another client of the trainer who witnessed the incident, it seemed that she did not know how to stop the treadmill since no adequate explanation of that process had been provided by the trainer. When she lost her balance and was thrown off the treadmill, her head hit the back wall causing a severe concussion and internal bleeding inside her skull.

The 72-year-old grandmother's life was maintained on life support while her husband and family pursued the personal trainer in a personal injury suit seeking several million dollars to sustain her prolonged and indefinite care. The trainer had been certified through a mail order educational course that took approximately 20 hours of study time and consisted of an "open-book" written test composed of 50 true-false questions. No practical exam or demonstration of his skills was required.

The trainer's prior employment had been in a machine shop. Any fitness training he had previously received had been accumulated sporadically over a ten year period following the trainer's high school graduation. Several experts in the fitness industry were expected to testify against this trainer.

With no state laws in place to use in any effort to establish that the trainer failed to adhere to state stipulated and required standards of care, it seemed that the trainer's new career really might not be in jeopardy. Liability insurance was limited and the trainer, like Tony, had few assets. Actual recovery on any verdict against him was therefore very doubtful.

Frank Lapri also knew that in California, a 46-year-old man spotted a male individual in a furniture store who the middle-aged man thought was very fit and "buff." He approached the fit male and learned he was a personal trainer. One thing led to another, and the next day the man, now a "client," wound up at the personal trainer's health club studio to begin his first session to get buff himself.

When the client arrived, the trainer had him sign a training contract but failed to screen the client to determine what his general health might be. He failed to weigh the client, record his height or age, ask him what he did for activity or even if he had a doctor. Instead, the trainer put him on a treadmill set at 4.0 mph and urged him to work hard.

The client was able to walk/run at that speed for some 14 minutes but then begged to stop. The trainer reluctantly agreed to let him stop but then had him do a series of weight lifts, push-ups, sit ups and more. The client implored the trainer to let him rest, but the trainer told him, "Get going, work overtime," pointing to a strikingly fit young woman working out in the studio nearby and said, "Don't you want to get some of that kind of ass? If you do, stop being such a pussy and get moving!"

With that incentive, the client tried to keep moving like he was told. But his heart seemed to be racing out of his chest. The pain in his neck and then the pain in his left shoulder and arm was becoming increasingly intense. It was very hard for him to breathe. It seemed that he was gasping for every breath through a chest that seemed ready to collapse under tremendous pressure and weight.

The trainer continued to demand that the client work even harder. He added more weight to the client's dumbbells and told him to pick up the pace. When the client could do no more and begged for a break, the trainer told him to keep moving. The trainer told him to start on a series of leg lifts, and when the client could do no more and gasped for breath through each attempt, the trainer raised the client's legs up and manually pushed them to work. The client's situation became worse, and he could no longer breathe. Finally, as he collapsed, the client stammered out, "Call 9-1-1. I'm having a heart attack!"

The trainer called 9-1-1 and after 6 minutes, the EMS Squad arrived. The client had indeed suffered a severe and debilitating myocardial infarction, a heart attack, due to the stress of the activities the trainer had developed and "supervised" for the client. While the client survived, it turned out that the client had a history of heart problems, was overweight, smoked a pack and a half of cigarettes per day and had never engaged in any program of physical activity outside of his previous high school gym classes which he attempted to skip every chance he got.

The client sued the trainer for negligence and asserted that the trainer failed to screen him for activity or to require medical clearance for activity. The client also alleged that inappropriate activity was prescribed for him, that he was improperly supervised and that the emergency response was not properly provided to him.

In response to the client's suit, the trainer moved for summary judgment contending that the client's claims were not legally recognized since the client had waived and released his right to sue and had assumed all of the risks associated with the training activity. The trainer simply contended that he could not therefore be liable because the client had expressly assumed the risks of a heart attack. Almost unbelievably, the court agreed with these assertions and determined that the activities carried on by such trainers were not legally actionable without legislatively mandated requirements imposing specific duties upon personal trainers to be performed by such trainers during client activity. The judge ruled that the client assumed all the risks associated with such activities, including those which turned out to have occurred to this client.

In a Washington state case which occurred some years earlier, Senator Lapri also learned that another personal training client in his twenties suffered a debilitating heart attack after working out under the supervision of the trainer. At that time the client, a computer operator, was 6' tall and weighed over 300 pounds. He had a history of high blood pressure, back problems and sporadic physical activity. He joined a health club which did not screen him for any health problems, and he started a program of exercise activity under the supervision of the personal trainer.

The client was told to run on a track. After completing 3½ laps, he became exhausted and very warm. He was then told to begin sit ups on a slant board; as he was doing the sit ups with difficulty the instructor told him if he couldn't do the exercises to just pay his money and don't bother with any further exercise since he would not train some "pussy."

The client defiantly continued but became further exhausted, left the exercise floor and threw up. When he returned and told his instructor that he was sick, the instructor told him that such a result was normal after a period of exercise activity and to go on with the routine.

As the client began to use the exercise machines that he was told to use, he became further nauseated and simultaneously threw up and defecated in his pants. He was then put on another machine to exercise and told his responses to exercise, which now included dizziness, were normal and to keep going.

Ultimately the client was told to go into a hot sauna which he did after he cleaned himself up. At that point, he became more dizzy, disoriented and lacked depth perception.

As he attempted to leave the facility, he began to experience chest pain and then suffered a heart attack. Suit was later filed based upon the client's proposition, among other things, that the trainer who had been represented as having degrees and advertised as being competent and qualified, had misrepresented himself and was not qualified. The case was settled out of court for an undisclosed sum since the settlement included a confidentiality agreement executed by the parties and a gag-order judgment entry issued by the court prohibiting any discussion of the case or its resolution.

Senator Lapri also learned that in Nevada, a rock star determined to make a comeback to his career after a hiatus of nearly ten years. He was nearly 52 at that time and thought he needed a personal trainer to prepare him for a grueling upcoming concert tour. He found a trainer in the Yellow Pages and asked for private and discreet lessons at his home. The trainer readily agreed and collected $500.00 for daily two-hour sessions. When the client asked for faster results, the trainer upped the sessions to two-a-day and collected $1,000.00 per day, six days a week. This went on for five and a half weeks until the client, the comeback star of the decade, was found dead in his bed. An autopsy showed he was anorexic, had suffered a cardiac arrest and had died as a result. Traces of amphetamines as well as pain killers and marijuana were found in the star's system.

While the client had several obvious risk factors which mandated that a competent trainer refer him for medical clearance, no such referral was made. Had it been made, the referral would probably have disclosed the serious conditions which led to his cardiac arrest and death. The family sued everyone who had cared for the entertainer, including his physician – who he didn't even consult, his manager, the comeback concert promoters who had encouraged the star to secure a trainer, the fitness organizations which had "certified" the trainer and even the responding EMS service which took more than six minutes to arrive at the entertainer's home when he was found unconscious in bed. As to this last defendant, the entertainer's family contended the star was deprived of a chance of survival due to the service's slow response.

The trainer did have some liability insurance which would soon be offered in settlement in exchange for a release and a confidentiality agreement. Eventually everyone associated with the case consented to a non-disclosed settlement agreement and the litigation was dismissed.

In another case from New York, a personal trainer's client suffered a broken ankle on her first session with the trainer. It seemed that the trainer left her unattended on a treadmill set at 3.5 mph and failed to instruct her on how to stop the machine, how to adjust the speed or even how to properly operate the control panel. Ultimately, she was thrown off of the machine and injured.

In yet another case, this one from Nevada, a middle-aged man was exercising on a treadmill under the supervision of a personal trainer. The client fell down face first on the treadmill during exercise. The trainer approached him to see if the client would sit up; when he didn't, the trainer checked the client's pulse and determined that he had an irregular pulse and was breathing, but weakly. By this time, other club members approached and gathered around the downed client. The trainer advised them to step back to give the client air; however, the trainer did not start CPR and eventually after several additional minutes had passed, the trainer, at the behest of one of the bystander members asked another employee to call 9-1-1.

By this time an off-duty police officer who had been working out at the facility told the trainer to start CPR. The trainer advised the policeman not to interfere and the trainer would simply monitor the client's breathing till EMS arrived.

When the downed client began to turn pale and as his skin grew cold, the policeman pushed the trainer aside and started CPR after he turned the downed client over on his back. By the time EMS arrived, there had been a significant lapse in time since the client went down and the police officer started CPR. The client died at the hospital.

In still another case, Lapri heard that a trainer pushed a 37-year-old Connecticut client so hard to engage in repetitive weight lifting and circuit training activities that she suffered rhabdomyolysis, a rapid breakdown of muscle tissue causing a release of damaged cells into the bloodstream, that in turn leading to kidney failure, hospitalization and sometimes even death. Apparently, the trainer just didn't know what was appropriate exercise activity for the client who nearly died.

Stories like these and resultant lawsuits were relatively easy for Lapri and those under his direction to find. Senator Lapri also heard that many other similar cases occurred which never made their way to the attention of the media or resulted in any lawsuit, judgment or court determination. While some of that was changing, the lack of relevant and applicable statutory law at the state level made the pursuit of such cases very difficult. Personal trainers' lack of adequate liability insurance and almost always no assets also made such defendants difficult to hold accountable. Something more was needed.

All Frank Lapri thought he really had to do was gather the evidence, present the case and make a closing argument in support of the legislation. His belief in this regard turned out to be very naïve indeed.

CHAPTER 24

Hank Curtis was sick of the pressure. He was tired of being told to generate more sales in all categories: sell more memberships, supplements, drinks, energy bars, clothes, massages, aerobics classes, personal training sessions and even fitness boot camps. His continued performance in all of these categories was evaluated and judged each month by the regional VP at FitAgain corporate.

It seemed to Hank that he had to justify his very existence as manager of the Upper Arlington FitAgain Club each and every month. Exceeding or at least maintaining established quotas was required. Three successive months of shortfalls in any two categories would reduce his salary and bonus. Six months of inadequate performance would result in his termination. While there were no time clocks to punch, not for managers like him, headaches took the place of any such requirement and came with the job. His hours were long, from 5:30 a.m. each day often until 7:00 p.m. each night, sometimes longer.

Hank really longed for the loose "job" framework which he had previously enjoyed when all he did was provide personal training services, not to mention the added benefits provided by his interaction with many of his former clients. Now it seemed that all he dealt with were whining, often unqualified employees, so-called independent contractors, aerobics instructors, floor personnel and personal trainers.

Some of these defined professionals didn't show up for appointments on time and some were living on facility provided energy drinks, supplements and even drugs. Some were always trying to hit on their clients, and some of these clients didn't always like the attention. Most of Hank's charges always had their hands out.

Hank tried to have all of his employees/contractors walking a fine line. While Hank had some training outside of FitAgain and even a certification from an established fitness training group, all of his UA employees and independent contractors were trained and certified in-house by FitAgain. Some had additional certifications in CPR, but most did not. None at the moment were trained in automated external defibrillator (AED) use. This deficiency, however, didn't really matter though since the UA facility had not yet ordered an AED, even though it seemed to be clearly foreseeable that such a device was potentially needed in the club.

The past record for FitAgain clubs indicated that a cardiac event requiring an AED occurred in each club the size of the UA facility about every six months or so. Since the local EMS unit's response time to the UA facility once a call to them was placed was about six minutes, the need for an AED onsite was even greater than would otherwise be the case since survival with normal function after six minutes from the onset of a cardiac emergency requiring an AED was very doubtful. If a real chance for survival was to be provided, AED use within four minutes was necessary.

At the last Regional VP visit to the UA club, the AED issue was brought up as a topic of consideration by Hank. "Mr. Parks," said Hank, referring to the Regional VP, "I would feel a lot better about our ability to respond to emergencies here if we had an AED on site. Any word on that yet?"

"No," responded Mr. Parks. "Corporate is still evaluating the issue. The units, even in large numbers, cost about $2,500 each. Then we would need to establish a maintenance program for each unit, train at least one person on each day's shift to use them and then integrate their use into our emergency response planning. That's a lot of extra cost, time and effort. We're not sure it's worth it to our bottom line. The battery maintenance/replacement program alone for these AEDs would cost at least $500.00 per unit, per facility, per year"

"But, you know our local EMS unit is about six minutes from here once we call them for any cardiac response. That may be too long to save someone the chance for a normal life."

"Well," said Parks, "AEDs are not required by law here in Ohio, at least in this kind of facility. Until they are, are you willing to pay for the costs out of your salary, your commissions or your year-end bonus?"

"Of course not," retorted Hank. "I don't own this place, I just work here."

"Maybe that's part of your problem. Your performance is borderline here anyway! You need to get your supplement sales up, your personal training fees up, and your membership sales are pathetic. What do you think the problem is here other than your own ineptitude?"

"I'm doing the best I can. I need more corporate support, more television and radio advertising and some good looking but competent trainers. You give me those things, and I can move ahead."

Parks was about to respond when Tony Piccini walked into the office. "Hank, I need some new blood," said Tony. "I have time slots open at least three days a week during the period from 7:00 a.m. to 9:00 a.m. I can do two women in that time and still serve my 6:00 a.m. time slot, even as I look forward to the 10:00 a.m. time slot. How is that advertising campaign from corporate coming along?"

"Your timing is great, Tony. This is Mr. Parks from corporate. Why don't you ask him?"

That being said, Tony turned to Parks and extended his hand with a smile, "Well, what can you tell me, Mr. Parks? I need some clients so all of us can earn more money."

"Tony, is it? I'll get you more clients if you push our supplements, energy drinks and products harder. Can you do that?"

"Of course," said Tony, "I have been selling and will sell more of our juice and supplements than anyone here. You get me the bodies, and I'll sell it to them. After all, it won't kill them and neither will we, right?"

"Not with people like you, we won't. Keep up the good work, Tony." Parks said as he extended his hand to shake Tony's. "It's good to meet you. How are you doing with our MP33s? We need to push those energy stimulant products to get these people moving and using our equipment and facilities. We need sales and referrals. "

Tony responded: "My sales are great. I push our products as hard and as fast as I can and set an example by using them myself."

On that comment, Tony left and hit the floor to meet his next client. He had a smile on his face. He liked what he did and apparently so did management. Of course however, there was no record of this meeting, nothing to trace the issues which were discussed back to the corporation. In the corporation's "eye", the meeting never occurred.

CHAPTER 25

In the course of attempting to silence all of the lawyer's cell phones which his Honor Charles Davis had previously told him to do, Bill Morris looked at them and wondered at the diversity of phone types and controls. While proceeding to do what he thought was necessary to turn all of them off, he pushed a number of control buttons and really hoped for the best. Some of them were too complicated to really assure that he was turning them off. However, he did what he could.

As he was finishing up this task, Judge Davis came out of his chambers and approached Bill's desk. Davis then asked Bill, "Did you go through the jury room and get the juror's notes? I want to know what they are thinking and how they are leaning so I can get these lawyers to settle this case without any of them knowing what I did."

"No," said Bill. "I haven't had a chance. I'm going now. I'll let you know in a minute."

With that, Bill left the judge, went to the jury room and began to see what had been left in the room.

Bill found some note tablets on the table and a series of crumpled notes discarded in the wastebasket. He took the tablets, then pulled all of the notes out of the receptacle, took them to the copy room in the court reporter's office, un-crumpled them, straightened them out and copied them.

Once copied, he returned the pads back to the jury room table and the wastepaper basket notes, duly re-crumpled, back into the basket. He then left the jury room and began to study the notes at his desk.

As Bill did so, it looked like the jury had made up its collective mind that FitAgain was Piccini's employer and that at least FitAgain, Piccini and SlimLine were going to be hit with some verdict. It looked to Bill as if the jury's notes in that regard were collective, perhaps unanimous, but that the amounts to be set and awarded were not yet established or agreed upon as to the various defendants. The figure, however, appeared to be in the $3 million to $5 million category against FitAgain and SlimLine; no specific dollar amount against Piccini could be gleaned from the notes.

Based upon Bill's analysis of the jury's notes, he gathered his thoughts and the jury notes and he took all of them with him to see Judge Davis.

Once in Davis' chambers, Bill said, "Judge, it looks like the jury is unanimously in favor of the Lawrences and against FitAgain and SlimLine and maybe Piccini for about $3 million, perhaps as much as $5 million against FitAgain and SlimLine. Can't tell what specific amount they are thinking of awarding against Piccini."

Bill continued, "They apparently believe that Piccini was FitAgain's employee. Couldn't find any notes about the pharmacy, the pharmacist or his company or the good doctor. Here are copies of the notes. I have put all of the original notes back in their place where I found them. All ends are covered."

"Great," said Davis. "I can use all of this to get this case settled." As he said so, he pulled a blank legal size manila folder from his desk drawer and labeled it "Juror Notes – Piccini Case." He put the notes in that folder and then put the folder in his top right-hand desk drawer.

"Bill," said Davis, "get the lawyers back in here. Let's do what we do best, and get this case settled. I have other things to do." Some years before that particular comment was made to Bill, that meant going to a nearby Columbus tavern to hoist a few with some of his lawyer friends. While those days were now behind him, at least for the moment, Davis had experienced a wild ride in years past.

DAVID L. HERBERT

CHAPTER 26

Once Davis and Morris reviewed the jurors' notes, Davis instructed Bill Morris to bring the defense lawyers into his chambers, one at a time, starting with Ms. Childs. Bill did so, and the settlement "negotiations" with the Judge then started.

"Ms. Childs," Judge Davis began, "I am concerned as to how this case is going, particularly for your client. While I don't know what the jury is actually thinking at this point [which, due to his bailiff's dictated actions, was a lie], I watched them closely during the trial. They may have some sympathy for Piccini but not your client."

"I don't think they have bought into your argument about Piccini not being your client's employee. In fact, based upon what I have heard, I may well direct a verdict on that particular issue because the facts are overwhelmingly in favor of Piccini on that matter. He worked by the hour, he wore your client's required uniforms, he used their facility, he used their equipment, they collected all the money from the clients and FitAgain paid him each week and by the hour."

"But your Honor," Joan Childs began, "his contract with FitAgain clearly provides that he was an independent contractor despite all of that. He agreed to and did secure his own insurance. He agreed to indemnify and hold FitAgain harmless in that contract from anything he negligently did or failed to do with his clients, FitAgain members, while he contracted individually with them."

"I know all that," responded Davis, "but I am inclined to set the contract aside and to decide that it lacks mutual consideration between your client and Piccini. Moreover, I believe the contract in that regard to be illusory. While the court of appeals might not buy into these arguments without a trial court ruling on them, I am inclined to do so. As you know, I have a great law clerk who recently graduated with honors from the Case-Western Reserve University Law School, and I am sure she can find sufficient law on that subject to support my decision."

Davis continued, "I strongly suggest that you get on the phone with your insurance carrier and advise them of what I said. I would suggest that your client throw a seven figure number into the settlement pot I am building. You have an hour. Get to it."

On that cue, Joan Childs stood, straightened her skirt and walked out of Davis' chambers absolutely fuming inside. There was little she could do but call the carrier and tell them the bad news.

Davis next told Morris to bring in the lawyer from New York, the one that Hatfield had originally vouched for – Matthew Reuger – but without Hatfield. Davis also left Vince Harper out of his request. Davis didn't think Harper was necessary for what he intended to do, and he didn't want any additional witnesses in any case at least as to what he was about to say and do.

When Morris brought Reuger into Davis' chambers, Davis began, "Mr. Reuger, sit down. Tell me what you think about this case and where we are. I, for one, think that the jury is leaning rather heavily toward the Lawrence family. What does your client think? Surely, you have given them some insight into the possibilities here. I know you are closer to them than Harper. After all, you are their in-house counsel."

Reuger listened and understood that Davis instinctively knew that Reuger had engaged in extensive conversation with his company's CEO, Mitchell Malloy. Malloy had carefully considered what was transpiring in this Midwest town. He wanted to keep the attention on this case as low key as possible so as not to disrupt the sale of any of his ephedra-laced products or, God forbid, to get the FDA cranked up to ban the sale of the ingredient in his supplement products. He wanted to avoid such possibilities at least until something equally effective could be put on the market by SlimLine to replace that ingredient or those products.

While Malloy had two possible products that were independently working their way toward commercial sale, citra-aid and at some point in the future, the exercise pill, neither was ready to be taken directly or indirectly to the public market. At least six months, if not more, were needed and necessary just for citra-aid. As a result, Malloy had instructed Reuger to work on a settlement through the company's insurance carrier and through the lawyer the carrier employed to defend the case, namely Jason Hatfield.

Reuger considered the judge's question and responded in a New York lawyer's fashion, "You know, Judge, I am not sure that the jury likes me here. I know that you probably wish I wasn't here but I am here to help.

"I have traveled all over this country for my employer, and I know that people need and benefit from SlimLine's products. However, I'm not sure that has come out or been presented adequately in this case. Therefore, I believe there may be some exposure here to SlimLine. That's why we have insurance. We need to get Hatfield in here and his carrier's adjuster to put forth a real settlement effort. I am prepared to get them in here and to encourage them to contribute to a global settlement but with the lion's share being paid by FitAgain."

"Well," said Davis, "I will deal with Hatfield and the respective contributions for each defendant if we can get this case in a position to settle. Go out and tell just Hatfield to come in, but first tell him that I'm about to hold you in contempt of court for again attempting to tell me what to do. That should stir him up a little. Then I'll work on him and get his adjuster in here if need be.

"I really have no intention of finding you in contempt since you agree with my assessment of this case but probably for different reasons. Hatfield doesn't need to know that. Just send him in."

With that instruction understood, Reuger left Davis' chambers and sent Hatfield in with the news that Reuger was about to go to jail for contempt.

Hatfield didn't take that news well. "What did you do this time?"

he asked.

"Nothing," responded Reuger, "except to tell him what we would do in New York. I think you had better talk to him about attempting to resolve this whole case or at least for us to get us out of this case by the payment of some insurance company provided sum."

Hatfield heard these comments as he went into Davis' inner sanctum and began to apologize to Davis as he went in. "Your Honor, I am sorry about Reuger. He's a different kind of advocate and believes that the New York way of doing things is the only way."

"I don't care; we are going to settle this case. I want you to get your adjuster down here, and I want $5 million on the table from him to put into a settlement," Davis directed.

"Judge," responded Hatfield, "That's the maximum potential insurance coverage my carrier has for this case."

"Not if the jury returns a verdict for more and your carrier did not, in the exercise of good faith, genuinely made efforts to resolve this case within the limits of the available liability insurance coverage. In fact, if we don't settle this case, I will put on the record your carrier's unreasonable failure to do so," said Judge Davis.

Hatfield didn't like what he just heard. "Judge, we all need to be reasonable here. I will do my best to accommodate a good faith opportunity to get this case resolved as I always do when I believe my client has some exposure. But at the same time, I won't lay down and forget who I am or what I am here to do.

"If necessary, I will get my adjuster and his boss down here to consider all that's going on. I might even recommend some settlement authorization, but only after I talk to them and Reuger and the CEO for SlimLine. Ethically I can't do anything less."

Davis didn't like all that he heard from Hatfield, but he respected his skills as a lawyer and knew he could only be pushed so far before he would demand a record of all case proceedings, including settlement negotiations in chambers.

"I think the jury is lined up principally against FitAgain but also against SlimLine. Your client is selling a dangerous product, especially for people like the poor decedent in this case. If asked on a proper motion, I might need to rule on such an issue; and if asked in the right fashion, I would have to do so."

"That motion has not been put to the court to my knowledge, and it certainly would not be appropriate for the court to do so unilaterally. I would seek an immediate appeal."

"Which," Davis angrily replied, "You would not get until this entire case was over. Go out and talk to Reuger and that novice, Harper, as well as your insurance carrier adjuster, his boss, SlimLine's CEO and anyone else you need to talk to. Then come back in here to see me.

"In the meantime, I will talk to the attorneys for the other remaining defendants," Davis said. "Send all three of them in as you go out, and start making contacts and calls."

Hatfield agreed to do so and knew the judge was on a roll and would do all he could to get this case settled. On his way out, he added, "I will need my cell phone back as well as those for Reuger and Harper so we can make some calls."

The judge responded, "I will tell Bill to get them for all of you so that you can make your calls. Then when you are all done, give them back to Bill until this case is over."

Davis told Bill Morris to return the three phones to SlimLine's lawyers. Bill did so and turned them over one at a time to each of them. He also gave Childs her phone but kept the others, at least until the judge was done with each of them.

Reuger turned on his phone and dutifully called Malloy. Hatfield also turned on his cell and called the insurance carrier. He told his adjuster and his boss to come to the courthouse. Harper examined his phone and determined it was in the on and locked position and was connected to his office voice mail. He unlocked the phone and then proceeded to call his voice mail to retrieve his messages, disregarding his own introductory voice mail comments. It was a new phone for him and one which he was just learning to use.

Harper had several messages. As he listened to them, he wrote each down along with the caller's numbers so he could return the calls. When he got to the last supposed message, however, he didn't have a caller leaving a voice mail but two voices, both of which he recognized as Judge Charles Davis and his bailiff, Bill Morris. Apparently, one or both of them had not properly turned off his phone but had inadvertently connected to Harper's voice mail which recorded all that the cell phone picked up.

Harper soon heard the judge telling his bailiff to engage in prohibited, ex-parte eavesdropping on the jury, to violate the sanctity of their jury room, their deliberations and their very constitutional function in the American system of jurisprudence.

Harper could barely control himself. He kept the clandestine conversation between Judge Davis and his bailiff on his cell phone voice mail to preserve and protect it. He remembered how the Honorable Charles Davis had treated him in Davis' chambers earlier in the case and decided that he could now even the score. He wasn't quite sure what he would do in that respect since he had ethical obligations to SlimLine, his client and his employer, as well as to the general bar.

Harper was licensed as an attorney in both Ohio and New York. He felt that the Ohio rules pertaining to judges and lawyers in that state would apply to evaluate the conduct of the judge and his bailiff, not to mention the application of the criminal statutes of the State of Ohio to both of them, which prohibited anyone, judges and bailiffs included, from tampering with the deliberations of a jury or in any manner attempting to interfere with their function and the sacrosanct nature of their deliberations. Such conduct was a serious felony in Ohio, and both the judge and his bailiff were clearly in violation of the law due to their conspiratorial actions. Harper would have his revenge, but he also had a duty to protect his employer as well as the sanctity of the judicial process and the jury system in general. All he had to do was figure out what to do with the information he had and the evidence which he had locked into his voice mail system.

While Harper weighed his options, Judge Davis met one at a time with the lawyers for the pharmacist and the company which employed him, the nutritional supplement store and the good doctor who treated Meri Lawrence. Counsel for the pharmacy and its pharmacist were on board for some amount to contribute to the settlement pot, but the good doctor's lawyer indicated to the judge that he could not get her to budge on any amount to put into the settlement.

This revelation infuriated Davis who had been at the settlement effort for a couple of hours by the time he got this disheartening news. Who did the doctor think she was anyway? This wasn't her office, any examination room or an operating venue; this was Davis' courtroom. He would control what happened here. He instructed her lawyer, David Taylor, to bring the doctor into his chambers.

Once she arrived, Davis began, "Dr. Janowitz, I need your attention and your cooperation. I am trying to get this case over and resolved. It's gone on too long, and I think the jury has absolutely no choice but to find against you and the others. A verdict against you will become public, but a settlement need not be so. It could be kept quiet and confidential by court order. I am told that you need to consent to any settlement, and I think you should do so. I need your cooperation."

"No," said Dr. Janowitz to Davis. "I did nothing wrong. Meri never even told me what she was doing or that she had stopped taking her full dose of medication. I am innocent of any wrongdoing. You can keep me here all day and all night, but I am not going to budge. Period."

"Obviously you need to know who you are dealing with and what is at stake. Your license could be at stake here, especially if the jury returns a verdict against you or if I refer the case to the State Medical Board with a request to review what you did or did not do here."

Dr. Janowitz responded, "You can refer this to anyone you want. I did nothing wrong, and no health care provider will ever say that I did so. My practice group is represented by one of the largest and most powerful law firms in the country – Poll, Davis and Wagner. If you insist on continuing on this course against me, I'll call them to come down here to deal with you. Shall I do so?"

Davis was now incensed at this threat. He turned to her lawyer and told Taylor, her insurance company provided lawyer, "Get her out of here now. Put her on a leash and take her for a walk."

At that same moment, Vince Harper just got off the phone with one for his former law professors from the law school he had attended at The Ohio State University. Professor Richard Aherns agreed, on Harper's request, to provide some pro-bono advice to Harper as his lawyer but only over the phone. If more was needed, despite their prior teacher-student relationship, he would need to be formally retained. Aherns listened to Harper's account of the voice mail exchange between Davis and his bailiff which had been recorded on Harper's voice mail.

Aherns analyzed the situation and began, "First, you have an ethical obligation to report this misconduct. That duty arises out of the Ohio Rules of Professional Conduct as well as the Ohio Code of Judicial Conduct. Moreover, what has happened here is a criminal act and you, my friend, are a witness to it who possesses material evidence of a crime which has not only occurred but which is on-going. As a consequence, you have an obligation, to report it to the authorities. If I had not agreed to act as your lawyer in this mess, I, too, would have had such an obligation to

DAVID L. HERBERT

report it. Even now, I may have such an obligation but since no one else is listening as this moment, I can at least give you time to do so."

Harper listened intently and began to review in his mind what all of this would mean. He knew that Malloy wanted SlimLine out of this case and if it took a settlement to do so, it had to be a confidential settlement and it had to be made confidential by a judgment entry issued by the Honorable Charles Davis. If Harper had to report what had happened and was continuing to happen, he first had to communicate with his client and employer to obtain consent and then somehow he would have to get the case settled and the final entry signed by Davis issued before all hell broke loose once Harper formally reported the jury tampering incident to the proper authorities.

Harper could spill the beans to the authorities right away while the jury was still out, but that would undoubtedly result in a mistrial, a new trial and more publicity than anyone at SlimLine, including especially Mitch Malloy, would ever want. Harper would probably be fired if that happened. Despite doing the right thing as far as the ethical rules were concerned, he would be hard-pressed to find another job with an employer who would then scarcely believe, despite his years of football, that he was a team player; his integrity would be suspect in that regard.

Since Harper had gotten Aherns to act as his lawyer and an attorney-client relationship between them was thus formed, he knew Aherns was bound to preserve the attorney-client communication in their telephone conference. The only possible exception to that absolute rule would be if Harper failed to act; that would amount to a failure to report ongoing criminal activity to the proper authorities. In that event, under Ohio's rules, Aherns would be obligated to make a report despite the attorney-client privilege which existed between them.

Upon gathering his thoughts, Harper replied to Aherns. "Ok, I will do what is required, but first it seems to me that I need to have a conference with my client to tell him what has happened and what I need to do. Otherwise, I will have violated my duty to inform my client."

Aherns replied, "Good answer. You're right. I'll give you till tomorrow to report all this. Call me just before you do so, and I will call the Presiding Judge of the Franklin County Court of Common Pleas to arrange an appointment for us to see him. The two of us can meet with him, play a tape of the voice mail and expand on what happened.

"Until then," Aherns continued, "you have a lot to do. Tape

162

record the voice mail over the phone, make two copies and get one of them to me. Talk with your clients, and then call me."

Realizing the gravity of the situation and what he was about to do, Harper could only sum up with, "Okay, I'll call you as soon as I can," and hung up.

Harper wondered if he should then tell Hatfield or Reuger, the latter of whom was really his boss at SlimLine. He considered the options and decided that if he told Hatfield, Hatfield would probably report what happened to the insurance carrier. If that happened the insurance company would want the matter reported to Ohio authorities right away, and Hatfield would probably do so. Since the company could only benefit by more delays to the prospect of paying out any money from the reserve it had established for this case, it would earn more money while a retrial was discussed and the case ultimately set for a retrial. Hatfield would also benefit some. The delay would allow him and his firm to earn more money while the case was held in abeyance for any retrial, even if it was ultimately settled.

So Harper decided that Hatfield was out of the loop on this issue. That left Reuger. Harper didn't particularly like Reuger. Reuger was an arrogant, pompous ass – a New York, smart ass lawyer, not a team player. He was an outspoken narcissist who thought he could do no wrong and needed all the praise himself. If Harper told Reuger what had happened, Reuger would take all the credit and leave Harper in the cold. No, he would not tell Reuger.

Harper decided to call Malloy himself. He had had previous contact with Malloy, and Malloy liked him. Malloy had played football in high school and at a small Division III college in upstate New York. He had been a linebacker like Harper and loved to hear Harper's stories about Ohio State football. Harper could talk to Malloy directly.

First Harper decided to secure his portable tape player, call his cell from a private location and tape the conversation between Davis and his bailiff. He grabbed his briefcase and made his way to an area on one of the upper floors of the courthouse where land lines were reserved for lawyer use only.

Harper entered the booth, closed the door, attached the tape recorder microphone to the land line phone and called his voice mail. Once he quickly passed through the other messages on his office phone, he turned the recorder on, taped the judge's illicit conversation with his bailiff

163

and then repeated the process for a second copy. He then saved the voice mail and turned the recorder off.

He then called SlimLine's executive offices, identified himself and asked to speak to Malloy. He was transferred to Mary Stone, Mitchell Malloy's personal assistant who answered knowing it was Vince Harper on the phone. "Vince, this is Mary. How are you? What's going on with the trial?"

"Mary," said Harper in a near whisper despite the seeming privacy of the booth he was in, "I need to talk with Mr. Malloy. It is urgent, and it's important."

Mary knew that Reuger was in Columbus as well, and she certainly knew the chain of command. "Vince," she said, "why are you calling directly? Is everything okay? Where is Mr. Reuger?"

Harper realized now that he would have to work to get beyond Mary and to Malloy directly. "Mary," he said, "he is tied up with the judge. I was only able to slip out for a few minutes. I've got to talk to Mr. Malloy. Now."

Mary wondered not only why Reuger wasn't calling but also why there was such urgency. "Mr. Malloy is in a very important meeting with some fellows from Washington. He gave me strict orders not to disturb him. I will have him call you later when he is free. Where can he reach you?"

"Mary," responded Vince, "I need him to call me back on my cell right away. I will wait here for a half hour. Then, I will have to go back. I would have him call me on this land line, but it only allows for calls to go out, not for calls to come in. Also tell him that I need to talk with him about Judson Trapp. Write it down, the Ohio State football coach, Judson Trapp. He will know who he is."

"I'll see what I can do to get him to call you back. Will Mr. Reuger be joining that call?"

"Probably not, just get Mr. Malloy to call me. The judge doesn't allow cell phones in his courtroom, his chambers or in his presence for that matter. I only have a half hour."

Mary was certainly suspicious by now but remembered the last attempt Mitch Malloy had made when he had tried to reach Jason Hatfield on Hatfield's cell phone. It had not gone well because of Davis. Mary would try to oblige and accommodate Vince Harper's request. Mitch Malloy liked him, and Mary knew it. No harm; no foul, she thought. She would put them in touch. But she might also try to call Matthew Reuger to get a fuller perspective on what was going on in Columbus.

Just then, however, Mitch Malloy hustled out of the main conference room all smiles. His meeting with the Washington folks had gone well. They were SlimLine lobbyists and research contract personnel. This latter group had made confidential contact with Dr. Barnet, and Barnet was ready to sign on to a new contract to provide essentially most all of the licensing rights to the citra-aid formula to Malloy's company for new SlimLine products.

Once Barnet and his formula were on board, Mitch could begin worrying less about the FDA action to remove Ma Huang and all ephedra products from the market. Until the citra-aid deal was closed and all said and done, his lobbyists would work Senators, Representatives, White House administrators and even DC bureaucrats at the FDA to delay any action to take ephedra off the market.

Overall, Malloy's plans were moving ahead regardless of what happened to SlimLine's ephedra-laced products. He could just replace the ephedra with citra-aid, perhaps rename the products and move ahead with a new and improved formula which could be marketed as such. "God," he thought, "what a great plan." The development of plans and strategies were always foremost in his marketing mind.

When Malloy said good-bye to his afternoon conference attendees Mary told him of Vince Harper's call. She told him it was important and it also included something about the Ohio State football coach whose name she had forgotten. While she wondered out loud to Malloy about why Reuger or Hatfield had not also called since Vince was in SlimLine's legal department and under Reuger's supervision, Malloy wanted to talk with him. He liked Harper, and he liked the fact that they had both been football linebackers. They had a lot in common. That was one of the reasons Malloy liked him, one of the reasons he hired him in the first place.

"Mary," Malloy said, "get Vince on the phone. I'll take it in my office."

At precisely 18 minutes after Vince had hung up with Mary, Mary called Vince's now properly activated cell phone and said, "Vince, this is Mary. I have Mr. Malloy ready for your call. Please hold while I transfer you to him."

As Vince Harper waited for the call to be transferred to Mitchell Malloy, he sensed the gravity of the situation. While he did not know how Malloy's conference had gone, he knew that too much adverse publicity arising out of the <u>Lawrence</u> case could spell disaster for SlimLine and for his own future. He would have to be careful.

"Vince, this is Mitch. How are you? What's happening in that hotbed of Midwest football, even though I still consider it a hick town?"

"It's fine here. I haven't yet had a chance to call to see Coach Trapp, but I am going to see him today while I am here. I will try to bring back an autographed poster of Jack Carter or an autographed ball for your office."

"That would be wonderful. Carter was a great All-American linebacker for the Buckeyes last year and will certainly be one again this year before be continues on to the NFL draft. I would really like to have an autographed poster or ball for my wall or desk."

"I will see what I can do," said Harper. "It should be no problem."

"Great. Why are you in such a hurry to talk to me, and where are Reuger and Hatfield?"

"They are both with the judge trying to see what to do with this case. The judge wants a lot of money out of us, and Hatfield will need to work on the insurance company along with Reuger and me to see what we can get."

"Well, I want you to get it. A big verdict in favor of the Lawrence family at this point would not be good. A quick settlement complete with a confidentiality agreement and an order surrounding that hush-hush settlement will keep more cases from being filed and should help me in my dealings with the FDA and Congress to keep our stuff on the shelves."

"I agree," said Harper. "But there's an additional wrinkle, and it has put me in a bad place." With that, Vince Harper explained to Malloy the entire cell phone event, the judge's tampering and interference with the jury function, Vince's own ethical obligations and the judge's insistence on settling the case.

When Harper was done, Malloy started, "Well, let me tell you what we are going to do. If I understood what you told me, we have this afternoon and at least several hours tomorrow before you need to tell anyone else. Right?"

166

"Well, that's pushing it some, but it should be okay until then."

"Good," responded Malloy. "I will need to talk to Reuger so he can push Hatfield to get some money on the table from the insurance company. But we should be able to use the judge's little indiscretions to knock off how much we have to kick in and keep our insurance company happy and our own insurance paid premiums on an even keel."

"Well, I'm not sure it's a good idea to get another lawyer involved given the ethical indiscretions of all this. I can handle it without Reuger, and I don't think Hatfield should know at all. He is completely above board, even somewhat square. If he knows about this, it may adversely impact our options. I can do this without them."

Malloy liked Harper, but he was a mere two and a half years out of law school, just two years since passing the bar. He had worked for a trade association before coming to SlimLine, and he had never tried a case like this. He didn't interact with judges as a usual matter at all. This first experience was to be a learning experience – a breaking in to this side of the law.

While Malloy knew that Reuger had not tried cases for SlimLine, at least on his own, he was a savvy, streetwise negotiator. He knew how to apply leverage and how to resolve seemingly insolvable situations usually in his or his client's favor. Malloy would have to involve him somehow in all this.

"Ok, Vince," Malloy said, "we will do it your way, at least for now. Do what needs to be done to get this case settled, with a confidentially agreement in place before you go to anyone to expose the judge and his bailiff. No matter what, that is how this needs to be done and in that order. No deviation. No slipups. Got it?"

"Got it," responded Harper. "I will get back with you."

Malloy concluded with a short comment, "Don't forget my autograph."

"Don't worry," said Harper, "I won't. In fact, don't worry about any of it."

Harper hung up and headed off to see where Hatfield and Reuger were in their negotiations and settlement authority. As he walked back to Davis' chambers, he saw another lawyer type pacing outside Davis' courtroom as if he were waiting for a baby's delivery.

When he went by this man, Harper said, "Hello. Anything happening in there?" referring to Davis' courtroom.

"Not that I know of," responded the man. "I wanted to know myself, but both the bailiff and the court reporter are rather mum. I'm not sure what will happen to that supposed trainer. Do you?"

"No, I don't," said Harper. "Have a good day."

The man was agitated and upset. By the tone of his voice and the wording of this question, he didn't seem to like Piccini. He must have watched some of the trial and heard some of the testimony. Harper just didn't recognize him.

With that, Harper walked into Davis' courtroom and then to the court's anteroom just beyond the courtroom, in-between the judge's office and the court reporter's space. In that area, he found Hatfield on his own cell phone with the insurance carrier for FitAgain and Reuger standing by and listening to what was said. As he approached them, he decided to listen to what was said on Hatfield's end.

"Listen," said Hatfield to the insurance adjuster on the other end, "I need you to at least authorize me to use the entire liability insurance limits of $5 million, if necessary. I won't go above $3 million unless I absolutely have to and even then, I will do it in increments, not all at once." With that, Hatfield went still and was intent on listening to the conversation from the other end which Harper could not hear. Soon Hatfield said, "That won't work. I can't call you while I am in the judge's chambers. He has an unbending rule about no cell phones in his courtroom or in his chambers. I need the authorization now. If I have to use my cell, I will excuse myself if I can and call you before I go to the limits. Otherwise, I will do what I can. In fact, the Judge wants you here. I suggest you get down here with your boss if need be, and we will approach this effort as a team."

Then Hatfield's end of the conversation went silent again but ended with Hatfield saying, "Okay, thank you, I will go to the $5 million but only if I have to, only in increments and only after we talk about it. You need to come here. The judge may or may not let you in on all this, but come now. He may demand that you and your boss, if necessary, be here. I know you are an important company to my firm. I won't let you down. Bye."

At that moment, Hatfield turned to Reuger and said, "Well, I have the limits of insurance coverage - $5 million if I need to use them, but only if I have to. The adjuster and maybe his boss will be here shortly."

Reuger responded, "Our CEO will be happy if the case settles within the limits but not so beyond that since it will then come out of his own pocket. I trust we are all on the same page about that."

Vince Harper then saw the need to enter the fray and added, "I think they will go for the offer. They, Mr. Malloy in particular, called me to get something out of the Ohio State football coach. But during that conversation, he told me to remind you both of the need to get this case settled quickly and with a confidentiality agreement backed up by a court order making sure the agreement is enforced. He said that under no circumstances were the assets of the company to be exposed, and the case should be settled within the insurance coverage limits."

Both Hatfield and Reuger were agitated with the messenger, not necessarily the message. Reuger spoke first, "What are you doing talking directly to Mr. Malloy? You are supposed to go through me. I will speak to him, not you."

"But," said Harper, "he called me."

"Next time, notwithstanding who calls who, you come and get me to talk with him. I'm Chief Legal Counsel for SlimLine. NOT YOU!!"

"No problem," said Harper.

At that point, Hatfield joined in and said, "No matter who called who, we need to get these other fellows to kick-in some money since I don't really want to use all of our insurance limits to settle this case. Any suggestions? The Judge was intent on me getting $5 million on the table from SlimLine's insurance carrier but I'd like to get some of it from the others."

Reuger considered the question but was only concerned with saving SlimLine's assets, not the insurance company's settlement reserves. Harper, however, felt he could play a decisive role in getting the judge to get the Plaintiffs to accept just $3 million as opposed to $5 million from SlimLine. After all, he had something he could use in that regard to encourage the judge to do so.

Harper asked, "Why don't you let me try to talk with the judge alone? He's an Ohio State football fan, and I'm not sure he remembers me or even associates me with Ohio State football. Once I communicate those facts to him, I'm sure I can do some good with him."

With that comment, Reuger looked at Hatfield, and both of them looked at Harper and smiled. Hatfield said, "Vince, Ohio State football and football stories will only get you so far in court, especially with his Honor Charles Davis. For God's sake man, he's got connections in the White House. Do you really think you can move him in this case with stories about football? He didn't even like you looking at the pictures on the walls of his chambers."

By then Reuger was laughing out loud. Hatfield joined in. Harper obviously didn't like their joint reaction and began to turn a shade darker than Ohio State scarlet. He said, "Laugh all you want. I'm going in there and will get the judge to sell $3 million to the Plaintiffs. Period. You stay out here and laugh all you want."

Harper turned and walked toward the judge's chambers. Reuger instructed him. "Don't screw this up. It will be your ass and your career. It will be over before it gets started."

Harper turned and walked into Judge Davis' chambers with but one knock and no reply. At that moment, Judge Davis was popping a piece of hard candy into his mouth while secretly wishing it was a bourbon, a gin, a whiskey or even a scotch. It had been several years since he had a drink. He missed going to the place he had called home for so many years after four or five gin and tonics or whatever he had then chosen to drink. It was a warm and friendly place, where there were few disruptions, good results for all concerned and happy thoughts at least until the next day. Regardless of the next day's assaults, it was, he then thought a good place to be.

At the same moment Harper walked in and Davis was popping a piece of candy into his mouth, he was also reviewing the copy of the Piccini jurors' notes that he had put in a labeled file in his top right-hand desk drawer. When he realized Harper was coming in, he quickly folded the file and put it back in his drawer.

Davis turned to Harper and said in no uncertain terms, "What are you doing in here? Don't you ever come in here until I tell you you can. Do you understand?"

With each syllable of each word, Davis' voice became louder and louder. Hatfield and Reuger heard the last part and turned to walk away shaking their heads in disbelief. Inside the judge's chambers, the legal fitness and conditioning of the participants to this conversation were about to be tested.

Harper walked toward his Honor Charles Davis and began quietly and deliberately, "I'm here because I know what you have been doing with the jury in this case. I have irrefutable evidence. It's your ass that's on the line here, not mine."

"You," screamed Davis, "have nothing. Do you really think you can come in here and threaten me, you novice pissant?"

Harper said, "Push me too hard, and I won't even give you a chance to do the right thing here. I'll go straight to the Presiding Judge and turn over the evidence I have. I will do it right now. Is that what you want?"

Before Davis could reply, Harper slammed his tape recorder down on Davis' desk and turned it on. The judge listened intently. Once he knew what it was, he immediately realized that he had a problem. He looked at the recorder and quickly grabbed it off the desk. Harper laughed and told Davis, "Don't get too excited here, I have another copy, and it's with an unimpeachable third party."

"What do you want?" asked Davis.

"First, I want you to treat me with respect now, in this case, and hereafter. I certainly don't deserve your singling me out in these chambers to scold me as if I were some child in front of all the others in this case. That was just wrong, and I don't want it to happen again."

"Then," responded Davis, "you should focus your attention on this case and this case alone."

"I always do," said Harper. "I was just looking at your pictures. I can listen, think and look at the same time. If you don't want people to look at what you have in here, why do you have those pictures on your walls?"

"Alright, alright. I can treat you like I treat everyone else. That's not why you're here, is it?"

"No, but it's part. Don't do it again. I am a lawyer from Ohio, I graduated from Ohio State. I played football for Coach Trapp, I was All Big Ten, and if I hadn't gotten hurt, I'd be in the pros now. I deserve some respect."

Davis tried to remember Harper's active football days but just could not place him.

Harper then continued, "Aside from that, I have $3 million to kick into the pot to settle this case. But that is it. We won't be putting in $5 million. The $3 million is all you'll get from us. Sell it to the others and the plaintiffs, or I will walk out of here to the Presiding Judge's office with this tape right now. You have sixty seconds to decide. Sell this settlement, or face your own humiliation, your demise and your esteemed position. I wonder what the Vice-President would say with you stripped of your robes even though all you judges look like men in dresses. You now have 45 seconds to decide."

"Don't push me too hard," said Davis, "or I'll . . ."

"You'll what? Find me in contempt while you're behind bars? Tampering with the jury process won't be allowed by anyone. You now have only 30 seconds."

"Who has a copy of the tape?" asked Davis.

"At this moment," responded Harper, "just you and my impeccable and trusted advisor."

CHAPTER 27

Many months before the drama began in Judge Charles Davis' courtroom, a different phone call had set a different scenario into motion. That call had been for Meri Margaret however. The phone call was innocuous enough, something Meri hadn't planned on. But it came at what ultimately turned out to be the right moment, or at least she thought so. The call might have led to something very good if things had turned out differently.

The caller on the other end, Jason Landau, worked for an employment recruiting company located in Cleveland, Ohio. He specialized in the women's fashion industry, particularly in the executive and marketing categories of that trade.

Jason began the conversation simply, "Hi, Meri, this is Jason Landau with Executive Recruiting in Cleveland. We have been doing some research into the Midwest fashion market, and I wanted to talk with you because I know you are a key player in the women's' fashion industry in this area of the country. My records indicate that you came to this area from the South and returned home to work for one of the big players in the market. I am in the process of completing a rather comprehensive and confidential search for a person who can provide the right fit for one of my clients. I was wondering if you would be willing to help me?"

Meri just half listened at first while she was reviewing a series of ad composites for Flair but began to pay attention to Jason's comments once he seemed to know more about her than she thought he should. In any case, she responded, "I would be glad to help in any way I can. I have been in this industry for many years and believe that I may be in a position to provide the kind of information you need. What kind of a person are you looking for?"

With that, Jason began to describe the opportunity in such a way that he felt Meri might have some interest. "Well, I'm looking for someone who can fit right in and hit the ground running with one of the foremost fashion leaders in women's clothing. In particular, my client is looking for someone who has a background in the petite women's wear category. They are looking for someone who can coordinate buyers and retailers, and who has a flair for merchandising. Someone who can bring a certain expertise to the market."

He continued, "The client is willing to put together a rather comprehensive salary and benefit package for the right person so that the group's executive leadership will be recharged for many years to come. We are looking for someone to fit this bill. Can you make any suggestions to me?"

With those comments, Meri's heart began to beat a little faster and wondered whether or not the unidentified company might be a right fit for her. She really felt that she had to have more information in order to secure some insight into what was really being asked of her. "Well, I might be able to provide some suggestions to you. What kind of a person are you actually looking for and what could they expect?" asked Meri. Jason realized that he had her ready for the bait and then the hook.

He said, "I'm looking for someone just like you who would be interested in this kind of position. I know that you have been with Flair for many years. Surely you have come across someone you could recommend who is, in essence, a clone of yourself." Then Jason cast out the hook, duly baited, "I am not sure, but would you even be willing to consider such a position yourself? It might be something that would be very attractive, not only for someone you could recommend, but perhaps even for you. What a benefit it would be to my client if someone like you, someone exactly like you, you in fact, would be interested. May I at least meet with you and provide some information to give you some insight into the kind of opportunity that is available? We are looking at a six figure salary, performance-based bonuses, a luxury automobile, an expense account, a very generous 401k plan, stock options, use of a private jet, clothing – you name it, it's all there for the right person."

Meri thought there was no harm in meeting, and no harm in getting together to see where this might lead.

She said, "Well, of course, I'd be willing to sit down with you. If I am not interested myself, I surely could provide a name of someone who may be interested and available. When would you like to get together?"

With that, Jason smiled and began to set a date and time, realizing that he may have a great opportunity not only for Meri, but for his client and for himself as well. The bonus for finding the right someone in this situation exceeded $25,000 in commissions. Jason could do very well. A good call, he thought, and a potentially great result.

CHAPTER 28

Davis was absolutely incensed that Harper, a young, inexperienced and totally unsavvy rookie lawyer would try to blackmail him by using Davis' own breach of ethics, not to mention the requirements of law, to Harper's advantage.

While Davis had been able to yank the tape from Harper's tape recorder, Harper told him he had another tape in the possession of some trusted third party. He wondered who could be such an "impeccable" source. Another judge? Some other office holder? An appellate court judge? Who?

In any case, Davis needed a plan to deal with Harper's threat. And he needed to get all copies of the tape under his own control. He wondered how Harper could have taped him and his bailiff in a private conversation with no one else present. At that moment he used his phone intercom and summoned Bill Morris, his bailiff, to his office. "Bill," he said, "get in here. I need to talk with you."

When Bill arrived in Davis' chambers, the judge started: "Bill, one of the lawyers on this Piccini case has a tape recording of the conversation you and I had at your desk in the courtroom – the one where I told you to get information about the jury's deliberations so we could use it to push the parties along to settle the case. How could he have gotten that conversation on tape?"

Bill thought back to where they were at the time of that conversation. There was only the phone on his desk, and it rested the entire time in its cradle. No one could have bugged it, he thought. Just then, however, on a hunch, he ran from the judge's chambers to his desk. There, on the corner of his desk, sat the judge's candy dish with a number of cell phones on it. One was still flashing – one he did not know how to turn off.

Morris quickly returned to Davis' chambers with the dish and said, "I'm not sure, but maybe one of these phones was on when we were talking. I'm never sure how to deal with some of these. Perhaps I pressed the wrong button."

"My God, Bill! How could you be so stupid?" responded Davis, "My ass is on the line now!"

Morris felt bad. He had let his boss down. "What can I do?" he asked Davis.

"Let's get all of the lawyers into my chambers, have each of them deposit their phones in the dish and go through them in detail. See if any of them have recorders or answering devices that can pick up conversations. If so, erase them and let me know. I'll keep the lawyers in my office long enough for you to do it. Do it quickly but correctly. Concentrate on Harper's phone."

With that, Morris assembled the lawyers for a further conference in Davis' chambers and gathered all the phones as he usually did. No one would be the wiser.

Once he had all the phones, he grabbed Harper's and studied it carefully. He called a local electronics guru he knew and told him he was having a problem with his own new phone. The expert walked him through the phone's options, and soon Morris was able to connect to Harper's messages and listen to the clandestinely recorded conversation between himself and Davis which had been recorded on Harper's voice mail. As soon as he heard it, Morris followed the voice prompts and his expert's advice to delete the message from Harper's office phone.

Morris then barged into Davis' chambers to surreptitiously convey the news of his successful venture to Davis.

"Judge, I have resolved your scheduling conflict. You are now oaky to conduct that pretrial conference call." Davis knew what the message really conveyed to him.

Davis then released the lawyers from his chambers with new instructions to get the case resolved. When Harper lingered too long without the others, Davis told him, "I will do what I can, but you'd better get your so-called advisor in here with that tape."

Harper replied, "I will, but only after this case is settled for the sum I specified and you put it in the court's record. If not, you'll be the one making a record – just a different one."

"Get out," replied Davis. "I'll call you when I get there." With that instruction to Harper, Davis reflected on the trial that had just concluded.

CHAPTER 29

Prior to the completion of all the evidence in the <u>Lawrence</u> case, prior to giving the case to the jury for its decision, prior to the efforts to settle the case and Davis' discovered improprieties, the trial started and continued for many days.

On one of the initial trial days, once opening statements were completed, His Honor, Charles Davis, entered the courtroom. As he did so, everyone rose to their feet. After Charles Davis entered the courtroom in full judicial robes (formal paraphernalia for a judge's courtroom wardrobe) and once the bailiff Bill Morris barked for all to stand, the bailiff announced: "This Honorable Court of Common Pleas is now in session, The Honorable Charles Davis presiding. This is a continuance of the Plaintiff's testimony, their case in chief, in the case of <u>Lawrence v. Piccini, et al</u>. Please be seated."

The judge, the Honorable Charles Davis, then called on Frank LaPorte to start, "Mr. LaPorte," he said, "call your next witness."

Frank LaPorte, the Plaintiff's counsel stood and called out: "The Plaintiffs call the Defendant, Anthony Piccini to the stand on cross-examination." With that, the bailiff walked toward Tony and asked him to stand and walk to the witness chair. That chair was located next to the judge's bench, between that bench and the jury. The chair was surrounded by a three-sided wooden structure composed of panels, one on each side coming up from the floor to about waist high. It was designed to "box" in the chair, except the part where a witness was required to enter the "witness box," as it was often called and to sit in the chair.

As Tony approached the witness box, he thought it looked more like some kind of confinement chamber, a small, tight cubicle, something like a place where he could be kept, where he could be held. He believed sitting in it would make him feel confined and nervous. He was right.

Before Tony could slip into the box and onto the chair, the bailiff told him to place his left hand on a Bible the bailiff held, a King James Version, and raise his right hand. The bailiff then clearly stated for all to hear: "Do you solemnly swear to tell the truth, the whole truth and nothing but the truth so help you God or as you shall affirm under the pains and penalties of perjury?"

Tony answered affirmatively and was then instructed by Morris to be seated. As he did so, Tony looked around at the judge, the bailiff, the jury and finally at LaPorte who stood at the lawyer's podium some twenty feet away. LaPorte began, "Good morning, Mr. Piccini. As you know, my name is Frank LaPorte. I represent the Plaintiffs in this matter, the surviving family members of Meri Margaret Lawrence, namely Meri's husband, Ben, and her two small children, Kimmy and Chase. For the record, your name is Anthony Piccini correct?"

"Yes, sir."

"You are one of the defendants in this case correct?"

"Yes, sir."

"In 2006 you provided personal training services at a FitAgain facility, a so called 'health club' in Upper Arlington, located in Franklin County Ohio, just outside of Columbus, correct?"

"Yes sir." (With that question and answer, the Plaintiffs had established and proven two essential elements of the case – the venue or the place where the wrongful death had occurred and the territorial jurisdiction of the court.)

LaPorte continued, "It is my understanding that you provided services at this facility as a fitness instructor or as the position is sometimes called, a personal trainer, correct?"

"Correct."

"So that we may all know just what a personal trainer is, at least from your perspective, would you mind telling us?"

"A personal trainer is a fitness professional who trains a client in a one-on-one, personal relationship to help the client get in shape and attain his or her fitness goals."

"While Meri Margaret Lawrence was alive, did you serve as her personal trainer at the FitAgain facility in Upper Arlington, sir?"

"Yes I did. "

"Why don't we examine your definition of a personal trainer and see where you fit in in reference to the service you provided to Meri. To start, please tell us in your own words what experience or training you had to be a 'professional' personal trainer?"

"Well FitAgain trained me to perform in their company as a personal trainer. I had a week of training sessions with them and became certified by them as a personal trainer."

"Mr. Piccini, it's true, is it not, that you are not licensed, for example, by the federal government, the United States of America as a personal trainer?"

"Well no; no one is."

"And you are not licensed by the State of Ohio as a personal trainer, are you?"

"No. There is no such license." Tony was beginning to be perplexed. Surely LaPorte already knew all this.

"You aren't licensed by the City of Upper Arlington or the City of Columbus to be a personal trainer, are you?

"No."

"Aside from the so-called "certification" you received from FitAgain what training did you have elsewhere?"

"I have been in athletic programs, gyms, and fitness facilities all my life. I was on the swim and gymnastics teams in high school ..."

"Mr. Piccini, listen carefully to my questions. I didn't ask your life story. I asked you what training you had at any place before you went to FitAgain to become a personal trainer."

"None like that, but ..."

"Thank you. You've answered my question. Why don't we review your prior employment history prior to your going to FitAgain?"

Ms. Childs, FitAgain's counsel stood and said, "Objection. May we approach the bench?" Judge Davis took a second or two to respond. In his hands, out of the jury's sight and below the oak rail that surrounded his bench and the top of his bench, he was reading that morning's paper, the *Columbus Dispatch* about The Ohio State University football team and didn't want to lose his place.

As all of the lawyers rose to walk the nearly 15 feet to the judge's bench to have a "side-bar" discussion with the counsel, one so characterized because it took place at the side of the judge's bench and away from the jury's hearing, Davis glared at Ms. Childs.

Once the lawyers' arrived at the side of the judge's bench and Childs began to speak, Tony tried to make eye contact with the jury as he had been told by his lawyer to do. The jury was composed of five women, three men and two alternates both of whom were women. One of the men in the front of the jury box and at least four of the other jurors looked like they never had seen the inside of a gym. Tony didn't know if that was good or bad. But as Finestein had instructed him and as Tony already instinctively knew anyway, he made every effort to have eye contact and smile with as many of the female jurors as he could during the side bar the lawyers had with the Honorable Charles Davis at the "side" of the judge's bench, on the record but outside of the jury's hearing.

As soon as Ms. Childs got to the side of Davis' bench away from the jury, she began: "Your honor, I object to Mr. LaPorte's verbal reference here to Mr. Piccini's alleged employment in such a way so as to make it seem by his questions and Mr. Piccini's upcoming answers that Mr. Piccini was employed by FitAgain. As the court knows he was not so employed. He was an independent, non-employed contractor. Nothing more. Mr. LaPorte's effort here to cast him in another light, as if he was employed, is improper."

Before Davis could respond and before even LaPorte could answer the allegations, the New York lawyer, Matt Reuger quipped in: "Judge, in New York, we would solve this by having the court rule in advance of any testimony on this issue by conducting a hearing on that issue, making a ruling and then proceeding with the case on that basis. Why don't we do so here?"

That was all Davis had to hear "Off the record," he bellowed at the court reporter sitting in front of his bench who dutifully and immediately dropped her hands to each side of her stenographic machine to comply with the judge's order.

"Mr. Reuger, I don't give a good damn about what you do in New York. This issue has nothing to do with you, and I suggest you let Mr. Hatfield do most of the lawyering for your client in this case and in my courtroom."

The judge continued, "This is not even your objection. As I already mentioned when I denied FitAgain's summary judgment motion on the Piccini employment issue before we started this trial, I will leave it up to the jury to reach and determine that issue with their verdict."

"So," the judge continued, "Mr. Reuger, do you get it? New York has nothing to do with this case. Don't raise that kind of issue here again ever." Davis then directed his comments to the court reporter: "Back on the record." Looking directly at Ms. Childs, he said: "Objection overruled. All of you return to your seats."

LaPorte smiled as he turned and walked back to the podium to continue his cross-examination of Tony Piccini. He never had to say a word, but Davis was pissed, at least at some of the Defendant's lawyers; LaPorte instinctively liked that. It made him feel good.

LaPorte then started questioning Tony Piccini anew, "Mr. Piccini what was your answer to my last question? Were you employed anywhere prior to going to FitAgain?"

Ms. Childs, needing to make a record, again started to rise out of her chair and stated, "Objection." Before she could even elevate her body completely out of her counselor's chair, her objection was loudly and forcefully overruled by Judge Davis.

"Sit down Ms. Childs, I have already ruled on your objections." Directing his stare at LaPorte, he concluded, "Proceed."

185

LaPorte began again. "Mr. Piccini, your answer is?"

"I worked for a downtown business establishment."

"Which one? What kind of a fitness establishment was it?"

"Well, it wasn't a fitness club. It was a restaurant establishment."

"Did you act as a personal trainer to the waiters there or the folks who came into eat?"

"No, I was a waiter, but…"

"You answered the question; no need to elaborate. Your lawyer can ask you questions later if he so desires…"

"Objection," said Allen Finestein, Piccini's lawyer. "Tony wasn't able to finish his answer before Mr. LaPorte interrupted him."

Referring to his client by his first name, not his last name, was an effort to have the jurors recognize, at least hopefully, that Tony was a regular person not just a "Mr. Somebody," a somebody who was just a defendant, someone to be judged instead of just being a regular person whose conduct should be evaluated.

By now the interruptions to Davis' own attempt to read the *Dispatch* were extremely annoying to him.

Instead of ruling, Davis simply stated, "It appears that Mr. Piccini did answer what was asked. Move on."

La Porte continued, "Where were you a waiter in the downtown area?"

"Lucita's Steak House."

"I take it then the place specialized in steak, red meat, no?"

"Yes, they served steaks."

"Did you have any training there in a personal, one-on-one, way to deal in meat like you later dealt with clients?"

Four of the seven defense lawyers immediately rose and nearly simultaneously objected. Before Davis could even gather his thoughts to determine what was at issue, LaPorte stated: "I will withdraw the question."

LaPorte's efforts had been to lay the groundwork for one of his potential later arguments to be made to the jury during closing arguments when the evidence was in and the case was over. He had hoped to make a comparison between Tony's qualifications as a personal trainer and the training he had received at Lucitas Steak House to serve red meat. The idea in the back of LaPorte's mind was to somehow equate Piccini's training with the serving up of meat or clients whether steak or individuals. Perhaps he would use it later, perhaps not.

LaPorte continued, "How long were you at Lucitas?"

"Three years off and on."

"Did you receive any training at Lucitas Steak House in personal training?"

"No, but I worked out at several gyms while I was there."

"Which gyms?"

"Sam's Weight Club on Broad over by the University and a few others."

"That's a weightlifting and power lifting facility almost exclusively frequented by men, is it not?"

"Well, I did see some women there on occasion."

"I bet you did. How many?"

"A few," responded Tony.

"Ever train any of them?"

"I wasn't employed there."

"You considered yourself employed at FitAgain following your career as a waiter at Lucitas, did you not?"

By this time, Ms. Childs was on her feet and objecting again. Davis looked at her and narrowed his gaze: "Ms. Childs. Did you not understand my last ruling on this issue?"

She answered, "Yes, sir, but I do need to represent my client's interests here and to make a record." By that she meant she must preserve through the record being transcribed by the court reporter, all that was said and done in court to make a snapshot, of sorts, to what was happening in the courtroom. The reporter was diligently recording on her stenographic machine all that was said and all that was done so that if anyone appealed the final verdict and rulings in the case, there would be a transcript of what had transpired for an appellate court to review. A review of the record could determine if any errors were made during the trial which could result in a ruling and a mandate for a reversal of the trial court's decision or rulings on objections and perhaps even a new trial or a different verdict. Making a record was done all the time.

Davis determined to solve Childs' interruptions to his morning reading: "I will let you have and I will note for the record your continuing objection to all questions about the employment of Mr. Piccini at FitAgain. Otherwise, there will be no more objections on that issue as I will allow the inquiry to take place. The jury will ultimately determine whether FitAgain was Mr. Piccini's employer."

With that LaPorte continued, "Did you consider yourself to be an employee of FitAgain?"

"Absolutely. They recruited me out of Lucitas to come work in their club in Upper Arlington. They told me where in their club I could work. They told me what I could do and with whom. They gave me clients to serve. They gave me a name badge and shirts and shorts to wear. They assigned me a locker. They had me use all of their forms and all of their documents. They let me use their floor, the facility and all the equipment in it to train their members, my clients. They had me sell the products they had on their shelves including energy drinks, energy bars, supplements, clothing and other things. They took 40% of my fees, and they collected all of the payments that were made by my clients. They gave me a check on a weekly basis and computed the compensation I was due by the number of hours I had worked. They even took note of the times that I came in and left their facility. They were my employer. I worked for them."

"By the way, prior to going to Lucitas, where were you employed?"

"I worked for several Columbus area restaurants as a waiter, not as a personal trainer. I also was at Kent."

"I assume you are referring to Kent State University, is that correct?"

(LaPorte already knew the answer since he and all the other lawyers had taken the deposition of Tony over several days after the case was originally filed but he had to get out all the information from Piccini which he considered to be important for the jury to hear.)

"Yes."

"When were you at Kent?"

"I was a student there."

"I understand, but when?"

"After I graduated from high school."

"Were you taking classes in fitness or exercise or biology or anything akin to what you later did as a personal trainer?"

"No. I was in business."

LaPorte then asked certain other questions but already knew the answers. This effort was to show the jury Piccini's lack of formal education.

LaPorte continued, "When did you graduate from Kent?"

"I didn't graduate."

"How long were you at Kent?"

"Two semesters."

"Why did you leave?"

"My grades."

"Your grades were not good enough for you to continue at or even graduate from Kent State University?"

"No, I guess they were not."

"Did you graduate from high school, Mr. Piccini?"

"Yes, I did. I previously told you that I was on the swim team and the gymnastics teams there. I ..."

"Mr. Piccini, not to interrupt you, but I am going to ask you a series of questions that require you to answer what is asked. Your lawyer will have an opportunity to ask questions later. But for now, I would like you to answer the questions that I ask and only those questions. I asked you whether or not you graduated from high school and you answered that you did. Your response answered the question. Do you understand? Let's proceed."

"It is my understanding that you were certified by FitAgain and received certain training from them to be certified as a personal trainer, is that correct?"

"Yes, I did."

"It's also my understanding from what we know based upon your previous testimony when I deposed you prior to this trial that the class work you received at FitAgain was in interpersonal relations, sales, and similar topics without any particular training in exercise except for general exercise activities. Is that correct?"

"Well, yes, that is correct."

"Did you have any particular training in physiology?"

"No."

"Did you have any particular training in kinesiology?"

"No."

"Mr. Piccini, do you even know what kinesiology is?"

"Well, I know it deals somehow with human movement."

"Did you have any training in exercise recommendations or exercise prescriptions?"

"Not any formal training, no."

"Did you have any training in human anatomy?"

"Well, not really other than what I know just from my general experience."

"Did you have any particular training in the responses of humans to particular forms of stress including exercise?"

"No."

"Did you have any formal training in weightlifting or weight-training techniques aside from what you may have picked up at the gyms that you went to yourself?

"No."

"Did you have any form of training in the operation and utilization of an Automated External Defibrillator, a so-called AED?"

"No, there was no defibrillator at the FitAgain facility."

"Do you have any current certification in Cardiopulmonary Resuscitation commonly known as CPR?"

"I have in the past."

"Mr. Piccini, my question was whether or not you have any current certification in CPR and your answer is?"

"No, I do not."

"Did you have any current certification in CPR when Meri suffered her stroke and ultimately died while she was under your care at the FitAgain facility in Upper Arlington?"

"I had just let it expire before that point in time."

"So Mr. Piccini your answer to my question was that you didn't have any CPR certification at that time, correct?"

"That is correct. I did not."

"Am I correct then that you are a high school graduate who attended but flunked out of Kent State University after trying a business program of studies, and during that time then and thereafter you served as a waiter in Kent and thereafter at several Columbus, Ohio restaurants, including most recently, restaurants serving, among other things, red meat?"

"I guess so."

"Your profession as a personal trainer came out of your one week of training and so-called certification by FitAgain and out of your prior personal involvement in your own weight training at various other gyms. Correct?"

"That's right."

"And you have no license in personal training?"

"No. I do not."

"And you have no license in medicine, do you?"

"No."

"And you have no license in Dietetics from the Ohio Department of Dietetics?"

"No."

"Nor any training or license or certification in any health care area, do you?"

"No."

"Going back to your relationship with Meri, it is my understanding that you began personal training activities with her in early January, 2006. Is that correct?"

"Yes."

"At the time that you first began to train Meri, did you have an opportunity to receive a health history questionnaire from her?"

"I did not personally, but I know that one was taken by staff members of FitAgain. I was told there was no particular problem with any of the activities that I could perform with her. I knew as of that time that she had recently given birth to a child, that she was in need of some weight loss activities and counseling, but other than that, I did not know of any specific health conditions when I started training her."

"Did you ever look at any health history form that Meri signed?"

"Yes."

"Did you recognize the handwriting above her signature?"

"Yes, I did."

"How could you possibly recognize the handwriting if you had just then met Meri?"

"It wasn't Meri's handwriting. I knew the handwriting because I had seen it before. It was Nanette Nelson's handwriting on the form."

Ms. Child's was once again on her feet. "Objection. Mr. Piccini is not qualified to testify as a handwriting expert."

By then Davis had finished the morning *Dispatch*. Davis turned to Tony and asked him directly: "Had you ever seen this person's handwriting before?"

Tony looked up and said, "Yes. Many times."

Davis then asked, "You are then familiar with her handwriting?"

"Yes I am."

"And you know it from having seen it before as Nanette Nelson's handwriting?"

"Yes," said Tony. "I know it as well as my own."

Davis looked up, away from Tony and directly at Ms. Childs with a blank but cold stare that really went beyond – if not through – Childs' eyes, as if she were not really there and said, "Objection overruled."

At that point, Ms. Childs should have made a request to approach the bench to make a statement for the record objecting to the judge's direct questioning of the witness. However, she was certain the effort would not change what had just happened and that any effort to make it a point for appeal on the record would be denied by an appellate court. She believed that any appellate court would determine in all probability that Davis' questioning of the witness was not prejudicial. She thought to herself, "No need to continue to get on Davis' bad side any more than I already am." So she sat down instead. It was undoubtedly for the best, given her lack of status with Davis.

LaPorte gathered his thoughts, chuckling inside at what had just again happened in his favor once again and then continued, "When you first began these fitness activities with Meri, did you learn that she had high blood pressure, was overweight and had been smoking for a number of years?"

"Not when I first started training her, although during the course of our relationship I did learn those things."

With that answer, Tony began to think back about his first sessions with Meri but the questioning continued which required some answers from him.

LaPorte continued, "Do you consider those factors to be important based upon the activities that you would ultimately recommend to her and in fact prescribe for her, despite your lack of specific knowledge regarding her conditions and despite your lack of any particular training in exercise prescription?"

"Well, I think they might have had an effect, but I am not a doctor."

"I know. That's obvious. When you first started with Meri, did you perform any kind of fitness test to determine what her level of fitness was at that point in time?"

"No, other than watching her perform as we began."

LaPorte knew that Tony had done nothing, but asked, "Did you test her flexibility?"

"No."

"Did you see the number of push-ups she could do?"

"No."

"...or sit ups?"

"No."

"Did you weigh her at any time during your training of her?"

Tony quickly replied, "No, she did that frequently and told me how she was doing?"

LaPorte pressed on, "Mr. Piccini, did you do anything to assess her fitness level other than merely looking at her?"

"Well, no, there was no need."

"Mr. Piccini, once you began training Meri without evaluation of her fitness level, what did you do?"

"Well, I put her on a treadmill for a specified amount of time which I don't really recall now, and based upon what I was able to see and from asking her questions as to how she was feeling while she was doing it and taking a pulse reading, I pretty much determined that she was not very fit. She was out of breath during the treadmill activity. She was overweight, and she smoked. I learned that as we started and continued with her program. It was no wonder that she was out of breath and that her heart rate was high."

"Did you take any body or body fat measurements from Meri?"

"I generally eyeballed her during her initial session, and I considered what she told me about her height and weight."

"Based upon that initial watching of Meri while she performed on the treadmill and knowing what she told you about her height and weight, what was your evaluation of her overall state of fitness as a result of that first session?"

"Well, based upon that first session and her stated lack of exercise prior to our meeting, I determined she was not very fit muscularly or cardiovascularly. That's basically it."

"Did you make any kind of record of the observations that you made at that time?"

"What do you mean by record?"

"Did you make any written notes?"

"No, I did not."

LaPorte continued to stalk Piccini, "How many clients did you have when you started with Meri Margaret Lawrence?"

"I had at least 50 people I was then training."

LaPorte knew then that he was about to establish a major point, "Mr. Piccini, can you even recall the names of half of them?"

Tony was then embarrassed. He could not name even ten of them. That was some time ago. He was in trouble. "Well, Mr. LaPorte, that was a long time ago. A lot of those folks aren't with me anymore."

"If you can't even remember their names, can you tell me who was overweight, who smoked, who had diabetes, who had any disabilities, who lost weight and who didn't – anything about all of them?"

"I can tell you some of that."

"Did you keep notes about any of these folks?"

"No, I did not."

"Did you even keep a folder about Meri?"

"Well, I kept some notes about some of the sessions that we had and some of the suggestions I made to her."

"Was there any requirement while you were performing these services at FitAgain for Meri that you take those kinds of notes or that you maintain a record of her progress for a file?"

"No."

"Was there any form of policy at FitAgain requiring you take notes and to continue to provide a record of an individual client's progress during your training activities with her?"

"Not that I am aware of."

Since LaPorte had obtained copies of some of the notes Piccini kept on his clients including Meri, he had Piccini's notes about Meri marked as Plaintiff's Exhibit 28 and handed the copy to Tony. "Would you tell the good folks of the jury what that is a copy of?"

"It's a copy of my notes of my training sessions with Meri."

"Is that one piece of 8½ x 11 inch paper with writing on both sides?"

Looking over both sides and confirming what he was asked, Tony replied, "Yes."

"Read the first note on the form for the jury, Mr. Piccini."

With that question, Alan Finestein rose to his feet and directed his comments to Davis, "Objection, your Honor, the exhibit will speak for itself and the jury will get to see it later."

"Judge," responded LaPorte, "the jury may see it later but Mr. Piccini won't be in front of the jury to answer my questions about these notes later."

Davis saw no harm in the question despite the fact that the objection was technically correct. "I'll allow it," said the judge. "Mr. Piccini," said Davis, then directing his attention to Tony, "please read out loud your very first note on your records of Meri Margaret Lawrence to the jury."

Tony knew he was in trouble but had to answer, "The note stipulates that I spent 50 minutes with her and the charge for that session was $150.00"

"Mr. Piccini," asked LaPorte, "Isn't there anything else on that first note?"

"No," replied Piccini, keeping his eyes on the paper.

"Well, Mr. Piccini, what was your very last note in Meri's records from the day she died?"

Tony did not know what he had written.

"It's the last note on the page," said LaPorte as he drove home the issue. "Mr. Piccini your last note on the day of her death was written by you, was it not?"

"Yes," said Tony.

"What did you write in that note Mr. Piccini – the last note in Meri's record on the day she died?"

Tony looked down and had to read what it stipulated and said, "I wrote, Meri Margaret needs to work hard today. I will push her to her limits. It won't kill her."

Upon Tony's response, LaPorte paused his questioning and asked for a recess to give the jury time to think about what they had just heard.

Davis granted the request and as the jury left the courtroom, all of them cast their eyes downward and away from Tony. It seemed, at least to LaPorte, that none of them could look Tony Piccini in the eye. It might reveal too much of their own disgust at what Piccini had noted on the very day Meri died.

When the jury returned, LaPorte continued.

"Well, when you started with Meri, did you take any information from her as to whether she had previously been hospitalized, whether she

197

was taking any kind of medication, whether or not she had been diagnosed with any particular medical condition – anything of that nature whatsoever?' asked LaPorte.

"Not initially, but I did ultimately learn during the course of our relationship that she was under the care of a doctor for high blood pressure, that she had recently had a baby and that she wanted to lose weight. I do remember she said she had been treating for high blood pressure and that she was taking a particular medicine for it.'

"Do you know what that medication was?"

"I didn't initially, but I believe it was called lisinopro."

"You mean lisinopril?" asked LaPorte.

"That may have been it," Tony replied.

"Do you know what the chemical composition of that particular prescription is?"

"Not really."

"Do you know who prescribed it?"

"I assume her physician."

"Do you know who that was?"

"No, I do not."

"Then I presume you never consulted with her doctor?"

"No," replied Tony.

"You now know who was Meri's doctor, correct?"

"Yes. She is a defendant in this case, too. She's sitting right there," Tony replied as he raised his right arm and pointed to the defense table where Dr. Janowitz was seated.

"Prior to this case, had you ever even met or talked to Meri's doctor?"

"No."

"Do you know what the effect of the high blood pressure medication was on Meri?"

"Well, not really; but I do know that it interferes with weight loss and makes it more difficult for someone taking it to lose weight. That is what I think happened with Meri even after several weeks of my working with her. She just couldn't seem to lose any more weight after the first few pounds."

"Well the truth of the matter, Mr. Piccini, is that Meri died because of what you recommended and suggested to her – namely that she stop taking her medication, isn't that correct?"

At that point all the defense attorneys were on their feet objecting. Davis reacted instantly shaking his head and then shouted, "I know he's not a physician and not qualified to express an expert opinion on causation. But I'll allow it with that caution to the jury."

LaPorte continued, "Your answer, Mr. Piccini, is?"

"Well, I gave her information regarding the weight loss products I recommended to her. What happened beyond that I have no idea."

"During the course of your personal training for Meri, did you have her engage in any weightlifting activities?"

"Yes, I did."

"And how did you determine how much weight she was to use for these exercises?"

"I always start, for females, someplace around 5 – 20 lbs. depending upon what exercise they are performing and their level of fitness."

"Did you make any notations during Meri's activities with these weights as to how she was handling them? For example, did you note whether Meri was shaky while using the weights?"

"Well, I did note that, but I didn't write it down," Tony replied. "She was shaky at the beginning and but I thought maybe it was just nervousness. I told her to relax and not worry about it. We finally came to the conclusion that it was her condition, the high blood pressure that was causing her to shake while using the weights."

"Did you then or even now have any knowledge as to whether individuals with high blood pressure become shaky while lifting weights?"

"No, not really."

"Or even, Mr. Piccini," LaPorte continued, "whether such individuals, like Meri, should even engage in weight lifting activities at all?"

"Well not really."

"Did you ever have any training or certification in that area at all?"

"No."

"Did you ever consult with anyone, anyone who was knowledgeable, to determine whether or not it was appropriate for Meri to engage in weightlifting activities knowing she had high blood pressure?"

"No."

"While under your direction and supervision, did you note during the course of Meri's weightlifting activities or observe whether or not she was holding her breath while engaging in those activities?"

"Well, I suppose she might have been."

"Do you know whether or not breath holding during weightlifting activity may adversely impact blood pressure?"

"No."

"Do you know if the effects of breath holding on blood pressure may be more serious in those who already have high blood pressure?"

"No."

"Do you even know in personal training vocabulary what breath holding during weightlifting activity is called?"

"No. I guess I don't."

"If you did not personally get a health history from Meri, didn't take notes of her personal training efforts, didn't make personal, written observations of her measurements or her weight, didn't know at least at first what her medical condition was and at that time, did not know what her medications were, what did you, as a professional personal trainer do to develop a personal, one-on-one relationship with Meri, another aspect of the terms which you used to define that profession?

"I did lots of things; I talked to her, I tried to become acquainted with her, to become her friend. I inquired about her family, her relationships with various family members like her husband and her children, how long she had been married, how much weight she wanted to lose, what size dress she wore, and what size she wanted to wear, what kind of job she had, how much stress she had – those kinds of things."

"Sounds like a great deal of very important information that any professional needs of any personal training client."

"Objection," said Alan Finestein as he rose to his feet. "That's not even a question."

"Sustained" said Judge Davis. "Mr. LaPorte, ask a question; don't testify."

Directing his eyes to the jurors, Davis stated to them, "The jury will disregard Mr. LaPorte's comments."

"At last," Finestein thought, "Davis has at last granted one of our defense objections."

LaPorte continued, "Mr. Piccini that kind of personal information from Meri didn't help you form a professional opinion about what you should prescribe for her as part of a personal fitness program, did it?"

"Well it helped me to get to know her better."

"Getting to know your clients is what you do best. Isn't it, Mr. Piccini?"

With that question Tony's thoughts began to drift back in time, out of the courtroom and to the weeks and days before Meri died. He remembered what she had told him. She had revealed some of her innermost thoughts. He would remember.

It was a Friday, Tony remembered or so he thought. Meri then told him, "I've got to meet with some executives at Le Petite Parisian International. A headhunter named Jason Landau set up the meeting for me. If I get the opportunity, the challenge as well as the rewards will be enormous. It will help me and Ben obtain a better life for us and for our kids."

"Great," said Tony.

Meri was worried, however. She had only lost some 15 pounds while with Tony. She needed to lose more and fast, another 25 pounds to get back where she had been before Chase's birth. The executive team at Le Petite Parisian International would expect Meri to look the part of a high fashion women's executive. Meri knew it. Jason had told her as much, and she only had four weeks to lose the weight. She would demand that Tony do more.

"Tony," she then said, "I've got to lose another 25 pounds in the four weeks I have left before my meeting for the potential new position at Le Petite Parisian International. You've got to help me." With that remembrance Tony was jarred back into the present, to LaPorte's questions. Back to the witness box. Back to the confining space. Back to the box and the never-ending questioning.

"Mr. Piccini, did you hear my question?" asked Frank La Porte.

Tony could hear the question but couldn't get his thoughts off Meri.

Meri approached Tony on a Friday several weeks before her last workout with him. She presented him with what seemed like an impossible request. She was stressed. Nervous. Overweight. She was intense, and she needed Tony's help. "Please, Tony, I need your help and I need it now!"

Tony said, "Meri, it has taken us months for you to lose 15 pounds. It will be near impossible for you to lose another 25 pounds in a few short weeks, unless…"

"Unless what?" Meri asked with a real need to know the answer to her question.

"Unless you start with some proven weight loss products," Tony continued, "I want you to start on some Extra Lean today. It will curb your appetite, keep you on your game, give you energy and enough fuel to keep you going at work. You'll need some extra workouts each night before I see you the next day."

Tony continued: "If we combine that with some natural weight loss pills called MP33s, we might, just might, achieve your weight loss and make your goal."

Meri became excited and asked, "How can I get those? Do I need to run these pills by my doctor? Are they safe?"

"Absolutely," said Tony. "I take them myself. No need to see your doctor. If they didn't hurt me how can they hurt you?"

"Ok, what do we do?" asked Meri.

"After we are done today, I'll take you over to a drug store around the corner, Pharmette, where we will pick up the MP33s. Then we'll go to the Natural Food Store to get some Extra Lean shakes."

Tony knew these products. Both were manufactured by SlimLine. The MP33s (Metabolic Poweraids) contained 33 mg. of Ma Huang, ephedra, while the shakes also contained a somewhat smaller dose but were sweetened with an artificial, zero calorie sweetener. They came in vanilla, chocolate, strawberry, boysenberry and other assorted flavors. They were sold at FitAgain too but Tony made more from product sales if they were purchased at Pharmette because Tony got a higher percentage of the sales.

"You will take three pills a day, one when you wake up, one at noon and one at 4:00 p.m.

"For breakfast you will have one of the Extra Lean shakes and another for lunch. I'll set up a number of very low calorie, low carbohydrate and high protein menus for your dinners. Then we will get you on track to a new body, a new job and a new life."

"In between if you're still hungry, you will eat one of the energy bars we will get for you at the front desk. They will even help you burn more calories and give you greater energy. They are loaded with a natural Chinese herb called Ma Huang and have been used for at least a thousand years. Great stuff. "

Meri reached out and embraced Tony with a big hug. He reciprocated and then told her, "Ok, let's get back on track with some leg lifts, but let's add some more weight."

Tony didn't bother to tell Meri that he would get a percentage of the take on all these products from FitAgain, from Pharmette and from the Natural Food Store where he had separate deals with store managers based upon all of his clients' total monthly purchases at those stores.

Thereafter, on another Friday several weeks later and on Tony's directions, at least as he now remembered them, Meri got on the leg lift machine and struggled, really struggled to complete three sets of lifts, 12 repetitions each with 160 pounds of weights. By the last set she gave it all she had, holding her breath as he visualized what he remembered, through every repetition until she saw spots before her eyes and became dizzy. Tony knew it. She knew it, but she worked through it anyway as Tony encouraged her to do so: "It won't kill you," said Tony. "Keep going."

With that remembrance, Tony's thoughts were diverted back to the courtroom, the box he was sitting in and the questioning by Frank LaPorte.

Tony responded to LaPorte's question: "I got to know Meri very well. I knew she had a great opportunity with a potential new job. I knew it meant a lot to her and I knew she had to lose 25 pounds to be considered for the job. I tried to help her do so."

Tony continued, "Clients often tell their trainers lots of personal, private, often very private information. They think of us as personal advisors, not just trainers."

LaPorte then knew he had Tony. Letting him talk had now paid off. "Mr. Piccini, if you were Meri's personal trainer in fact, her personal advisor, why didn't you tell her to see her physician before starting products literally laced with ephedra?"

"I took these products for years; they didn't hurt me."

"You didn't just have a baby, you weren't overweight by at least 25 pounds, you weren't under a great deal of stress, you weren't taking medicine to control high blood pressure, you didn't smoke and you didn't have a personal trainer pushing you to lift more and more weights and to do more and more repetitions, did you?"

"No, I guess I did not."

"Mr. Piccini, the truth is that in the weeks after receiving these products and during the two weeks before her death, you decided to cut Meri's blood pressure medicine in half, didn't you?"

Once that question was asked and put to him, Tony again drifted back in time. He did tell Meri to cut her medications but only after she had lost just another 7 pounds in two weeks. At that point she only had two weeks to go before her interview, and she had to lose 18 more pounds. She wasn't sure what to do. She asked him: "Tony, are you sure that the blood pressure medicine makes it harder for me to lose weight?"

Tony replied, "It does, FitAgain trained me to know this, and it does. You need to cut back if only until you lose more weight and get through that interview. Surely cutting back by half for only two weeks won't do any harm. It won't kill you."

"I don't know," Meri said.

"Well, it's up to you," replied Tony, "but if you don't cut it, I can't make all this work for you. The key is to let these products kick in to rev up your metabolism, to get you going in double time."

"Tony, those shakes, particularly with the pills and then the bars make me shaky, and I get even more shaky when I lift weights with you. It makes me feel as if my heart is going to race out of my chest. I even sometimes get dizzy."

"Meri, don't worry," said Tony. "That's what happens; that's how you get used to these exercises. I've been taking these products for years, and I've been lifting weights almost all my life. Look at me. I am *fine* - am I not?" Tony emphasized the "fine" part and posed for Meri.

She laughed and said, "Ok. I'll do what you say. I trust you. I know you know what you are doing; and yes, I know it won't kill me."

"Ok," said Tony. "Let's get going. I want you to get on the treadmill for at least 30 minutes now and again when you get home tonight before you go to bed. We will set it now at 6 and then 7 mph with an incline program. I want you to run hard and work through each session. Let's go."

With that Meri got on the treadmill. She felt it begin its continuous movement and then increase in speed and elevation beneath her ever faster moving legs and feet. She began to feel hot and then to sweat. As she did so, Tony stood in front of the machine and encouraged her to put forth maximum effort.

"Move," said Tony. "Run off the fat. Come on, you can do it. Let's go and go hard."

She felt breathless but continued on as Tony reminded her of what was at stake.

Tony remembered she finished that day and each day for the next week and a half, with several sets, repetitions, on several weight machines to work her arms, shoulders, abs, core and legs. Tony increased the weights every other day for the sessions which had become daily sessions rather than every-other-day workouts. They only stopped on Sundays. Even then Tony told her what to do on Sundays, how long to work out, how far to run, what to take, how many MP33s to ingest, how much food to eat, how much water to drink and how little of her blood pressure pills to ingest. He promised it would work.

"Mr. Piccini," said His Honor Judge Davis. "I don't know exactly where your mind is at this moment, but Mr. LaPorte has asked you a question. I am telling you to answer it, do you understand?"

Tony looked up at the judge, almost in surprise. He had been deep in his thoughts about Meri and was really jarred back into the reality of the courtroom and what seemed like never-ending questioning. "Sorry Judge," said Tony. "I was just trying to remember. I guess I need the question repeated."

With that Davis looked at LaPorte to prompt him to continue, at which point LaPorte then began his questioning anew, "Mr. Piccini, let's get to May 16, 2006, the day Meri Margaret Lawrence died. Do you remember that day?"

"Yes. Of course."

"Meri worked with you that morning, the morning of May 16, 2006 before she died, correct?"

"Yes."

"In fact, Mr. Piccini, Meri Margaret Lawrence died in the FitAgain facility in Upper Arlington, here in Franklin County, did she not?"

"Yes."

"And she died while she was in the facility and under your care during one of these professional personal training sessions with you at FitAgain at a rate of $150 per hour, correct?"

"Yes."

"In fact, Mr. Piccini, from January 2, 2006 when Meri Lawrence started with professional personal training sessions at FitAgain under your care, she paid over $18,000 to you and FitAgain for these sessions, did she not?"

"I would have to look. Perhaps you could ask FitAgain."

"Do you dispute that figure?"

"No, but –"

"You answered the question, Mr. Piccini. You also received a number of tips from Meri for your "good" service, did you not?"

"Yes, Meri was very generous."

"She thought you were helping her, did she not?"

"Objection," said Ms. Childs just before Alan Finestien raised the same objection. She stated, "How could Mr. Piccini or for that matter anyone else know what Meri's brain was thinking?"

Once again, even before Judge Davis could rule, Frank LaPorte said, "I'll rephrase the question. Mr. Piccini, did Meri Lawrence ever tell you at any time that she believed you were helping her?"

"All the time."

"Did she tell you she trusted you?"

"Repeatedly."

"That happens frequently with your clients, doesn't it? They come to trust you and believe that you are helping them?"

"Yes, we form close relationships with clients."

"Do clients follow your suggestions, your recommendations, your exercise prescriptions and diets?"

"Yes that's what we do with them. That's why they contact us in the first place."

"On the day Meri died, did she follow your directions and instructions?"

"Yes."

"As I understand it, Mr. Piccini, on that morning she told you she had not slept well the night before, correct?"

"Yes."

"She told you that she felt really stressed and worried over her upcoming job interview, correct?"

"Yes," responded Tony beginning to look down at his feet instead of at the jury, contrary to what his lawyer had told him to do. There was not much for him to smile about during this phase of the trial. He didn't feel like it. It would be inappropriate to smile at the jury at this point.

"Did she tell you she felt as if her heart was racing and working very hard?"

"Yes."

"Did she tell you she had been having headaches nearly continuously?"

"Yes, I just attributed all that to worry and stress."

"Not to the ephedra-laced products you got her to take?"

"No"

"Did you then know what these products did to her metabolism, her blood pressure, her spirits, her heart rate, her headaches and even her ability to sleep normally?"

"I never had these problems."

"I'm sure you didn't. But she told you about the problems, correct?"

"Yes."

"And in regard to these expressed concerns – those worries on top of worries – you never once, not on any day and not even on the day Meri died, ever told her to go and see her doctor, did you?"

"No, I'm not a doctor."

"If you weren't a doctor, why did you ever tell her to alter her blood pressure medication?"

"I only told her that taking it was interfering with her weight loss."

"Did you tell her, did you warn her that by reducing the medications that action could kill her?"

"No," responded Tony, feeling and looking very dejected and peering down at his feet once again.

"When Meri showed up on May 16, 2006, she told you she was tired, hadn't slept well, was shaky, that her heart had been racing, that she had had a number of headaches and that she was stressed. Did you then tell her to take it easy?"

"She wanted to work out."

LaPorte quickly responded, "That wasn't my question. Answer my question."

"No, I did not tell her to take it easy."

"Mr. Piccini, when you showed up that morning, the very morning of Meri's death, you were late. Is that correct?"

"Only 5 minutes."

"And when you showed up late, Meri told you how she felt and all the problems she was having, correct?"

"She told me those things."

"And despite all that, you put her on the treadmill, cranked it up to 7.5 mph and at an incline of nearly 25%, correct?"

"Yes."

"You made her run for 30 minutes at that speed and incline, correct?"

"Well, it was started somewhat slower at first."

"Mr. Piccini, essentially what I asked you is correct?"

"Yes."

"And when she was done, you put her on the weight machines, did you not?"

"Yes."

"After working out on several weight machines doing several sets of repetitions for over 20 minutes, you put her on the leg lift machine, lifting 175 pounds of weight for numerous repetitions. Correct?"

"Yes."

"And Meri struggled with those lifts didn't she?"

"She did it, but I felt she had some difficulty."

"In fact she was shaking, was she not?"

"She did some shaking."

"How many shaky repetitions did she do before she could do no more?"

"7 or 8."

"Did you have a chance to look at her during this time while she was doing these leg lifts?"

"Yes."

"So you did see that she was holding her breath and forcing the lifts with all the might she could muster. Correct?"

"I did. I could see that was what she was doing."

"And then Mr. Piccini, during the last repetitions she gasped, her eyes rolled back in her sockets, and she lost consciousness. Is that also correct?"

"Yes," said Tony, looking even more dejected than before and staring at the floor.

"You then called to her, did you not?"

"Yes, I did, but I couldn't arouse her."

"What did you do?"

"I picked her up and carried her to the front desk. She never came to. The front desk called 9-1-1. The EMS people arrived several minutes later."

"And Meri never regained consciousness?"

"No."

"Did you later learn that she had died?"

"Yes."

"You were the last person to see her, the last person on this earth to talk to her, correct?"

"Yes."

"And if I remember correctly, according to the statements that were given to the police, the last thing you told her was, 'Meri, keep pushing. Come on. One more. It won't kill you.' Is that correct?"

Tony didn't answer, at least not right away. All he could think of was Meri's face as he remembered carrying her to the front desk. She had looked so strained, so distraught. Tony was so scared. So sorry. So very, very sad. He had killed her. He just didn't know any better. After all, he was only trying to help her.

Not getting a direct reply, LaPorte said, "Mr. Piccini, I think we all know your answer." LaPorte then sat down as Tony continued to sit in the cubicle, the box he did not like, for what seemed forever. All eyes were on him. He didn't like it. He didn't like it at all but he was very sorry for what had happened. He never meant for anything like it to occur. He was so very, very sorry. He began to cry and then to weep. Meri had been his friend, someone she trusted. He was her professional personal trainer, and he had failed her. She died in his care, in his arms.

Eventually, his Honor Judge Davis called for a recess. He told Tony to step out of the witness box. He instructed the jury to take a break and not to discuss the case in the meantime. He asked his bailiff to have the jury return to the jury room and await further instructions.

As everyone stood, except the Judge, the jury was led out. Judge Davis called all the attorneys up the bench. He then told the lawyers that he would allow them three more days of testimony on top of the three days they had already been at it.

He also then told all of them off the record that they had better start trying to settle the case.

At least some of the lawyers didn't listen. The case went on for three more days of testimony. The plaintiff's case in-chief included the introduction of the coroner's report and his testimony. The cause of death was an aneurysm, a stroke brought on by grossly elevated hypertension, extremely elevated blood pressure, caused and aggravated by a decrease in Meri's blood pressure medication which was below a therapeutic level. Her condition was further compromised by the ingestion of Ma Huang through her ingestion of a number of ephedra-laced products, breath holding and straining during heavy lifting.

The coroner was very critical of what had happened. Over Alan Finestein's very vigorous objections, all duly denied by the Honorable Charles Davis, the coroner labeled Tony Piccini's actions and recommendations as "criminal" in nature. That characterization was really the kiss of death for Tony and for FitAgain as well.

Coroner Pieter Gothe's testimony was in some respects routine, dull and matter of fact. While on the witness stand, he testified that Meri had died of an aneurysm, specifically an aneurysm in the Circle of Willis. This was an especially dangerous site he opined, because the interior carotid arteries branch off from this area and supply more than three-quarters of the supply of blood to the brain. In Meri's case, the aneurysm had burst due to the stress placed upon her body and her circulatory system while she was doing strenuous leg lifts under Tony's instruction and supposed guidance. Her death was logged in by him on her death certificate at 7:07 a.m. on Wednesday, May 16, 2006. Her time of death exactly matched the recorded time of her birth. No one who testified knew that. No one knew but Meri's father and mother and neither of them testified.

Dr. Gothe's ultimate opinion as to the cause of Meri's death was that the stress of Tony's prescribed exercise for her, coupled with the massive doses of ephedra she received and the reduction in her blood pressure medication inexorably led to and proximately caused her death. When her breath holding during the stress of the heavy leg lifts was not corrected by her trainer, Dr. Gothe concluded that her impending death was then and there sealed. Tony's lack of proper education in human anatomy, kinesiology, physiology, exercise, weight lifting and personal training ensured Meri's fate. FitAgain's promise and Tony's reiteration of that promise to Meri "not to kill" her was breached. FitAgain's sloppy hiring practices and grossly inadequate in-house training really laid the groundwork for Meri's death.

The coroner's expression of opinion was followed by the testimony of representatives of the local police department, the EMS service providers who attempted to revive Meri at FitAgain, and the triage nurse who logged her in at the hospital and the emergency room physician who ultimately coded her when he could not secure any positive response from her in basic life functions.

Once the emergency personnel testified, Meri's husband, Ben, provided the final testimony necessary to stir the jury. He did so in part by identifying a family picture of Meri, Ben and their two children. This was done to demonstrate Meri's life and her importance to the family.

"Ben," Frank LaPorte asked him during his testimony, "how old was Meri when this picture was taken?"

"She was 32. Chase had just recently been born. Meri wanted the picture taken for posterity. She never realized it would be her last photo with me and the kids."

LaPorte continued: "What did Meri do as a matter of daily routine for the family, for you and the children?"

"She did everything for us even though she worked sometimes 60, 70 or more hours a week. She was loving, attentive, caring. She never missed a beat, never skimped in providing for all three of us. I really don't know what we will do without her," Ben responded in a cracking and wavering voice. "She was the bedrock of all we were from the moment she got up in the morning till she tucked Chase into bed and went to sleep next to me each night. I miss her even now and can't seem to get from one moment to the next without a feeling of dread and hopelessness in the pit of my stomach."

The jury was obviously moved. Meri Margaret Lawrence was someone who was essential to this family. Someone who could not be replaced. Someone who would never be forgotten.

While Chase might miss her the least since he would never really remember her independently of what Ben and others would tell him because he was so young, he would always later wonder what he missed every time he looked at her pictures.

Allen Finestein, Tony's lawyer, decided not to ask any questions of Ben. He just didn't see the point in trying to attack either Meri's husband or his memory of this young woman. There was nothing to be gained by attempting to smear Meri's memory or Ben's view of her or her role in the family.

Joan Childs, FitAgain's counsel, however, had other ideas and decided to cross examine Ben on issues she felt would help her client.

She began with legal niceties, "Mr. Lawrence, my name is Joan Childs. We met previously. I am very sorry we are here today; and I am very sorry if anything I ask you will cause you any pain or heartbreak, but it is my job to do so. I am obligated to proceed. Do you understand?"

"Yes, I do," responded Ben in as matter of fact a tone as he could muster up.

Ms. Childs continued, "Mr. Lawrence, it is my understanding that your wife was under the care of a doctor, Alice Janowitz, prior to her death, correct?"

"Yes," Ben answered.

"In fact," she continued with her questioning, "Mrs. Lawrence had been under Dr. Janowitz' care for a number of years, correct?"

"Yes, she was."

"She came under the good doctor's care before your second child was born, did she not?"

"Yes, she did," answered Ben. Through her questions, Ms. Childs was doing her best to stay away from the first names of Meri or her children in order to make them seem more formal, more distant than the message that otherwise would be conveyed by using their more personal first names. It was a small but potentially important psychological tactic which was often used by defense attorneys in their questioning of witnesses – especially family members providing testimony in personal injury cases or wrongful death filings.

"Mr. Lawrence, it's true, it is not, that Mrs. Lawrence worked hard, kept late hours, was under a great deal of stress at work and usually didn't take proper care of herself, isn't it?"

"Meri worked very hard at everything she did," Ben said. "She was competitive and goal oriented. She saw Dr. Janowitz to get help. That's also why she went to FitAgain."

"And yet, Mr. Lawrence, Dr. Janowitz is a defendant along with everyone else in this case, correct?"

"Yes, Dr. Janowitz is a defendant. Meri is gone, and we believe Dr. Janowitz had a role in causing her death along with everyone else here."

"Mr. Lawrence, isn't it true that Dr. Janowitz was attempting to treat Mrs. Lawrence's high blood pressure and trying to get her to take better care of herself through lifestyle changes and weight loss?"

"Yes, she was."

"Did Mrs. Lawrence follow the doctor's advice to reduce her hours at work and the stress that went with it?"

"She was trying."

"Is that why she agreed to consider taking on additional responsibilities with a new and even more demanding and stressful job, so she could reduce her work related stress?"

"Meri would have had a better position, more benefits, more people under her care, all of whom would have reduced her personal load. Meri loved to work."

"Mrs. Lawrence also smoked, did she not?"

"Yes, unfortunately she did. She was trying to quit. She was on the path to doing so when she died. I was helping her in that effort"

"Mr. Lawrence, you weren't with her 24 hours a day, were you?"

"No, I wasn't."

"So, obviously you don't know how much she smoked at work or even when she was outside your presence, do you?"

"No, I don't. But, I know that she had to go to a smoking lounge at the office or outside to do so and she was too busy to do much of that."

"That's speculation on your part, isn't it?"

"No, I don't think so since I knew what Meri did each day at work."

"Regardless of that issue, your wife smoked, she had considerable stress at work and she was being treated by Dr. Janowitz for high blood pressure. Correct?"

"Yes, she was trying to get help. To improve her life so she could be with the children and me for many years to come."

"Mr. Lawrence," Joan Childs continued, "Mrs. Lawrence decided to reduce her blood pressure medication without consulting even her doctor, didn't she?"

"Meri eventually told me that when I noticed that she seemed to be getting headaches on a basis which I considered to be too frequent. She told me she had temporarily reduced her medication at the suggestion of her trainer, Tony Piccini."

With that, Ms. Childs turned toward the judge and stated, "Your Honor, Motion to strike the witness' unresponsive answer. I asked him if he knew that Mrs. Lawrence had reduced her blood pressure medication, not who may or may not have suggested that she do so."

While Judge Davis knew that Joan Childs was technically correct, he saw little harm in letting the answer stand, given what Tony Piccini had already admitted doing. He decided to let the answer stand.

Davis stated, "Ms. Childs, you opened the door here. You asked a very broad question, and Mr. Lawrence answered it. Mr. Piccini has already admitted to making that recommendation to Meri Lawrence. I will let the answer stand."

Joan Childs was incensed but she was not surprised at the ruling, given all that had transpired in the case to date. She was simply pissed.

"Judge," she stated, "note my exception."

"So noted. Move on, Ms. Childs," the Judge stated rather distastefully. Davis didn't particularly like Ms. Childs. She was on the "other team," as he liked to refer to female lawyers whom he felt were too masculine in their demeanor and approach. Her team, he felt, was from the wrong side of the street. Even if she was a decent lawyer from a good firm, she was much too "butch" for Davis' liking.

Joan Childs knew how Davis felt about her. He rarely let his true feelings spill over and onto the record in any case when she appeared before him. However, he held her in some contempt because of what he perceived her sexual preferences to be. She knew it, and she didn't like it; but she was forced to be in Davis' courtroom for this trial and some others. Sometimes she had to accept his style of dealing with her personal preferences. If she were a trial lawyer in Franklin County, Columbus, Ohio, she would on occasion draw a case in Davis' courtroom. That was a given.

Returning to her questioning of Ben Lawrence, Ms. Childs continued, "Mr. Lawrence, once you became aware of your wife's own decision to reduce her blood pressure medication, did you call her doctor to tell Dr. Janowitz what she was doing?"

"No, I did not. I told Meri . . . "

"Mr. Lawrence, you have answered the question," Ms. Childs said, cutting off his full answer.

"Did you call Mr. Piccini and talk with him about Meri's decision to reduce her medication?"

"No, I did not. He was the one . . . "

"Mr. Lawrence, just answer the questions that I ask," said Ms. Childs, not wanting to repeat the previous opportunity she gave Ben Lawrence to answer her questions as he saw fit.

"Mr. Lawrence, did you call anyone at FitAgain to complain about Mrs. Lawrence's decision to cut her medication?"

"I saw no point in doing so."

"Did you counsel your wife regarding the decision she made to reduce her medication?"

"I don't agree with your characterization of it being 'her decision' to do so. Tony Piccini, who worked in your client's facility, told her to do so."

"Mr. Lawrence, I will remind you again of the need to answer the questions and only those questions which I ask."

"Okay, I told Meri that I didn't want her to reduce her medication. But she trusted Piccini and told me she would not continue with the reduction once she completed her new job interview."

"Did you, Mr. Lawrence, consult with anyone at FitAgain about this issue of reducing her medication?"

"No, I did not."

"Did you talk with anyone at all, other than your wife about this issue?"

"No."

"Did you tell your wife of the potential dangers in reducing her medication?"

"We discussed whether she should do so, but I did not discuss the dangers with her. I didn't know what those dangers were."

"Did you even tell Mrs. Lawrence that continuing to smoke was bad for her?"

"Yes, I did."

"But she continued to do all the wrong things, didn't she?'

"No; she was seeking help from those who were represented to her as being qualified, professional people."

"Mr. Lawrence, did you ever go to FitAgain's facility yourself?"

"No"

"How much weight did your wife gain from the time you got married until the time of her death?"

"I am not sure."

"It was considerable, was it not?

"I don't know."

"It was nearly 50 pounds, was it not?"

"I don't know."

"Mr. Lawrence, if we can examine the records of her physician from when she started seeing the good doctor, before the birth of your first child, until the last time she saw the doctor, several months before her death, the patient chart for your wife shows that she gained 48 pounds in that period. Is this true?"

"I am saying, it shows what it shows. I loved her. I didn't check her weight."

While Childs was making these points, at least in her own mind through such questioning, the bottom line appeared clear. Meri Lawrence had sought help from those who were represented to her and in fact to all the public as qualified, well trained professionals working in a facility which vouched for their qualifications as "certified" professionals and properly prepared trainers, under circumstances where the facility promised "not to kill" them when, in fact, they had done so, at least with Meri Margaret Lawrence. No amount of questioning from Ms. Childs would change any of that.

Once Childs finished her questions, LaPorte called a medical expert, as well as a physiologist, an economist, and a real professional in exercise and personal training all to testify. After those four testified, LaPorte rested the Plaintiffs' case – in other words he stopped calling witnesses or presenting any further evidence to support the family's claim of wrongful death.

The various defendants then offered their own experts to testify as to their respective theories about the cause of death, which they attempted to attribute to Meri's obesity, her stress, her smoking and generally her unhealthy habits. They offered little, however, to refute Tony's obvious lack of real training and qualifications. There really wasn't much to be done about that aspect of the evidence.

After all of this was over and done, the case was submitted to the jury on the instructions of law as provided by the good Judge Charles Davis.

CHAPTER 30

Once the jury was instructed on how to apply the law to the facts as they would find them to be in their deliberations, they began their first effort at reaching a verdict. However, they were at it for three days without reaching a verdict.

On the third day, Davis decided to keep the jury beyond 4:00 p.m. After there was no verdict by 5:30 p.m., Davis determined to let them have an evening meal. They were sent out for dinner by order of His Honor Charles Davis at 6:00 p.m. They would not formally deliberate at dinner. But they were still undecided and otherwise would have to deliberate once they returned to the jury room in a continuing effort to reach a decision. After their dinner recess and another two hours of deliberation, Davis sent them home for the night with instructions not to read about the case in the newspaper or to watch or listen to any media coverage reported on the case that evening. He instructed them to return at 8:30 a.m. the next day.

Despite the fact that the jury was still undecided, there really wasn't much for anyone to be positive about. Tony was at a standstill in the civil litigation, waiting for the jury to make some decision. By the next day, the fourth day of deliberations, Tony was frustrated. All he wanted was to get on with some semblance of his former life. No easy task.

More waiting would be required. At least that is what Finestein told him.

Meanwhile, Tony was also waiting for some word from his criminal case defense lawyer on when he would be retried in that case, where his freedom and future were at stake.

While Tony waited outside of Davis' courtroom on the civil jury to make some decision, his criminal case lawyer, Walt Manos, came out of the courthouse elevator and saw Tony sitting alone at the end of the hallway. Tony sat on one of the long benches located just outside the three civil courtrooms on that floor. He seemed very much alone and dejected, at least from Manos' perspective.

"Afternoon Tony," said Manos. "How are you holding up?"

"Not good," said Tony. "But I'm still here, and I guess no news in this situation is better than it could be."

"Well," chirped Manos, "I have some news. Maybe some good news. The Prosecutor, James Urban, is under consideration for possible appointment as Ohio's next Attorney General. I don't know if you heard what happened this morning but Mitchell Daniels, the present Attorney General for the State of Ohio, resigned over the so-called sex and financial scandal which has been brewing in that office for the last several months. I know you have been tied up first with your criminal trial and then with this litigation so you may not have heard what's going on; but that's the word on the street. Urban may be appointed Attorney General yet today."

"So what does that do for me?" asked Tony.

"It could help," said Manos. "It could pave the way for Urban's chief assistant, Sally Goldfarb, to then be appointed as the next Franklin County Prosecutor. If those appointments come through, given all that has happened in the Attorney General's office and it could happen quickly, it may help us with your case. Golfarb has very little interest in this criminal case of yours. She and I worked together previously. We are friends. It may be time to call upon her to do the right thing here and put this whole matter in proper perspective. If the jury in this civil case reaches a verdict in favor of the family, that may well cinch it and make her feel that everyone involved has gotten their pound of flesh. In your civil case, that's potentially a million or more such pounds. No pun intended."

Tony felt a sense of hope that he had not experienced for many months. Perhaps the long downward spiral might be working its way for the better.

"What can I do?" asked Tony.

"Wait," responded Manos, "We will just have to see how it unfolds. If it happens as I expect, we might know more in a very short time. I'll be back later today or tomorrow to fill you in. In the meantime listen for the news as it transpires."

With that, Manos walked off down the hallway and toward the steps located on the other end of the building. As he did so he walked past a group of others in the hallway. Most of them were dressed like lawyers, mingling with a number of people who were surely clients, witnesses, court personnel or other lawyers.

Tony had noticed some of them previously. One of them he had noticed in particular. This man had been in the criminal courtroom where he stood trial, at least during parts of the testimony in that case. Tony also remembered that this man had been inside Davis' courtroom for parts of the civil trial. He had noticed him talking to Ben Lawrence at one point. The gentleman was older, in his early 60s. Tony was sure he was a lawyer, probably someone with some interest in the case. Tony was just not sure who he was or where he fit in, if anywhere.

As Manos walked by the group of probable lawyers, witnesses and others, Tony noticed how the one Tony had designated as a probable lawyer and the one he had previously seen in the courtrooms during his trials, stared intently at Manos, Tony's criminal case protector. He obviously didn't care for Manos, but Tony was not sure why. If he remembered, he would ask Manos when they next met. Perhaps the two of them had some history; maybe they had been opponents.

At that very moment, however, Finestein emerged from Charles Davis' courtroom and approached Tony. Finestein said, "The judge is putting a lot of pressure on us to settle this case. I've got to call your insurance company's adjuster to see if I can get the full amount of your insurance policy's coverage to throw into a possible settlement pot or at least some of it. If I need to, the judge has ordered me to bring the adjuster here to appear before him.

Finestein continued, "The insurance carrier for SlimLine has just

223

put an offer of three million dollars on the table toward a possible resolution of this case, and the judge made it clear what we should do. It seems that SlimLine, for whatever reason, really wants this case over and done. They have been pushing everyone here to work towards doing that, perhaps more so than even the judge. In fact, the judge is now starting to warm up to Reuger, the New York lawyer, who seems to be the one leading the settlement charge. If this happens, it may well help you work out something with your criminal case."

"Do what you can" said Tony. "I just talked to Manos who also told me not to give up hope. I need something good to happen to make the carrier understand what all this is doing to my life, at least what is left of it."

Finestein promised to do so. He walked down the courtroom hallway as Manos had previously done just a few minutes earlier. He got the same cold look from the same lawyer type that Tony previously observed looking at Manos. "I wonder what's up with that guy," thought Tony. At that moment, however, the presumed lawyer's cold calculated stare focused off of Finestein and riveted onto Tony. It sent a chill down Tony's spine. He felt as if someone had just walked on his grave. Tony thought the guy might just be having a bad day.

He had enough to worry about without adding more worries to his stress.

CHAPTER 31

Finestein reached Tony's insurance carrier by his cell phone which had been released to him by Bill Morris at the order of the judge. He called the carrier's adjuster, the one in charge of Tony's liability insurance coverage, and told him what was going on and to come to the courthouse. After considerable pressure from the judge and an order requiring the adjuster to come to the Court to appear before Davis, the company sent the adjuster to the courthouse.

Davis spent ten minutes with the insurance company's representative and with charm or threats, perhaps both, he had the company put the full one million dollar value of Tony's liability insurance on the table toward a settlement offer. He also got FitAgain to put in one million dollars despite Ms. Childs' attempt to circumvent the matter.

When the judge was able to get the pharmacy and the natural food store to each put in another $250,000, Davis had more than five million dollars to offer LaPorte and his clients. While not the full amount the plaintiffs had hoped to receive, they would wind up with over three million dollars tax free after costs and attorney fees. It would not make up for Meri's death and the agonizing emotions that her death had created for the family, but it would certainly help. A net of approximately three million dollars after costs and attorney fees, even in a dour economy, could potentially produce nearly $150,000 a year if the principal were left untouched. That should be enough with Ben's salary to take care of the kids and even send them to college when the time came. Meri was still gone, but some legacy from her early death would be left for the kids. Perhaps that was enough for the family. Perhaps not.

Meri's physician refused to contribute to any settlement because she felt she had done absolutely nothing wrong. Despite the judge's threats, she would not give in. Since the doctor had a provision in her professional liability insurance policy requiring her consent to any settlement paid on her behalf by her insurance company, the insurance carrier was contractually prohibited from doing otherwise. Such consent provisions were common in the medical malpractice insurance industry. Physicians demanded such clauses to maintain control over their often egomaniacal existences. No matter what, she would not authorize her carrier to kick in any sum.

The case settled anyway. No one but his Honor Charles Davis, Mitch Malloy and Matthew Reuger were completely happy about that fact. Tony was somewhat relieved but still concerned about his criminal case. However, Tony remained hopeful that the civil settlement would lead to a resolution of his criminal case as well.

CHAPTER 32

In light of the defendants' collective settlement offer as put together by Davis and the plaintiffs' agreement to accept the settlement so tendered, there was no need for Judge Davis to provide an answer to the jury's original question as put to the judge. It turned out that the jury's inability to reach a consensus on a verdict had led to some arguments and then their question to the judge.

Davis already knew what they were likely arguing about since Bill Morris, his bailiff of many years, had been able to pull some of their notes from the jury room wastebasket. While no one knew what Davis and Morris had done, except, of course, Vince, as well as Vince's own legal advisor, Richard Aherns and Mitch Malloy, Davis was able to get both sides to move toward a resolution of the litigation. He did it by subtly implying to some of the defense counsel that his bailiff had inadvertently heard things that the Judge thought defense counsel should know. Davis was a master at such deception.

Davis had also told Hatfield that his bailiff heard that the jury was considering an award of more than five million dollars. In the case of Ms. Childs, Davis told her the jury had already decided that Piccini was a FitAgain employee and that they were considering an award against FitAgain of more than ten million dollars.

Since such figures would have exceeded the primary and excess liability insurance that FitAgain had available to it, those numbers got Child's attention. She promptly called FitAgain with the news of these possibilities, the supposed suspicions and the need to consider the worst. FitAgain's CEO, Mark Trudeau, didn't take the news very well and immediately wanted to know, "How in the hell can the jury even reach the conclusion that Piccini was our employee? We have a contract that says he isn't our employee – that he's an independent contractor. Doesn't that explain it all?"

Childs responded, "Sure it matters, but it's only one piece of paper against a mountain of other evidence demonstrating Piccini's employment. Remember, I was able to keep out the evidence about the 'closed' classes you had for trainers at the club on the topics of supplements and energy drinks. If that information had gone into evidence, that would have put another nail in your coffin for sure," responded Ms. Childs.

Trudeau didn't like it, but at the same time he was dealing with dollars and cents. He decided it was best to let the insurance company pay and contribute toward the settlement or risk a verdict above the insurance limits which could cause his company to lose its assets – perhaps all of them. The risk was too great. Settlement for FitAgain was the only real option.

CHAPTER 33

As soon as His Honor Charles Davis completed reading the Piccini case settlement into the record, Harper was ready to spring his retaliation on Davis. All of this was done in the presence of and with the consent of all of the parties and their lawyers, in a completely confidential manner from observation by third-parties and in the judge's chambers. He quietly left Davis' chambers as soon as the settlement was read into the secret record and called Aherns so that they could meet at their prearranged time and place.

While Harper went to meet the Franklin County Presiding Judge to turn in Davis, he began to enjoy what was to come. It was something that Vince had been gearing up to enjoy, much like the pre-game warm ups he had experienced before one of the big football games he had previously enjoyed in high school and college. Adrenaline surges, a stimulated heart rate and the encounter to come was to be anticipated and savored. He enjoyed the feeling and looked forward to the meeting.

During the time he worked his way to the covert meeting with Richard Aherns and the Presiding Judge, Vince checked the voice mail on his phone so he could play back the taped communication between Davis and his bailiff just in case Aherns forgot the tape he had previously provided and entrusted to him. As Harper accessed his voice mail, he quickly learned that he had no messages on his phone – none at all! He repeated the entry to access his messages but all he heard from the unidentified voice mail messenger was, "I'm sorry; you have no new or saved messages."

He could not believe the previously recorded voice mail was no longer on his phone. What could have possibly happened? Thank God he had enough foresight to trust Richard Aherns with a copy of the tape. He knew it would be safe. At least he hoped so.

As Harper got to the Presiding Judge's office, he introduced himself to the receptionist and was ushered into the Presiding Judge's well-appointed office. Richard Aherns was already there and had filled in the Presiding Judge, Judge Michael P. O'Donnell, on all of Harper's allegations.

O'Donnell extended a hand to Harper and asked him to sit down. "Richard has explained to me what you believe happened here and what the issues may be. He has told me you came to him because of a tape you have of a private conversation between Judge Davis and his bailiff. Since their communications are of a very private and confidential nature, I need to ask how you acquired that tape?"

Harper was a little uneasy with the nature of the question but explained the matter about the bailiff's confiscation of his cell phone at Davis' order and how Vince had acquired the conversation by his cell phone voice mail system, probably by accident.

At that point, Judge O'Donnell asked Harper to let him hear his playback of the cell phone conversation.

"I'm afraid I can't do that, your Honor," replied Harper, "Somehow the message was erased from my voice mail system. Thankfully, however, I made a copy of the voice mail and gave it to Mr. Aherns. Mr. Aherns has it in his possession," gesturing toward Richard Aherns who was seated in a chair next to Harper, both of which were in front of the Presiding Judge's desk.

"Okay, Richard," said O'Donnell. "Let me have the tape."

Aherns replied, "Sure, your Honor. I have it right here in my coat pocket, next to my own cell phone." Aherns reached in and pulled out both his cell phone and the tape which had been resting in the same pocket during the trip from Aherns's office on the Ohio State campus to the Franklin County Courthouse. He believed the tape was safe there since he had felt it while he answered his phone several times on the way over to the County Courthouse.

"Here, your Honor," said Aherns, "Let's play it back." At that point, O'Donnell loaded the tape into his dictating equipment and pushed play. All three of them then heard the same thing: static. Several attempts to do more to illicit some recorded voices out of the machine resulted in the same noise but no content.

"What the hell is going on here with the two of you?" asked O'Donnell. "Richard, did you ever hear the tape?"

"Why, no," replied Richard, "I never did. I just took Vince at his word here. Vince, where is the other copy I told you to make?"

Harper looked at Aherns and replied, "Davis took it."

"What to do you mean, Davis took it?" asked O'Donnell, "How did he even know about it?"

Harper now knew he was the one in serious trouble. He couldn't tell Aherns or, God forbid, O'Donnell that he had used the tape to blackmail Davis or he would be the one going to jail. He simply stammered, "Somehow he found out about it and got it from me in his chambers."

"This is nonsense, Mr. Harper. I have known Richard Aherns for years. He trusted you enough to bring this matter to me, and it sounds like a fairy tale. Judge Davis has had some issues in the past but nothing like this. I suggest you get up, get out of that chair and get the hell out of my office. I'd also suggest that you keep your fantasies to yourself and move on with your life back in New York and not here."

Once Harper rose to leave, he glanced at Aherns whose own eyes were now downcast and staring at the floor. Harper then turned to walk out of O'Donnell's office. As he did so, he looked to his right at one of the Presiding Judge's office walls and saw a picture of four men, including Sam Wilson, the now Vice President of the United States. The picture was of four young lawyers – O'Donnell, Wilson, Davis and Aherns – taken when they were first sworn in as Ohio lawyers many years ago.

As he turned to look at the Presiding Judge and after O'Donnell saw Harper gaze at the picture and then at him, he simply told Harper, "Get out. You have no business being here at all."

Harper complied and learned what some would describe as the delivery of a New York lesson in Ohio. If only Aherns had known that a cell phone sometimes causes voice tapes to be erased. If only Harper had saved his own tape from Davis' grasp. If only Harper had known that these four lawyers had obviously been friends. If only.

CHAPTER 34

Once the settlement was reached and memorialized in the confidential record put together in Davis' chambers, Tony left Davis' kingdom feeling exhausted but relieved. He felt as if the weight of the world had been lifted from his shoulders. Hopefully he could now get on with his life.

He began the walk to where he parked his car, a parking deck inside a downtown mall that had once been "the" shopping place in Columbus – the Downtown Center City Mall. Now, due to an economic downturn in some segments of central Ohio and due in part to the proliferation of surrounding suburban malls, this Downtown mall was virtually empty. The only remaining stores included a watch and clock sales and repair store, a few fast food places and a lone health club on the street level, which still had a few members. A few of those members were also clients of some other personal trainers Tony knew.

Tony decided to stop in the mall's men's room before he got to his car in the attached mall garage. As he went into the nearly empty mall, he took a second to find and then enter the men's room to relieve himself. He walked into one of the stalls and proceeded to do what was necessary. He heard the restroom door open and the sound of footsteps signifying that someone was entering the room. Tony thought perhaps the mall wasn't so nearly unused as he believed.

Suddenly, the door to Tony's stall burst open. The disturbance caused Tony to miss his mark, but he put away what he had been using while trying to see who or what was standing in the stall's doorway. As Tony turned around to look, he learned the intruder was the same older, lawyer-like gentleman he had seen off and on during his criminal and civil trials – the one who had been in the courthouse hallway. It was the same one who made Tony feel as if that man had walked on Tony's grave.

In response to this man's sudden entry into his private stall, Tony blurted out; "What the hell are you doing? What do you want?"

At that moment, Tony noticed the barrel of a pistol pointed at him, slightly above waist high. Slowly, ever so slowly, however, the pistol was raised until it was pointed directly at Tony's face.

CHAPTER 35

John Allen David, the man behind the pistol which was squarely pointed at Tony Piccini's head, had been driven to this moment, to this end.

Meri Margaret Lawrence, who was first known as Meri Margaret David before her marriage to Ben Lawrence, was John's only daughter. He was the very first human being to ever hold her hand. She had grasped his little finger with her tiny hand within a moment of her birth and right after her Apgar coding by the delivery room nurses.

Meri was seven pounds, seven ounces and 17" in length, head to foot. She was born on July 7, 1977 at 7:07 a.m. John and his wife Linda had always told Meri that 7 was obviously her lucky number and that it would hold some special meaning in her life. Little did they then know how prophetic that number would be and not so lucky in the end.

John had doted on Meri. While he had a small but successful private legal practice in Canton, somewhat near Akron and Cleveland, Ohio, he always made time for Meri from the time she was old enough to walk. He would watch her for hours on end as she played fashion dress up. He would take picture after picture of her as she grew up – all with Meri "mugging it up" as they called it, which really amounted to nothing more than Meri posing for the camera. All of those pictures along with many others would someday be placed in a book labeled by John as "The Book of Meri - a Dad's book of love for his daughter." He had given it to her just before her wedding day when she married Ben.

John was extremely proud of Meri. She was the apple of his eye. She loved "mugging" for him, but she was a competitor. She excelled at gymnastics and cheered for years with a passion that could not be matched – not by anyone, not by her coaches, her teammates or anyone else. John always thought she would be an Olympian. But as she grew into womanhood, she became very beautiful and much sought after by a string of boys, at least until she met Ben. When she met Ben, John knew the Olympics would have to do without her.

Her drive and competitiveness continued through college and even when she began her fashion industry career. Once she met Ben however, she first became infatuated with him and then ultimately fell deeply in love with him. They married and had children. Meri's family and career were the center of her life. She had neglected herself for a time until she ultimately realized that she needed to take better care of herself first and foremost or she wouldn't be able to take care of anyone else.

John was pleased with Meri's decision in that regard. However, he had no idea that professionalism in the health club industry was meaningless and all too often run by ex-jock types who knew nothing about health or wellness, but rather spent their time looking out for their own self-promotion, financial well-being and fulfillment of their sexual desires with many of those clients under their care

CHAPTER 36

Tony was not new to altercations. He had engaged in some fights in high school. He even had some serious confrontations later with a few other trainers. He also had some very close calls with jealous boyfriends and husbands stricken with anger and rage who sought vengeance due to Tony's intimate dealings with their girlfriends and wives. However, this was the first time he ever had a gun pointed directly at him which was now held head high. This altercation could be one-sided. He dared not escalate it, at least at the moment.

Once he realized what was happening, Tony spoke in a shaken and quivering voice: "Listen, I don't know what's going on here, but I'm pretty sure I don't know you and you don't know me. My life has been in a real uproar of late, and I don't know what you want. If it's money, I don't have any. I haven't worked for months, and I'm living hand-to-mouth. If you are the boyfriend or husband of one of my former clients, I didn't do any harm. It just happened. A lot of the women I work with like me too much; they trust me. They want me to help them in many ways. I meant no harm to you. Who are you, and what do you want?"

By the time Tony got out those last few words, the older man on the other side of the gun, slowly, ever so slowly, pulled back the trigger. As the man pulled back the trigger with his right thumb, it made a distinctive and ominous 'click'. Tony looked at the gun and the eyes behind it, which, as they had done before, now made Tony grow cold. This time, Tony felt an immediate and very real fear. "What do you want?" Tony implored. "What have I done to you?"

The eye's behind the gun narrowed and somehow seemed even more ominous than before.

After what seemed like an eternity, the voice associated with the eyes and the gun began to pour out words which echoed in the bathroom stall: "You took the most precious, wonderful gift I ever had. You destroyed the most important life I have ever known. You killed my only daughter, Meri, through your stupid, selfish and thoughtless actions. You think your plea bargain and the payment made for you by your insurance carrier will make up for the misery and heartache you have caused? You are wrong."

Tony began to feel very chilled. A streak of cold emanated from his very essence up to his heart and into his throat. His heart began beating very fast. The voice continued, "You will not escape punishment for what you have done. You will pay for your stupid selfishness, here and now."

"But," said Tony, "I didn't mean any harm. I tried to help Meri, not hurt her. I would never have hurt her. It was an accident. I didn't know any better. I just did what I was taught to do. I'm sorry. You've got to listen …"

Tony began to sweat above his upper lip. His left hand and left foot began to tremble uncontrollably. He didn't know how he could get out of this jam – not this time.

"You're a lawyer, right?" asked Tony. "You can't seek vengeance in this way. You believe in the rule of law, in the system of justice, in the law of the land, don't you?"

Tony continued, "I was found guilty when I pled. The judge will punish me. He will impose sentence. I know I'm probably not going to prison but …"

"But nothing," said the man with the gun. "Justice be damned.

Justice will be served by what I do here and now, not by what the court may or may not do later."

The man continued, "No one will ever find out what happened here. When they find your body, they will think you died in a random robbery and shooting in a forgotten mall. They will think it's a simple homicide of a two bit punk who thought he could be somebody."

"No one will care what happened to you - no one. It's only fitting that you die in a dirty toilet stall in a men's room, in a nearly empty mall next to some unregulated, so-called health club that has nothing really to do with health. It's all about show. It's all about making money, not making people better. People like you have no business in a profession that really should be helping people. All you were trying to do was help yourself."

With that, Tony's mind began to wander. He thought back to Meri's death, to the look of loss on her face at the end and then the emptiness in her eyes as the life behind those eyes faded from this dimension of reality. Tony had been totally saddened as the sparkle in those eyes turned lifeless and flat. He wondered where the light in them had gone. Perhaps he had no need to wonder any more.

AUTHOR'S EPILOGUE

The fitness industry in the United States is big business. Total industry revenues recently approached $20 billion. Worldwide, the industry accounts for an estimated $68 billion in revenue from 117 million fitness facility members working out at nearly 125,000 facilities.

The nutritional supplement industry in this country is even bigger business, approaching $24 billion in sales. Worldwide, this industry accounts for perhaps as much as $228 billion.

The population in America is aging and with each passing year, becomes more sedentary and unhealthy. Some people, however, are seeking to regain their youth, vitality, vigor and "lasting" health benefits through activity, exercise and the ingestion of nutritional supplements. Health club memberships exceed 45 million in the United States. Nearly 200,000 personal trainers and perhaps as many as 400,000 such individuals, provide one-on-one fitness services, exercise prescription, instruction and supervision to these Americans. None of them are licensed by the federal government or by any state as fitness professionals or personal trainers.

While the vast majority of personal trainers are adequately and professionally educated and trained, many are not certified by accredited fitness certification organizations. Some personal trainers are woefully incompetent.

Until very recently, hundreds of organizations purported to prepare, educate, train and certify fitness professionals to enter the health and fitness marketplace to provide service. While responsible segments of the industry have acted in many respects to address training shortcomings and to improve the preparation of fitness professionals, particularly personal trainers for the provision of safe exercise activity to clients, no state has yet adopted legislation to see to it that these professionals are qualified, licensed and regulated. Even though the industry has acted to adopt standards and guidelines applicable to the delivery of fitness services, these statements are neither mandatory nor uniform. Many so-called fitness professionals don't even know of or apply these practice statements in their delivery of relevant services to clients. More importantly perhaps, the court system has not held many such trainers accountable for their alleged lack of compliance with industry standards.

In a country which often requires dog and pet groomers as well as their kennels to be locally licensed and/or regulated in some form, many authorities contend that more needs to be done to impose the force of law upon the regulation of these fitness professionals in order to protect the public from harm.

While the stories provided in this book are fictional in their entirety, nearly all are inspired by some semblance of what I have observed in the real world over the last 30 years. Ill prepared and poorly trained fitness professionals have in some situations caused needless injury, pain and even death to the populations they were supposed to help. State licensure may ultimately be the only way to really improve the profession. In the meantime, this book offers food for thought on this important topic. Ultimately, readers are free to draw their own conclusions.

David L. Herbert

2012

ABOUT THE AUTHOR

David L. Herbert is an Ohio attorney and principal member of David L. Herbert & Associates, LLC, Attorneys and Counselors at Law. He is a graduate of Kent State University where he was a student-athlete and a graduate of the University of Akron School of Law where he was a member of The Akron Law Review.

He was an Assistant Stark County Prosecuting Attorney (Canton, Ohio) in the 1970s. He is an author of over 40 books/book chapters and numerous articles written on the topics of trial practice, negligence, standards, guidelines and the law associated with health care, criminal and civil law, fitness, sports and sports medicine activities. Over the last 30 years, he has also helped write some of the most authoritative and respected standards and guidelines for the fitness industry. He has lectured before virtually every major fitness organization in the United States and provided service and representation to numerous fitness and sports medicine groups. He is considered an expert in this area of professional practice. This book is his first work of fiction.

35884950R00154

Made in the USA
Middletown, DE
18 October 2016